THE HANDKERCHIEF TREE

A Selection of Recent Titles by Anne Douglas

CATHERINE'S LAND
AS THE YEARS GO BY
BRIDGE OF HOPE
THE BUTTERFLY GIRLS
GINGER STREET
A HIGHLAND ENGAGEMENT
THE ROAD TO THE SANDS
THE EDINBURGH BRIDE
THE GIRL FROM WISH LANE *
A SONG IN THE AIR *
THE KILT MAKER *
STARLIGHT *
THE MELODY GIRLS *
THE WARDEN'S DAUGHTERS *
PRIMROSE SQUARE *
THE HANDKERCHIEF TREE *

* *available from Severn House*

THE HANDKERCHIEF TREE

Anne Douglas

This first world edition published 2012
in Great Britain and in the USA by
SEVERN HOUSE PUBLISHERS LTD of
9–15 High Street, Sutton, Surrey, England, SM1 1DF.
Trade paperback edition first published
in Great Britain and the USA 2013 by
SEVERN HOUSE PUBLISHERS LTD.

British Library Cataloguing in Publication Data

Douglas, Anne, 1930-
The handkerchief tree.
1. Edinburgh (Scotland)--Social conditions--20th
century--Fiction. 2. Love stories.
I. Title
823.9'14-dc23

ISBN-13: 978-0-7278-8196-0 (cased)
ISBN-13: 978-1-84751-448-6 (trade paper)

All Severn House titles are printed on acid-free paper.

Severn House Publishers support The Forest Stewardship Council [FSC],
the leading international forest certification organisation. All our titles that
are printed on Greenpeace-approved FSC-certified paper carry the FSC logo.

Typeset by Palimpsest Book Production Ltd.,
Falkirk, Stirlingshire, Scotland.
Printed and bound in Great Britain by
MPG Books Ltd., Bodmin, Cornwall.

One

The lady from the council was due at two. Ten minutes to go.

'Shall I see if she's coming?' Shona Murray asked from the door of Mrs Hope's house in Edinburgh's Dean Village.

'Might as well,' answered Mrs Hope, small and plump, her round brown eyes on the dresser clock. Ten minutes to go. How must the poor bairn be feeling?

Look at her now, moving into the street, wearing Kitty's black dress that was too big for her, only eleven years old and facing such change! If only she, Addie Hope, could have taken her in.

She'd wanted to, and not just because you got paid if you gave a home to a boarded-out orphan. She'd wanted to do what Emmie asked and had even sort of said she would – at which memory, Addie bit her lip. But what could she do? She'd five children of her own and little enough room as it was in the house in Baxter Row. What could she do but agree with her man, Jock? It just wasn't possible to give the lassie a home. So, it was the orphanage for Shona. What a mercy her poor ma would never know.

Outside, unaware of the guilt churning up Mrs Hope's mind, Shona was standing in the sunshine of that afternoon in May, 1919. Small, with delicate features, hazel eyes and a plait of auburn hair that could look gold in the sun, she was keeping watch on Baxter Row.

Baxter Row was a terrace of little houses designed for the workers of the flour mills in the Dean Village, which was in fact the surviving village of two, for one had been demolished to make way for a cemetery. Such a strange event, you might have thought, but now it was almost forgotten. All that was known was the place that was Shona's home, in the valley of the Water of Leith, beneath the famous Dean Bridge.

And, oh, how Thomas Telford's handsome bridge dominated the houses of Baxter Row and all the area! Built to carry the main road north over the Water of Leith, it had been a huge engineering success, as solid today as when it was opened in 1832 and, of course, busier than ever. Only half a mile away was Edinburgh's bustling West End, but down in the village, under the bridge, it was quiet, even peaceful, in spite of the grain mills and bakeries. Here was a place of tradition and character, and well beloved by its residents, Shona being one of them.

Of course, it wasn't much like the sort of village you saw pictured in books and calendars, being much more straggling and separated out, not built to any plan, but just developed as time passed. Though there was a school and a church, the important feature was not a village green but the Water of Leith, Edinburgh's nearest thing to a river. At one point it was lined with buildings, houses and mills, some of which were very old, with a history that could be traced back to the twelfth century. Elsewhere, it ran between grassy banks, where there were trees and shrubs – a delightful place to walk.

Shona had learned the history of her village at school. How the Ancient Incorporation of Baxters, or Bakers, had pretty well run everything in the early days, even though the weaving community had considered themselves important, too. But the weavers hadn't lasted as long as the baxters, baking still being a popular occupation. Why, Shona's own street even bore the baxters' name – her own dear street, her home, and seeing it in the sunshine, so peaceful, so much hers, she was afraid she might be taking her last look. Did they let orphans go visiting from orphanages? She shivered in the warmth of the sun, realizing just how little she knew of where her life was taking her.

If they did let her out, she'd come straight back. Not to see her old house – she couldn't bear that yet – but to visit all the people she knew who lived in her street, who worked at the mills, like Mr Hope and her dad (until he'd gone to war and never come back), and Mrs Hope who'd been so kind. She'd talk to all the neighbours, who'd been kind as well, and their children she went to school with, and played with after school in the street. She'd go walking with Kitty Hope in that lovely valley of the Water of Leith, so like being in the country, and feel at home again. If only she could.

Seeing no sign yet of Miss Lucas, Shona balanced on one foot, then another, keeping her eyes on the far end of Baxter Row, never letting them stray to the house next door to Mrs Hope's. That had been her parents' house, her home for her whole life – until some weeks before when Emmie Murray, her mother, had died from the Spanish Influenza. Died so fast she'd scarcely had time to ask Mrs Hope, her friend, to look after Shona. So fast, Shona had almost been too late to kiss her goodbye, but then her mother hadn't wanted her to, and had tried to push her away in case she caught the flu.

'I don't care about the flu!' Shona had cried, but her mother's hand had already fallen to her bed and her eyes had closed.

'Come away, pet, come away,' Mrs Hope had said, and packed a few things for her and taken her next door, where Jock Hope and the five Hope children were waiting. Since then, Shona had not been back to her old home, now locked with its curtains drawn, but she'd been told that new tenants would soon be moving in and tears at the thought stung her eyes.

Best brush them away before Miss Lucas came, she decided, for today she must be ready to face the future, which was an orphanage in Murrayfield. A fine house, Miss Lucas had said, in a very nice area of the city. As though Shona cared about the area if it wasn't the Dean, if it no longer held her mother.

She'd been so happy in the Dean, in that little house she couldn't yet look at, especially before her dad had been killed in the war. There'd been three of them then – her mother and father and herself. After the terrible telegram, of course, there'd been just the two, and Shona, at eight, had soon understood she must try to make her mother happy again. If she hadn't managed that, they had at least faced life together and become very close until, like a poisoned arrow, the Spanish flu had struck. Now Shona was the only one left, with no relatives except her Auntie Mona, her mother's sister, in Canada – someone she would never see.

She'd been told, of course, that the council had cabled her aunt, Mrs Mona Webster, informing her of her sister's death and asking what she would like to do about her motherless niece. Her aunt's reply had been brief. 'Regret Unable to Help *Stop* Letter Following *Stop*.'

But so far there had been no letter.

'Thank the Lord for the council, then,' had been Mrs Hope's comment – with which Shona could only agree.

Suddenly her eyes sharpened as she picked out a tall figure in the distance and her heart gave a lurch. Miss Lucas, at last! Wearing a blue walking out two-piece and a straw hat over her pinned up dark hair, she was smiling and waving, but Shona was already on the move.

'Miss Lucas is here!' she cried, running into the house Mrs Hope had spent so long tidying after her children had left for school that day. 'Mrs Hope, Miss Lucas has come!'

Her face turning pale, it was hitting Shona afresh that her time had also come. To say goodbye. To put on her coat, take her bag and go, away from the life she knew to something unknown, something she must face and didn't know if she could. But as Mrs Hope ushered in Miss Lucas, Shona swallowed hard, straightened her shoulders and even tried a smile. She'd always been a brave one, her mother had liked to say, even when days were dark, and she'd be a brave one now. For her parents' sake.

Two

'Good afternoon, Mrs Hope – hello, Shona.' Miss Lucas's tone was consciously bright. 'No children around today, then?'

'All at school, out o' the way,' replied Addie. Heavens, did Miss Lucas think they wanted Kitty, Biddy, Jamie, Dair and Pat all standing around, staring at poor Shona having to leave, then? Kitty would probably shed a few tears, being quite a friend of Shona's, which might set the others off, and then what a time they'd have!

'I told 'em I might be out when they got back,' Addie went on, 'in case I went with you and Shona to . . . to the house.'

Doesn't want to say orphanage, thought Miss Lucas.

'Edina Lodge,' she said aloud. 'It's a nice name, isn't it? And Shona is going to be very happy there. But there will be no need for you to come with us, Mrs Hope. I have to see Shona in, you understand, and introduce her to Miss Bryce, the superintendent.'

'Oh, well, then.' Addie lowered her eyes, so as not to show the relief she felt at not having to see the orphanage. Miss Lucas had said that it was a grand house, but who'd ever heard of a grand orphanage? It would be better to say goodbye to Shona here, eh? If only she didn't feel so bad about this whole business . . .

'Shona, if you're ready, I think we should be on our way to the tram,' Miss Lucas said briskly. 'Miss Bryce is expecting us and I don't want to be late. Mrs Hope, may we have Shona's bag?'

'Aye, it's here.' Addie hurried to fetch Shona's small canvas bag.

'There's no' much in it, mind, but we were told everything would be provided and Shona was just to take one or two things she wanted.'

Wanted . . . Shona looked up.

'My photos,' she said huskily. 'I'm taking my photos. There's one of Ma at the seaside and one of Dad in his uniform. They're what I want.'

'Very nice, too,' said Addie, 'but do you no' want your toy rabbit and your dolls, then?'

Shona shook her head. 'No, I'm too big for dolls now, and they'd probably no' let me have them, anyway.'

'But you always have your wee rabbit, Shona! You've had it since you were a baby!'

'The children are allowed some special possessions,' Miss Lucas put in. 'You could take your rabbit if you'd like to, I'm sure.'

But Shona was still shaking her head. She couldn't really put into words why she didn't want to take Master Bun to the orphanage. Perhaps because he was part of the old life and might not be safe in the new. Who could say how things would be at Edina Lodge, for her or her dear old rabbit?

'I'll leave him for now,' she said at last. 'Will you keep him for me, Mrs Hope, and my dolls?'

''Course I will, pet! I'll keep 'em safe and see nobody touches 'em. Now, shall I get Shona's coat, Miss Lucas?'

'Coats are provided, but Shona can take hers if she likes and it can be sent back later.'

'With Kitty's black dress,' Shona murmured. 'It was nice of her to lend it to me.'

'Och, she was glad to lend it,' said Mrs Hope. 'Never wears it, you ken. I'd to make it special for her gran's funeral.'

Her voice faltering and her eyes sliding everywhere, Addie helped Shona into her thin brown coat and stood back, her finger to her lip. 'It's goodbye, then,' she murmured at last, her gaze coming to rest on Shona's pale, set face. 'For today, anyway. But maybe we'll be able to come and see you?'

'Not at first,' Miss Lucas said hastily. 'Visits can be considered unsettling.'

'Unsettling?' Addie's eyes flashed. 'Why, the bairn's got a right to see her friends, surely?'

'It's really for Miss Bryce to say. Perhaps you could ask about it later? But now, Shona, we must be going.'

'Goodbye, Mrs Hope,' Shona said, clearing her throat. 'Thank you very much for looking after me.'

'No need for that, no need to thank me.' Addie, sniffing, threw her arms around Shona and kissed her cheek. 'Good luck, eh? Take care, and maybe drop me a wee line some time, if it's allowed. You'll no' forget?'

'I won't forget.'

Shona, from the door, looked to Miss Lucas, who was shaking Addie's hand and telling her not to worry, Shona would be happy, would settle in with no trouble at all. Now where was her bag?

As the two figures left the house, one tall, the other small, Addie suddenly ran after them. 'Shona, Shona! Wait a minute, eh?'

'Yes, Mrs Hope?'

'I just want to say that I'm sorry I couldn't take you. But you understand, eh? It just wasn't possible – with the best will in the world . . .'

'That's all right,' Shona answered quietly. 'I never thought I could stay. I knew you couldn't take me.'

'Shona!' called Miss Lucas and with a last quick hug for Addie, Shona turned and joined her on the steep walk up to the Queensferry Road. One or two neighbours came out as they passed to wish Shona good luck, but Addie said no more and after watching until the two figures were out of sight, went slowly back into her house.

Three

The tram could only take them a short way along the Queensferry Road before they must get off and begin walking to reach the orphanage.

'I'm afraid it's rather a long way,' Miss Lucas told Shona, who had already removed her coat because the afternoon sun was so hot. 'I hope you won't get too tired.'

'Och, no, I'm used to walking.' Though not in this grand part of the city, thought Shona. She'd never had occasion to come to such a wide, pleasant street where the few houses were large with their own private gardens laid out with grass and flowers. She'd vaguely heard that this was a place where rich folk lived, and of course she knew there were some grand schools around, where the pupils wore smart uniforms and could be seen sometimes on the trams, carrying hockey sticks or tennis rackets and satchels bulging with books. Where would she go to school now that she was too far from her old one? That would be another thing to find out.

'Is Edina Lodge really a grand house?' she asked Miss Lucas. She couldn't believe that it was.

Miss Lucas hesitated. 'Well, it was,' she answered cautiously. 'Outside, it still looks rather the same as when it belonged to Mr Hamer.'

'Who's Mr Hamer?'

'He's the wealthy man who left the house to the council in his will, specifically for children without families. He lost his parents when he was very young and lived in an orphanage himself for a time, before he was adopted. His aim, he said, was to give orphans the chance to grow up in pleasant surroundings.'

'So, it should be nice inside as well as outside?'

'Well, yes, but of course it's not been possible to keep it like a family house inside. If you think about the sort of use it has, I'm sure you'll understand that.'

'Oh, yes,' Shona replied, beginning to understand that perhaps Edina Lodge was not really as grand as Miss Lucas had originally made out. The nearer they got to it, the more she seemed flustered – but then, the day was so uncomfortably warm and it was very tiring, walking so far.

'At last!' Miss Lucas cried as she halted at a turning to a side street where there were more large houses. 'Shona, this is where we turn for Edina Lodge. It's just at the end here – what a relief!'

After only a short walk down the small street, they came to a pair of large wrought-iron gates set into a high stone wall with a notice affixed: *Edina Lodge – Please ring for admittance.*

'Can we no' just go through the gates?' asked Shona.

'Oh, no, that wouldn't do at all. It's necessary to know who's calling.'

Or who's leaving, Shona commented to herself. Maybe some ran away.

As soon as Miss Lucas had rung the bell, the gates were opened by a tall, heavily-built man, obviously the caretaker.

'Name?' he asked.

'Miss Lucas from the council, with Shona Murray.'

'That's all right, you're expected. Step this way, please.'

As they passed through the gates and the caretaker returned to a cottage-style house at the side, Shona thought they would see Edina Lodge, but there was only a drive stretching away though extensive grounds of trees and lawns. These were truly lovely, and she would have liked just to walk through them if she hadn't been feeling so desperately fluttery inside.

There was no hiding the fact that time was now running out. Soon she would have to discover what was waiting for her, what sort of life she was going to lead. Round the corner of this very drive she might for a start see her new home, the house Miss Lucas had told her about: Edina Lodge.

And . . . 'Oh!' she cried involuntarily. For round the corner of the drive, there it was.

Grand? A grand house? Well, it was big, no doubt about that. Big and grey, built, like so much of Edinburgh, of solid stone, with a dark tiled roof and rows and rows of windows that might have been shining in the sun if their glass hadn't been so dull. And surely, there were too many chimneys? More twisted chimneys than Shona had ever seen on a house before, but then, she hadn't seen many such houses as this.

'There it is then, Edina Lodge,' Miss Lucas murmured. 'Mr Hamer designed it himself, I believe. What do you think of it?'

Shona hesitated. 'I'm no' sure,' she said at last, telling a little white lie, for she was in fact sure that she didn't like it. Yes, it had been a rich man's house, she could tell that, and would have cost a lot of money to build and make his home. But . . . a home for her? She shook her head at herself. What had she been expecting to find here, anyway? Not a home, that was for sure.

'Ah, well, no doubt it seems strange to you,' Miss Lucas said with a resigned sigh. 'Perhaps you'll get to like it when you're more used to it. Now, we must ring the bell at the front door. Soon you will meet Miss Bryce.'

Miss Bryce. Shona's heart, already feeling heavy in her chest, plummeted. 'I'm wondering what she'll be like,' she said in a low voice.

'Strict but fair,' Miss Lucas told her firmly. 'And her fairness is what's important. You mustn't worry about her – she will make you welcome.'

'Will she?' Standing close to Miss Lucas as she rang the bell at the solid entrance door, Shona had lost her earlier resolve to be brave whatever happened. She knew she must retrieve it, but for the moment her will had left her. Even a warm welcome wouldn't make much difference, wouldn't bring back her old life. She was the only one who could help herself, but just then she was too much on edge to do it.

After a few moments the door was opened by a slim, fair young woman in a plain dark dress who, having taken their names and business, told them to step inside. Shona, clasping her coat and her bag and keeping her face as expressionless as possible so as to hide her nerves, followed Miss Lucas into the house.

'Please come this way,' the young woman said. 'Miss Bryce is expecting you.'

Four

First was a vestibule. Empty. A large, wide room, it led to a vast hallway, which showed every sign of having once been grand and now was not. Even before she'd fully taken in the linoleum-covered floor, the custard-yellow walls lined with pegs and the scuffed steps of the staircase, Shona knew how it would be, because she knew its smell. A smell familiar to anyone who attended school, it never seemed to vary, being a mixture of damp shoes, carbolic soap and children's bodies, with the addition, in this case, of something pungent cooked long before, now floating down like an unseen mist from the fine plaster ceiling.

It was no disappointment to recognize all this. In fact, everything about the hall was so familiar to Shona it made her feel a little easier for a moment or two. Until she remembered she still had to meet Miss Bryce.

'Through here,' their guide was murmuring as she pushed open a door at the back of the hall. 'Miss Bryce's office is on the right. I'll just tell her you're here.'

In response to her knock, a firm voice called 'Come in', and she opened the door.

'Miss Lucas to see you, Miss Bryce, with Shona Murray.'

'Thank you, Miss MacLaren. Please show them in.'

After the young woman had withdrawn, Miss Bryce came forward, smiling briefly. In cool Edinburgh tones, she greeted Miss Lucas, shaking first her hand, then Shona's. 'So this is our new arrival? Welcome to Edina Lodge, my dear.'

How strong the hand was, thought Shona. Just like Miss Bryce herself. Wearing a grey jacket and an ankle-length tweed skirt, she was tall – much taller even than Miss Lucas – with broad shoulders and a good-looking face. Her brows were dark and level, her nose straight, her eyes clear grey, and her light-coloured hair, looking as strong as everything else about her, was coiled into a great knot that would never, Shona was sure, dare to slip from its pins. How old was she? Shona had no idea. A grown-up was to her a grown-up, that was all she knew.

'Yes, this is Shona Murray from the Dean Village,' Miss Lucas was murmuring. 'I believe you have all the paperwork, Miss Bryce?'

'Yes, indeed. I have familiarized myself with Shona's case. Such a tragedy.' Miss Bryce's gaze resting on Shona was neither warm nor cold, though her words were sympathetic. 'I'm very sorry for your loss, Shona. It's hard for you to have lost your mother as well as your father.'

Shona, flushing, caught Miss Lucas's look and murmured a word of thanks.

'All I can tell you,' Miss Bryce was continuing, 'is that you will be made welcome here, and if you abide by the rules we have to have, you will do well. Now, you do understand that we have to have rules?'

'Yes, Miss Bryce.'

'Bells ring for certain things: getting up, going to bed, attending prayers and so on, and you will learn very quickly what they all mean. You will have certain tasks to do – everyone has to learn to be helpful here – but you will not find them too difficult. And then, of course, you will go to school, which will not be your old school but one equally good. My assistant, Miss MacLaren, will give you more details of life here, as well as providing you with your uniform.'

'Thank you, Miss Bryce,' Miss Lucas said. 'I'm sure Shona will soon find her way around.'

'Of course. And you will find all the other children very friendly and helpful. We have eighty residents here, equal numbers of boys and girls, all joining together for meals, tasks and so on, but the boys have their dormitories to the right of the building while the girls sleep on the left. Prayers are said every morning before breakfast and everyone attends the kirk on Sundays. Are there any questions?'

Still pink in the face, Shona hesitated.

'Don't be afraid to ask me anything you're not clear about,' Miss Bryce told her.

'Well, I was just wondering . . .' Shona hesitated. 'The lady who's been looking after me would like to visit me sometimes. Would that be allowed?'

Miss Bryce frowned. 'I don't care to say that visits are not allowed, but it's true that we don't encourage them in the early days of a new child's stay. They can be unsettling.'

'Perhaps Shona could ask about a visit later?' Miss Lucas suggested.

'That would be best.' Pressing a bell push on her desk, Miss Bryce shuffled some papers on her desk and stood up. 'And now, I think the time has come for Miss MacLaren to take you along to your dormitory, Shona. The young people are due back from school about now, and it will be a good time for you to meet them.'

'Thank you, Miss Bryce,' Miss Lucas said again, now rising with Shona. 'I'll leave all the paperwork with you, then.'

'Certainly. Everything is in excellent order. And – see – here comes Miss MacLaren.'

After her assistant had reappeared and been introduced to Shona, Miss Bryce turned to say goodbye.

'Shona, I'm sure you'll settle in well. Do your best and you'll be happy. Miss MacLaren, will you show Miss Lucas out?'

Five

Seemingly the first ordeal was over, then, and Shona was out of Miss Bryce's office and on her way to the front door to say goodbye to Miss Lucas: her last link, she was beginning to feel, with the outside world. Maybe it hadn't been so bad, meeting Miss Bryce? She might have been worse. All the same, Shona knew well enough that you had to tow the line with someone like her. Always obey the rules. Never answer back. Really, she was no worse than a teacher, and Shona was used to obeying teachers. The difference, of course, was that she was also used to going home at four o'clock and leaving her teachers behind. At Edina Lodge, they would always be there.

'Here's the front door, then,' said Miss Lucas, trying not to look too sadly at Shona while Miss MacLaren stood to one side. 'I'm afraid it's time for us to say goodbye.'

'I know,' Shona answered in a small voice. 'I wish it wasn't. You've been very nice to me, Miss Lucas.'

'And you've done very well. I'm proud of you. It's not been easy, but you've broken the ice; you know what Edina Lodge is like and you'll soon think of it as home.'

'Will you be coming back sometimes? I don't mean to see me, but, you know, looking in?'

'Of course. I often have business here.' Miss Lucas gave Shona a quick hug. 'And I'll certainly see you. Goodbye for now, though – I really must go. Goodbye, Miss MacLaren.'

'Goodbye, Miss Lucas,' said Miss Bryce's assistant, moving closer to Shona. 'Don't worry, we'll take good care of her.'

'I know you will.'

Away hurried Miss Lucas and as the front door closed on her, Miss MacLaren gave Shona a quick smile. 'Like to see your dormitory, then? We can just fit that in before everybody comes back from school. They're due any minute now.'

So Miss Bryce had said. Another hurdle to face then. And everyone knew other children could make your life difficult if they didn't like you. Will they like me? wondered Shona. Whether they did or not, there would be no getting away from them.

'Yes, I'd like to see the dormitory,' she said, putting the thought aside, and followed where Miss MacLaren led, up the staircase and along a landing, up more stairs and into a long room lined with neatly made beds.

'Here we are!' cried Miss MacLaren cheerfully. 'This is Stirling. All the dormitories are called after Scottish places, so the girls have Stirling, Kintyre and Aberdeen, and the boys have Cromarty, Inverness and Roxburgh.'

'I see.' Shona stood looking around, her heart once more descending to her boots. So many beds. How many beds? As an only child, she'd never shared her wee room with anyone, had never known what it was to be with other people until she'd moved to Mrs Hope's, and it had been strange enough then to share with her girls. But not like this. Not with so many beds.

'Where's my bed?' she asked at last.

'The fifth on the right. There are sixteen beds in all in Stirling, which is the largest dormitory for girls.'

'Sixteen? I thought there'd be more.'

'Seems like it?' Miss MacLaren smiled. 'No, eight on either wall. Quite enough, too, when you're scrambling for washbasins in the morning. But, come on, let's unpack your bag. Everyone has a locker, you see, where you can put your photographs and so on, with pegs behind and a place for a towel, plus in the centre of the room there are shared chests of drawers for your clothes. Now, we'll get you fitted up with your uniform. It would be nice, eh, if you could be ready before the others come?'

Too late. Somewhere doors were banging, footsteps thudding, someone was laughing and a woman's voice was shouting, 'Less noise, please! Less noise, or there'll be trouble!'

While Miss MacLaren was sighing and Shona was standing, uncertain where to go, the door of Stirling was thrown open and a crowd of girls in brown-check dresses and cardigans streamed in, some talking, some giggling, but all seeming cheerful enough. Just like any other lassies, really, Shona thought, even if they were orphans. But, of course, as soon as they saw her, someone new, they halted and stared.

'Who's this, then?' cried one.

'This is Shona Murray from the Dean Village who's come to join us,' Miss MacLaren said smoothly. 'Come and meet her.'

Six

'Why's she no' wearing her uniform?' a tall girl of about fourteen asked sharply, at which Miss MacLaren clicked her tongue.

'Because she hasn't got it yet, of course – you might have worked that out for yourself, Julia. Poor Shona's mother died recently and her father died in the war, which is why she's come to the Lodge. I hope you will all make her welcome.'

'Oh, we will, Miss MacLaren,' a pretty blonde girl said quickly, taking a step or two towards Shona. 'Hello – my name's Cassie Culloch. I'm very sorry about your ma, but you'll be fine here, eh? Is that no' right, girls?'

There were some murmurs of assent, though one or two girls were still studying Shona as though they'd have to make up their minds about her before they spoke, while she, in her black dress that didn't fit, was feeling as if she'd been put on show.

'Could I go and get my uniform now?' she asked desperately, and Miss MacLaren, nodding, clapped her hands and told the girls to scatter, put on their pinafores for tea and tidy themselves.

'Quickly, now! Shona, you come with me, but leave your bag by your bed first and hang up your coat. Cassie is next to you and will be very helpful, I'm sure.'

'Och, yes, Cassie's always *helpful*,' the girl called Julia said scornfully, keeping her voice down, but Cassie heard and flushed while Miss MacLaren frowned but made no comment, only hurried Shona along to her bed and then out of the dormitory.

'Don't worry about some of the older girls,' she said quietly as she unlocked the door of the uniform store. 'They like to show off, you know, because they consider themselves rather grand, being nearly ready to leave.'

'Ready to leave?' Shona was staring round at the rows of dresses and grey flannel skirts hanging up, the jackets and cardigans and piles of underwear, the socks, pinafores and nightclothes. Outside a shop, she'd never seen so many clothes, though there was a dreary sameness about them all that did not appeal. Still, she shouldn't complain – she should be grateful. After all, these clothes were new. Not many of Shona's clothes had been new in the past, for new clothes cost good money.

'Ready to leave?' she repeated, as Miss MacLaren took down a couple of dresses to check for size. 'Why? When do people leave here? No one's said.'

'At fifteen.' Miss MacLaren held a dress against Shona but shook her head and tried a smaller one. 'Fifteen, for both girls and boys. Usually, the girls go into service – that gives them a home, you see, and the boys are best going into the army, for the same reason. I think this one's your size, Shona. Like to slip off that dress?'

'Fifteen? Does that mean nobody stays on at school, then?'

'I'm afraid so. After all, many young people go to work at that age, or younger, and places are needed here. Everyone has to move on.'

'I'm no' keen on going into service,' Shona murmured, feeling very exposed in her liberty bodice and knickers until she was able to put on the checked uniform dress. She could tell at once that it fitted her very well, though Miss MacLaren was laughing as she held up a mirror.

'Oh dear, it's only your first day here and you're already deciding what you want to do when you leave! Let's cross that bridge when we come to it, eh? How do you like that dress, then?'

'It's nice, it fits.'

And she looked like everybody else, which meant folk couldn't point the finger, Shona thought, trying on a cardigan and watching Miss MacLaren sort out the rest of the things she would need.

'All these will require marking before they go to be washed, but I'll give you some marked tapes later and you can sew them on. Like sewing, Shona?'

'Aye, I'm no' bad at it.'

'That's a relief. The boys, of course, are hopeless, but we don't let them off. Now, there's no raincoat in your size at the moment, which means I'll have to order one and you'll have to wear your own coat for the time being. I'll return the black dress for you, though, if you give me the address, as you won't be needing that.'

'No,' Shona agreed, remembering Kitty and feeling a sudden rush of sadness overwhelm her, a sort of dull pain gathering strength in her chest.

'The address is number twelve, Baxter Row,' she said chokily. 'That's where Mrs Hope lives. I've got clothes of my own, but it was her daughter lent me that dress, because it was black.'

'I see,' Miss MacLaren said softly. 'Well, I'll make sure it's washed and returned. Now, when you've put your things away in the dormitory, Cassie can show you the bathroom where you can wash your hands before tea, and then she'll take you down to the dining room. You might find it a bit noisy, I'm afraid, with everyone there together.'

'I'll no' mind,' said Shona.

Oh, but she would. She knew she would, for the pain in her chest was no better and the feeling of sadness gripped her still. Folk had been kind – even Miss Bryce had been sympathetic – but it was all too different here for her ever to think of it as home. A place to stay was all it was, and a place to leave at fifteen, eh? To go into service? Not for her.

'I believe it's macaroni cheese for tea tonight,' Miss MacLaren told her as they returned to Stirling. 'Like macaroni cheese, Shona?'

'Oh, yes,' replied Shona, who didn't feel like eating anything.

Seven

Her first experience of having a meal at Edina Lodge was just as unnerving as Shona had feared. As Miss MacLaren had warned, the dining room was buzzing with noise and so large and so filled with unknown young faces that Shona had the feeling, when she entered with Cassie, of being quite swallowed up. It didn't help that half the faces belonged to boys – all, she felt, staring at her.

'Hello, here's a new wee lassie,' one cheeky-faced boy called across from the long table next to theirs. 'Where'd you come from, then, Carrots?'

And though a tall, frowning man with black hair and a black moustache immediately told him to be quiet, the damage had been done. As some of the boys sat grinning over their plates, Shona, sitting next to Cassie, couldn't help blushing, longing to show she didn't care what the boys called her, just wishing she were a thousand miles away. Or, at least, back home.

'Don't you be taking any notice of the laddies,' Cassie whispered. 'Some just like playing the fool, like Archie Smith there.'

'Hey, you two, where's your knives and forks?' asked Julia, slapping down plates of macaroni cheese in front of Shona and Cassie, and staring at them with hard, dark eyes. 'Might be my turn to dish this out, but I'm no' getting your cutlery as well!'

'Oh, my fault!' cried Cassie, starting up. 'I should've said: we collect our knives and forks when we come in. Stay there, Shona, I'll go for them.'

'And where's your pinafore?' Julia demanded fiercely of Shona. 'Did dear Cassie no' tell you we're all supposed to wear pinnies, to save our clothes at meal times? Another thing she's forgotten, eh?'

'She's been showing me round and very well an' all!' Shona cried. 'And why've we got to wear pinafores if the boys don't?'

'Aye, why?' some girls sitting nearby piped up, but the boys started laughing again at the very idea, and the man with the black moustache had to intervene to restore order.

'You the new arrival?' he asked Shona.

'Yes, I'm Shona Murray.'

'Hope you'll be happy here. I'm Mr Glegg – in charge of the boys. Just want to say,' he added, lowering his voice, 'not to worry about their teasing. They don't mean any harm.'

'That's all right,' she answered quickly, her high colour fading. 'I don't mind.'

As he moved away and Cassie breathlessly returned with their knives and forks, Shona hoped he was right about his boys. Probably he was, though she had her doubts about Julia's goodwill. What a bit of luck that she would be leaving soon!

'We should be wearing our pinafores,' she murmured to Cassie, beginning to eat her macaroni cheese, which wasn't too bad. 'So Julia says.'

'Our pinafores?' Cassie put her hand to her mouth. 'Och, no! I was that keen to show you round, I forgot all about 'em. Trust Julia Hammond to see! Just hope no one else notices.'

'Aren't we too old anyway, to be wearing pinnies?'

'It's Miss Bryce's idea – to cut down on washing.'

'So, where is Miss Bryce?'

Shona was gazing round at the once-handsome dining room, which still had its fine plaster ceiling and elegant chimney piece, above which was the portrait of an elderly man – probably Mr Hamer, who'd owned Edina Lodge and willed it to become an orphanage. Now, of course, his dining room was crammed with tables – two long ones and a smaller top table from where food was served and three women were now sitting over their meal. There was no sign of Miss Bryce or Miss MacLaren, as Shona remarked.

'They sometimes have meals in Miss Bryce's room,' Cassie told her, 'though they always have breakfast here and say prayers with us. The three ladies over there are on the staff. There's Miss Carmichael, who's the matron, and Miss Donner – she's in charge of the senior girls, and Miss Anderson, who looks after the younger ones. Miss MacLaren sees to our uniforms and pretty much everything else.'

'Am I a senior? I'm eleven.'

'So am I. No, we'll be seniors next year. For now we've got Miss Anderson.'

'So many names,' sighed Shona. 'I'll never remember 'em all.'

'You will, you will! But now I have to go and help with the rest of the tea. We all do a turn at fetching in from the kitchen, you ken, and serving.' Cassie smiled. 'It's treacle tart tonight.'

'Boys take a turn as well?'

'Oh, yes, they'll be bringing in the custard! But you'll be let off till tomorrow, I expect.' Cassie rose. 'Want to stay here then, till I bring the puds?'

'I'm no' sure I want any treacle tart.' Shona put her hand to her brow where a headache was beginning to beat. 'I feel . . . sort of weary, all of a sudden.'

'And you look awful pale,' Cassie said sympathetically. 'Why'd you no' ask if you can go to bed early?'

'Oh, no, I'd better not.' Be alone in that echoing dormitory, waiting all the time to hear the other girls come tearing in? No, Shona didn't want that. 'Do you think they'd let me go outside for a bit? I'd like to be in the fresh air.'

'Och, just you go! Nobody'll miss you if you're no' gone too long. Come on, I'll show you a side door.'

'Thanks, Cassie, you're very kind,' Shona said earnestly when Cassie had hurried her to a side door that led to the gardens. 'As long as I don't get you into any trouble.'

'No, no. If they saw us leave the dining room, they'll just think we've gone for the puds – and I'm off now. Go on, then, Shona. Have a wee walk round the gardens. They're lovely, eh?'

Oh, they are, thought Shona, moving out into the warm, scented May evening and looking at the lawns and shrubs, the trees in full leaf, the rose beds where the buds were just waiting to burst into flower. She would be sure to feel better now.

Eight

The awful thing was that she didn't. If anything, she felt worse. Not ill, but overcome with such yearning for home, for her life with her mother, for her mother herself, that she had to put her hand to her aching heart. Instinctively, she turned away from the windows of the house so that she would not be seen and, still holding her heart, moved across the drive to a bench under a tree, where she suddenly began to cry.

Oh, wasn't it the last thing she should be doing? Crying, so that when she went back into the house, everyone would see her reddened eyes and Archie Smith would probably shout something about it, and Julia would make remarks. But she couldn't stop, and didn't even have a hankie in the pocket of her new cardigan. How strange it was, to be sitting in this lovely garden and to feel so bad! Or, maybe not so strange, after all, for she had reason enough to feel as she did. Which didn't make her feel any better.

'Hallo,' a voice suddenly said, breaking into her desolation. 'This won't do, will it? There's no crying allowed, you know, in this garden.'

Through her mist of tears, she made out a young man standing before her. He was tall and thin, wearing a light jacket and flannels. He had dark brown hair, very thick and very unruly. His eyes were a vivid blue and his smile so friendly, her tears started up again and began to run down her cheeks, at which he passed her a large linen handkerchief. Coming to sit next to her on the bench, he watched her wipe her eyes but shook his head when she tried to return the handkerchief.

'No, you keep that. But tell me what's wrong, won't you? Can't be so bad to need all these tears.'

She looked away, dabbing again at her eyes. 'It's my first day here,' she whispered. 'I'm missing home.'

'Ah, I know what that's like. Went through all that at boarding school. Blubbed my head off.'

'But you weren't the only new one, eh?'

'No, but some of us minded more than others – leaving home, I mean.'

'Were your folks still at home when you went back for the holidays?'

'Only my father. My mother died when I was small.'

Shona stared intently into his pleasantly open face. 'So's my mother dead,' she said at last. 'She died of the Spanish Influenza. And my dad never came back from the war.'

The young man lowered his bright gaze. 'That's hard,' he said quietly. 'That's very hard. Listen, what's your name, then?'

'Shona Murray. I come from the Dean Village.'

'I'm Mark Lindsay. I live not far from here. My dad's the doctor for the orphanage.'

'Are you a doctor, too, then?'

'Me?' He smiled. 'No, I'm just a medical student – got back to studying after the war. Dad said I could come along to see one of his patients here, but then he told me to wait for him while he had a word with the lady in charge.'

'Miss Bryce.'

'That's the one. I've been looking round the gardens because I like gardens and this is a good one.'

He suddenly stood up and extending a hand to Shona pulled her up, too. 'Would you like me to show you something that I'm sure will cheer you up?'

She looked around, hesitating. 'I think maybe I should go back to the house. I'm no' even supposed to be out here.'

'Come on, won't take a minute.'

Giving in to the curiosity that seemed to have stemmed her tears, she followed him from the bench to another corner of the garden well away from the house. And stopped, staring in wonder at one of the strangest trees she had ever seen.

It was quite tall and beautifully shaped, its branches fanning out from a slender trunk as regularly as from a Christmas tree, but what made it different from any other trees Shona knew were the flowers that hung in rows from its branches. These were made up of pure white petals with a reddish centre, yet seemed to be not flowers, but leaves. How could that be?

She stared, she went close, she touched the flowers that were leaves, then turned to Mark Lindsay, who'd been watching her with a smile. 'I don't understand,' she told him. 'Are these leaves, or flowers?'

'You might say both. What you're seeing are something called bracts – they're leaves that bear flowers. And these remind some people of doves' wings and they call the tree the Dove Tree. But others think they look like handkerchiefs, and they call it the Handkerchief Tree. Which is what my father calls it and he has one in our garden – that's how I know about it.'

'It's beautiful,' Shona said, her large eyes still dwelling on the tree. 'I'm glad you showed it to me.'

'I wanted to. I thought it might take your mind off your troubles – at least for a little while.'

'It has. I do feel a bit better.'

'Time's what matters. With every day that passes, things will get easier, I promise you.'

She nodded, turning away. 'I must go back now. Hope no one's missed me.'

'We'll walk back together. I have to see if Dad's ready to go yet.'

'Do you think you'll come here again – to see people?'

'No. I'm in Glasgow, mostly, at the university medical school. Just happened to be here this weekend when Dad had this unusual case – rheumatic fever with complications. He's arranging for the patient to be admitted to hospital.'

'Oh.' Shona shivered, thinking maybe her troubles were not so bad compared with those of the poor orphan facing hospital. And it was true, she did feel a little better anyway, having seen that beautiful tree.

'Is it foreign?' she asked, as they neared the house. 'The Handkerchief Tree?'

'Yes, it comes from China. The first specimens were brought over in 1904. Folk probably thought they wouldn't survive, but they did. See how well the tree's done here, and ours is the same. My dad's pride and joy.' Mark grinned. 'And here's my dad now.'

An older man with a look of his son, except that his shock of hair was grey not brown, was coming out of the front door, a medical bag in his hand.

'Good timing, Mark!' he cried. 'Let's get the car.' His eyes moved to Shona, now desperately trying to remember how to get back to the side door, and he gave a kindly smile. 'But who's this?'

'This is Shona,' said Mark. 'She's feeling a wee bit homesick, and I've been showing her the Handkerchief Tree to cheer her up.'

'And I'll bet it did, eh? Grand fighter, that tree. Shona, I'll wish you all the best. You're in good hands here, I can assure you. Now, we'd better go.'

'Good luck!' Mark called, waving his hand. 'Remember what I told you.'

As the two Lindsays, father and son, made their way down the drive, Cassie came running round the side of the house to grasp Shona by the arm

'There you are! I thought you'd come back in, I've been trying to find you. Miss Anderson wants to see you – better no' keep her waiting.'

'Just tell me where to find the side door,' said Shona.

Nine

Miss Anderson, young and bright, seemed nice enough, if a little brisk in manner, but had so much to explain of life at the Lodge that Shona found her eyes glazing and longed to go to bed, even in the dormitory that had depressed her. So much to take in! So many rules and regulations! So many duties, from cleaning wash basins to serving porridge, from remembering to put your laundry out at certain times to making your bed before breakfast and not after.

As for going to school, a special effort must be made at all times to look clean and tidy with well-polished shoes, so as not to let down the Lodge's reputation. For Shona's first morning, Miss Anderson herself would escort her and see to the formalities.

'Be ready tomorrow at half past eight, sharp,' she ordered, 'and we'll walk along with the others. It isn't far, just down Murrayfield Road. A very nice school with a very good headmaster. You'll do well, I'm sure. But now, it's been a long day for you and I think it's time you were away to your bed. I'll check later to see that you have everything you need.'

'Thank you, Miss Anderson.'

'You're welcome, Shona.

'She's no' so bad, eh?' asked Cassie, on the way up to Stirling. 'Always been very helpful to me.'

'How long have you been here?' asked Shona.

'Since I was nine. My folks died when I was little and my auntie took care of me, but then she died too.' Cassie's pretty face was suddenly bleak. 'So, there was no one. I had to come here.'

'Same with me.' Shona explained her own circumstances. 'But you said it was nice here, eh? You told me I'd be all right.'

'Aye, that's right. I was so nervous at first, I thought I'd never remember all the rules and things, but it's funny, you soon get used to everything.'

Shona hesitated a moment. 'Is it true they expect all the girls from here to go into service?'

'Well, I don't know about expecting it, but most of 'em do.'

'How d'you like the idea of that?'

Cassie shrugged. 'Means you get a place to stay. Where else would you find that?'

'I don't know, but I'll find out. Going into service is no' for me.'

'You've plenty of time to think about it,' Cassie murmured with a smile. 'We're only eleven, remember?'

They had reached their beds in the quiet dormitory, where two or three other girls were sitting chatting. The bell would go at eight o'clock for under twelves, Cassie explained; those older got an extra half hour.

'So, Julia won't be here yet?' asked Shona.

'Oh, don't be worrying about Julia. We can always call Miss Anderson if she tries to cause trouble.'

'It's just that I've met her sort before, at school.'

'There's always one like her,' Cassie agreed. 'But, listen, while you were with Miss Anderson, an ambulance came to take a lassie to hospital. Queenie Turner, she's called. Used to be here in Stirling, but she's got a fever and they moved her out to be on her own.'

'Poor girl,' Shona murmured, but said nothing of having heard about the sick orphan already. Said nothing at all, in fact, of having met the orphanage doctor and his son. She unfolded her nightdress, which was of flannel and a standard pattern issued to all the girls, and rubbed her tired eyes.

'Think I'll get to my bed now, Cassie.'

'Aye, let's run and bag the washbasins before the bell goes, else we'll end up in a queue.' Cassie grinned. 'That's the trouble with living here – we're always in queues.'

Tired though she was, Shona couldn't sleep. There'd been too much happening in that long, long day, and still too much moving round her brain. Being May and in the north, the daylight had not yet completely faded from the dormitory, and she was able to see the photographs of her parents by her bed, taking some comfort in her memories. How quickly, though, she marvelled again, her life had changed! Who would have believed, only weeks ago, that she would be here now in an orphanage bed, wearing an orphanage night gown, surrounded by sleeping girls but feeling so alone?

No, she shouldn't feel that. Cassie, in the next bed, was already a friend, and no one had been difficult except Julia who, thank heavens, had gone straight to her bed when she came up to the dormitory. No doubt because Miss Anderson had been patrolling around, but at least for that night there'd been no more snappy remarks to cause upset.

And then, if Shona was counting friends, she thought she might number Mark Lindsay, even if she might never see him again, for he had made her feel better, talking to her and showing her the Handkerchief Tree, that lovely tree from China that could settle in strange places. Maybe it was like Shona herself? She hadn't settled yet, but she was beginning to realize she must. She had no choice.

Though her eyelids were growing heavier she was still wide awake, thinking of so many things, one being that the next day she would find out how she could post a letter to Mrs Hope and Kitty, for they would be worrying about her and had been so kind. She should be grateful: there had been so much kindness.

Why, she had a sign of it right under her pillow, which was Mark Lindsay's handkerchief. He'd said he didn't want it back, so maybe she should just keep it and put her own name on it? Yes, she'd do that, but now at last she was yawning and drifting, with all the beds around her receding and drifting, too . . . surely soon she would be asleep?

It occurred to her with sudden jerky clarity that she should, after all, have brought Master Bun to the Lodge as Mrs Hope had advised. She was so used to having him close she might have gone to sleep much more quickly if he'd been with her. Perhaps she'd ask Mrs Hope in her letter to bring him in when she was allowed to visit? She'd have to hide him from Julia, of course, but she could do that . . .

Suddenly, all thoughts stopped and she was asleep, just a girl amongst others in a dormitory, far away from the world until the rising bell rang in the morning, calling them to another day.

Ten

Time. Everyone said it had to pass, and pass it did: sometimes slowly, sometimes fast, but never standing still. Even so, Shona could hardly believe that within a few short weeks she would be fifteen. Fifteen! A momentous birthday, which meant that once again her life would change. How, she didn't as yet know, but sitting beneath the Handkerchief Tree on a fine Saturday afternoon in May, 1923, she knew she'd soon find out.

. Shona had been at Edina Lodge for four years. Four years during which she had moved from a child of eleven, small and anxious, to a girl of almost fifteen, confident and unafraid, her auburn plait replaced by a bob, her pretty face alert to the world around her. And she was tall. Yes, tall, for almost overnight she had seemed to grow like Jack's beanstalk and, at five foot seven, found it just as wonderful. That she, 'little' Shona, should be almost as tall as Archie Smith had been something for her and Cassie to laugh about, for Cassie was tall, too, and both were no longer teased but deeply admired by Archie and his friends. Not that Shona and Cassie were interested in them; they had other things to think about. One was the future.

If only they could persuade the authorities to help them find some sort of work that really suited, Shona sighed, something that might lead somewhere! But Miss MacLaren had never been hopeful that such a thing would be possible, and Miss Lucas, who had always been willing to listen when she visited the Lodge, was equally sure there could be no change.

Change had come to her, though, and Miss MacLaren, too, for both had forsaken their jobs to be married: Miss Lucas to a schoolmaster and Miss MacLaren to a businessman. Both were seen no more at Edina Lodge. For a while, Shona had felt quite bereft, for there could be no replacement for Miss Lucas and Miss Bryce's new assistant seemed still so different from Miss MacLaren. Nothing to be done about the changes, of course, except to put up with them.

At least, though, the gardens of Edina Lodge had not changed. They were still as beautiful as when Shona had first seen them, looking their best as in that other May, with blossom trees scenting the air, leaves bright with new green buds unfurling almost under her very eyes. And then there was the Handkerchief Tree, covered in its strange, fascinating flowers, holding Shona in thrall, as it always could, being her favourite tree. That was just the same, too.

She lay back against the bench, putting her hands to her throat for it was so sore, but Matron had said she might wait in the fresh air until someone called her to see the doctor. Not the 'old' Dr Lindsay, who was ill at present, but his son, Mark, now qualified, a part of the practice and standing in for his father as the orphanage doctor. Shona, in spite of her painful throat, was smiling to herself as she waited to be called. At present, Dr Mark was busy checking on other patients with similar symptoms, but soon would see her. And she would see him.

Still smiling, she sat up to wave to Cassie, coming through the garden towards her.

'Come to fetch me?' she croaked.

'Me? No.'

Cassie, blooming in her fifteenth year like one of the blossoming trees, sat down next to Shona and ran her hand through her damp blonde hair.

'So warm, eh? No, I just thought I'd come and see how you were before I go to dressmaking.'

'Thought you might have called me for the doctor.'

'Can't wait to see him, eh?' Cassie laughed.

'Course not! I just want something for my throat.'

'Come on, everybody wants to see young Doctor Mark, Shona. Might as well admit it.'

'As a matter of fact, I think his dad is very nice.'

'Aye, but he's no' well, is he? Lucky he's got his son to help out.' Cassie laughed. 'So all the girls have fallen for him. Trust me no' to get the tonsillitis – I won't be seeing him.' She stood up. 'I'll best away to my class.'

'No, wait a minute, Cassie. I was thinking – if you're doing well at the sewing, maybe you could do that for a living? I mean, get apprenticed to a dressmaker, have a proper job. You don't have to go into service.'

Cassie shook her head. 'I'd have nowhere to live, Shona. Apprentices get paid brass farthings – how could I pay rent anywhere? I'd be better off in service.'

'No, no, Cassie, you wouldn't! It's no life at all, and you're worth something better than that. We both are.'

'Who says so? We never stayed on at school; we never got the Leaving Certificate. That's what employers look for.'

Shona's brow darkened. Though grateful for all that the orphanage had done for her, she just wished that it could have done more and let her and those bright enough stay on at school to take the Leaving Certificate, the passport to better jobs. Too late now to change the system. She must just do what she could to find something better than domestic service for herself.

'Tell you somebody who's doing pretty well since she left here,' Cassie said, still lingering. 'Julia Hammond! She's already been promoted to parlour maid at her place in Heriot Row because she's got just the right manner for answering the door. That's what she told me, anyway, when I met her in Princes Street that day we had the outing. Would you credit it?'

'No,' Shona answered shortly, putting her hands to her throat again. 'If Julia Hammond has the right manner for anything, it'd surprise me. Surely you can do better than that, Cassie?'

'What I'd like,' Cassie said slowly, 'is to be part of a family. I'd like to try for work in a big house where there's a lot o' staff, and I could be part of it. Everybody'll know who I am and I'll have my special place.' For a moment, she held Shona's gaze. 'That's all that's wrong with the Lodge, eh? Nobody thinks you're special?'

'That's right,' Shona agreed, after a pause. 'They take care of you here, but you're no' special to them like you would be to your folks.'

But would working as a maid in a large household be any different? Shona didn't think so, though she said nothing to Cassie, who was already on her way.

'Here's someone come to fetch you, Shona!' she suddenly called back. And with an astonished look, Shona saw that it was Dr Mark himself.

Eleven

There he was, then, the idol of all the lassies, wearing a grey suit and white shirt, his medical bag in his hand, his smile as friendly as always. In the last year or so since he'd been standing in for his father, Shona had seen him around the Lodge, of course, and he'd always given her that same smile. But she'd never been ill and they had only exchanged a few words since their first meeting.

On those occasions, he'd ask her how she was, if everything was going well for her? And she'd answer, yes, it was, everything was fine. Only once had he asked if she remembered how he'd told her that as time passed things would get easier? Of course she remembered, she'd told him. And had he been right? Oh, yes, he'd been right!

No doubt about that. With the passing of each day, as he had forecast, things had certainly become easier. She had settled at the Lodge and become part of its life, though not forgetting the precious memories of the life she had left behind. She'd made friends, done well in her duties and at school, and had been allowed to have visits from Mrs Hope and Kitty, who'd brought Master Bun, as requested and, joy of joy, had been able to visit them in the village.

She'd even faced her parents' house again in Baxter Row, but had drawn the line at meeting the new tenants. At least they didn't have her parents' furniture – all her mother had been able to leave her – for that had been sold for thirty pounds, no less, which was now in her post office savings account. To her, it was a fortune, though she knew well enough that she would probably need every penny when she was alone in the outside world.

Still, she wasn't there yet. For now, she was facing Dr Mark, wondering why he'd come himself to collect her, and perhaps that showed in her face, for he said easily, 'Soon as I was told my next patient was you and you were waiting in the garden, I said I'd take a breath of air and find you myself.' Seating himself next to her on the bench, he laughed a little. 'Because I knew where you'd be, of course.'

'Under the Handkerchief Tree,' she answered, her voice sounding husky even to herself. 'It's very kind of you to come for me.'

'Not at all.' He grew serious as he put cool fingers against her throat. 'And there are no prizes for me to see that you've got the same tonsillitis I've been seeing all morning. Come on, let's get you back to Matron and I'll examine your throat.'

As they both stood up, however, he shook his head in surprise. 'My word, you've grown, Shona! You're not so far down from me as you used to be, are you? And have you done something with your hair? I thought you had a plait?'

'That was ages ago, Doctor Mark! Miss Bryce wanted all the girls to have their hair cut because she likes the new style; she thinks it's more hygienic.'

'Probably right, too, but takes a bit of getting used to, I expect.' As they began to walk back to the house, he added quickly, 'Suits you, though.'

Blushing, she made no reply, and after a moment, he asked what was coming next for her. 'Am I right in thinking that you might be leaving Edina Lodge soon?'

'At the end of the summer term.'

'Do you have any plans for what you'll do?'

'No' yet. All of us leavers have to see Miss Bryce and she'll fix us up with somewhere to go.' Shona's voice was not only hoarse now, but low as she brought out the dreaded words. 'Domestic service, that'll be. And I'm no' keen.'

'I should think not! You're a bright girl, Shona, you could find something better.'

'I want to.'

'You must tell Miss Bryce. I'm sure she'll have good advice.'

Shona's smile was wry, but they had reached the house and she said no more. There was no point, anyway, in telling Doctor Mark that she already knew what Miss Bryce's advice would be. 'Find a good situation, my dear, and you'll have work, three meals a day and a roof over your head.' What more could an orphan want?

In Matron's room, with the matron herself and her assistant nurse present, there could of course be no further opportunity for conversation with Dr Mark anyway, and Shona just had to stand patiently as he examined her throat and felt the glands of her neck. 'Not too bad,' he declared. 'There's no suppuration – that's a nasty discharge – which means you should recover fairly soon. I'm going to give you a linctus which will soothe the discomfort, and some tablets to relieve your temperature, as that's slightly up. Also, I'd like you to stay in the dormitory over the weekend. Rest is very important, isn't that right, Matron?'

'It is indeed, Doctor.'

'And either Matron or Nurse will superintend your taking the tablets, Shona, so no need to worry about that.'

'Oh, certainly not, we never let you young people take tablets yourselves.' Matron smiled at Shona. 'But let's give you one now, eh? Nurse, could you fetch a glass of water, please?'

'Well done!' Dr Mark cried when Shona bravely gulped down the tablet. 'Not easy for you, swallowing at the moment, I know.'

Her spirits now were sinking fast. It was time for her to go, time for someone else to be called in to see Dr Mark. Better go, then. Say goodbye. Surely, though, she would see him again?

'Thank you, Doctor,' she murmured. 'And thank you, Matron. When do I take the linctus?'

'Three times a day after meals,' said Matron. 'See, I have it here, it's on the label, but Nurse will bring it to you in the dormitory with your tablet. Doctor, shall we call your next patient?'

'Thank you, Matron.' Mark's vivid blue gaze, however, had moved to Shona at the door, and he suddenly strode across to join her.

'Just in case I don't see you again, Shona, I want to wish you the best of luck for the future. Stick to your guns, aim for what you want and you'll do well.'

'Goodbye, Doctor Mark,' she managed to say calmly as they shook hands. 'I hope your dad will be better soon.'

'Nice of you to think of him, but don't worry, I'll see that he is.'

'Shona, Nurse will be along soon to see you in your dormitory,' Matron called when Mark had left the door. 'And if Wilfred Hunter's out there, please tell him to come in now.'

'You can go in now,' Shona obediently told the scared-looking boy waiting in the corridor, and smiled as he scuttled in. The last person he wanted to see was the doctor. How unlike herself!

In the dormitory, she felt overcome by sudden weakness, as though her legs were made of wool, and sank down on her bed, lying back against her pillow. There were three other throat patients already in bed, two of whom appeared to be sleeping, while the third, another fourteen-year-old, named Mavis Maxwell, was reading *Jane Eyre*.

'Hey, Shona,' she called hoarsely, 'you'll get wrong, lying on your bed with your shoes on!'

'So who's going to tell anyone?'

'I'm just saying.'

'Well, don't say. Just read your book.'

'Think I'll leave it for now. I liked it when Jane was in that Lowood school and I kept thinking, oh, glad that's no' me, but now she's got mixed up with this awful Mr Rochester, I'm no' interested. I mean, what does she see in him?'

Not feeling up to a discussion, Shona closed her eyes but then the thought came – why were folk attracted to other folk? Why were all the girls attracted to Dr Mark? Because he was a nice-looking young man and they didn't see many of them, but if there were other nice-looking young men around, perhaps Dr Mark's charm would fade? Not for her. Right from that first day by the Handkerchief Tree, she'd felt a special bond with him, felt that he himself was special to her, and that she might even be special to him.

But now, as her head ached and her throat throbbed, she knew she must see the situation clearly. 'If I don't see you again', had been the words that had shown her why, for it was obvious enough that her path and Mark's were never likely to cross in the future.

There would be no point at all in thinking that she could ever be special to a man she would never meet, a man older than her who would have all kinds of interests and friends she could never share. To keep thinking about him was a piece of nonsense and could only lead nowhere, so take a stand, she told herself, stop thinking about him and think about what you want to do. Yes, about her future. That was what mattered.

Opening her eyes, staring at the whitewashed ceiling, Shona drew a long, heartfelt sigh. If only it were not so hard! To look into the future and to know, whether it contained a job or not, that it would not include Mark Lindsay.

'Here we are!' cried a voice at her bedside, and she opened her eyes to see Matron's assistant, Nurse Lawson, bearing a bottle of something dark, a spoon and a small white pill box. 'Now I've got all you need here, Shona. Sit up, then, you're the last to have it; the others have all had theirs.'

'I must have been asleep,' Shona said, slowly sitting up.

'And still dressed and in your shoes!' Nurse Lawson clicked her tongue. 'Shona, what were you thinking about?'

Better not say, thought Shona.

Twelve

As Dr Mark had prophesied, Shona did feel better after the weekend's rest and within a few days had quite recovered her health, if not her spirits. Though she concealed this pretty well, Cassie still asked her if she was feeling 'a wee bit low?' Miss Bryce had announced that she would soon be interviewing all leavers about their prospects. Maybe Shona was worrying about what she'd say?

'No, why should I be worrying?' Shona retorted.

'Well, I bet you're going to get into an argument with her, about going into service, eh?' Cassie gave a small shrug. 'If you do, she's sure to win, 'cos you've nothing else in mind, have you?'

'I'm going to state my views,' Shona said loftily. 'I've got the right to do that.'

'Oh, dear, sounds like trouble.'

'There'll be no trouble, Cassie. I'll be as polite as can be.'

'At least your birthday's after mine, so she'll see me before you. I'll tell you how I get on.'

'Cassie, I know how you'll get on, unless you do what I'm going to do and tell her you want something different from service.'

'No, thanks!' cried Cassie. 'It wouldn't be true, anyway. I'll be happy if she finds me a nice place where I can feel at home.'

Sighing, Shona said no more, but was glad to find that the thought of making her point with Miss Bryce had, oddly enough, cheered her up. Maybe it was true, what folk said: that if something occupied your mind, it stopped you brooding on other things. Who would have thought that Miss Bryce could exclude Mark Lindsay from her mind, then? The truth was that her birthday was coming ever closer and with it the reality of leaving Edina Lodge. The future that she'd thought so much about would actually be upon her, and she'd have to have something worked out. Much would depend, of course, on what Miss Bryce said, and whether she would come up with any suggestions.

'Roll on our interviews,' she said to Cassie firmly. 'Let's know what we're doing, eh?'

'Can't wait,' Cassie answered fervently.

In late May Miss Bryce began her interviews, Cassie being one of the first to be called. As soon as Shona saw her later that day, when they were in the kitchen at teatime, ready to carry in sausages and mash, she knew at once that Cassie was happy.

'Oh, Shona,' she whispered, her blue eyes shining, 'it's so lovely! Miss Bryce has a list of places willing to take us orphans as maids, and when I told her I wanted to work with a big staff and get to know folk, she picked out just the place!'

'That right?' asked Shona, wrapping a cloth round a hot dish of mashed potato. 'So where is this wonderful place?'

'The Hermitage. That's past Morningside, you ken, where there's the Hermitage Burn, and then you get to the Braid Hills golf course. Miss Bryce showed me on the map.'

'Very grand, then. You got the sausages?'

'Aye, it's grand, all right, the people are very well to do.' Cassie, her face flushed from the heat of the kitchen and her own excitement, was following Shona into the dining room bearing a huge platter of sausages, one of several to be placed on the top table, now used for self-service – Miss Bryce's latest idea – where a queue was already forming.

'Here they come!' cried Archie Smith, pushing people out of the way so that the girls could set down their burdens. 'Make way, let the lassies get through!'

'No need to push folk like that!' Mr Glegg shouted at him, but Archie, tall, cocky and looking ready to leave for work already, only grinned.

'Sorry, sir!' he cried. 'Only trying to help, but the lassies have to get back for more sausages, you see.'

'I'm bringing 'em in now!' Mavis Maxwell called, carrying in another great platter. 'Honestly, the fuss you laddies make about sausages—!'

'Our favourite!' one of the boys said. 'Should have 'em every day!'

It was some time before Cassie and Shona could sit down for their own meal and Cassie was able to say more about her new place.

'Seemingly, Shona, it's a wealthy businessman who's the owner of this house in Hermitage Circle, and then there's his wife and three children, all at school. There's a butler and two footmen, a cook and kitchen staff, two parlour maids and three house maids – at least, there should be three, but one's left, and that's the job that's going.' Cassie, almost too excited to get her words out, paused to eat some mashed potato. 'I'll be an under house maid, but they give you training, you see, and then you can move up.'

'And this job's yours for definite, is it?' asked Shona.

'Well, they want to see me, but Miss Bryce says they're willing to take me on her recommendation. They feel it's the right thing to do, you ken, to help orphans get jobs.'

Shona was silent for a moment. 'Should be all right,' she said at last. 'If it's what you want. Big house, plenty of people to work with and get to know.'

'And who'll get to know me! I'll have a home and all my meals, two print dresses a year and two black with apron and cap, and wages, of course.'

'Did Miss Bryce say how much?'

'No' bad,' Cassie answered carefully. 'Twenty-six pounds a year. The going rate – maybe a bit more.'

'Lucky you've got all found, as they say, or you wouldn't have much to spend.'

'You don't need much. Oh, Shona, I think you should consider it – I mean, being in service. You'd be a parlour maid in no time!'

Not if I know anything about it, thought Shona, rising.

'The others'll be collecting these plates any minute – we'd better go and get the puddings, Cassie.'

'Will you no' think about it, then?'

'I haven't been told to see Miss Bryce yet.'

'Your birthday's next month. I reckon you'll be called pretty soon. You'll have to think out what you're going to say.'

'Leave that to me,' Shona answered, wondering just when she would be called.

She didn't have long to wait. Two days later she was asked to report to the superintendent's office when she came home from school. Hastily combing her hair and straightening her dress, she caught Cassie's arm.

'Wish me luck,' she whispered.

'Och, you'll no' need it. You'll be fine.'

Shaking her head, Shona made her way to Miss Bryce's office and tapped on the door.

'Come in!' came the familiar, firm voice. And Shona went in.

Thirteen

There were the clear grey eyes fixed on her again, giving the impression, as they always did, that they could see right into her mind to read her thoughts. Everyone said that about Miss Bryce; it was never any use trying to hide things from her. But this time, just for once, she might be in for a surprise, Shona decided, for she would never expect one of her girls to refuse to go into service.

'Come and sit down, Shona,' Miss Bryce told her now, indicating the chair in front of her desk. 'You'll know why I want to see you, of course. Just a chat about your future.'

'Yes, Miss Bryce, I know.'

'I always like to talk to those leaving us to make sure they make the right choices. It's very important that people are happy.'

Right choices? There were choices, then? Her eyes widening, Shona stared at Miss Bryce who, seeing her look, smiled a little.

'Well, when I say choices, it comes down to choosing the most suitable places for those going into service – usually girls, but it can be boys, although they have the alternative of early entry into the army or navy. The council can't afford to keep anyone longer than fifteen and it's quite usual to start work at that age or, in fact, fourteen, so the extra year is a bonus.'

'Except that some folk stay on at school and take the Leaving Certificate.'

Miss Bryce sighed. 'You already know why that's not possible here; I have explained it to you before. Everyone must leave at the end of the school term in which they reach fifteen. You've always understood that, haven't you?'

'Yes, Miss Bryce.'

'Though people of fifteen are old enough to work, they still need support, which is provided in domestic service where all is found – food, clothing, shelter, and regular wages. The same, of course, goes for boys entering the services.' Miss Bryce cleared her throat. 'Now, I have here a list of vacancies in various types of household which I'd like to go through with you. Perhaps you'd like to read it first for yourself?'

'I don't think so, Miss Bryce.'

Shona, colouring to her brow, couldn't believe that she had just said those words. Had it been her voice? Oh, Lordie, yes, it had been her voice, all right. Just look at Miss Bryce, staring.

'I beg your pardon?' Miss Bryce's grey eyes fixed on Shona were as cold as a winter sky. 'I beg your pardon,' she repeated, 'what did you just say?'

'I said I didn't think I should look at the list, as I don't want to go into service.'

It was Miss Bryce's turn to flush, with two red spots beginning to glow on her cheekbones. 'I really can't believe you are talking so foolishly, Shona. You don't want to go into service? Haven't I just explained the advantages?'

'Yes, Miss Bryce, but I'd rather do something else. Train for something, maybe.'

'And how do you propose to keep yourself while you do that?

Agreed, it might be more rewarding, but it's just not practicable. You have no family here, no one to stay with. You never hear from your aunt, do you?'

'I've had one or two letters,' Shona answered after a pause. 'She said she was sorry she couldn't see me but she'd keep in touch.'

'And hasn't? So, how do you think you might manage, then? I understand your mother's friend can't take you into her own home. Just where would you go?'

'I've thought about it and I think I can get lodgings in the Dean. One or two people let rooms and don't charge much. If I could find a job, I could afford to pay something. And I've got the money from my ma's furniture.'

'Oh, Shona, Shona! That money is to be saved, not frittered away!' Miss Bryce was shaking her head, as though she was suddenly out of her depth, as though all her experience had never taught her how to deal with anyone like Shona. 'Why can't you see that domestic service would solve all your problems?' she asked. 'No one else has complained about it.'

Shona hesitated. 'I think, if I went into service, I'd – I'd no' be me any more.'

There was a silence in the room except for a clock ticking, and for some time neither Miss Bryce nor Shona spoke.

'The fact is,' Miss Bryce said at last, 'that I and the council are responsible for you, Shona. You are what's called a minor and we can't just let you go from here into the city, where who knows what might happen to you.'

'I'll be all right, Miss Bryce. I'll be near Mrs Hope, I'll be near folk I know. There'd be no need to worry!'

'Hmm, I wonder.' Miss Bryce sat, turning a pencil in her fingers and considering. 'Well, I'll tell you what I'll do. If Mrs Hope could put you up temporarily and be sure to find you respectable lodgings, I'm prepared to let you go into her care. As to finding a job, I'd expect to be informed if you are successful. That is the best I can offer, and you must do as I suggest.'

'Oh, I will, Miss Bryce, I will!' Shona cried, her face radiant. Never had she imagined Miss Bryce could be so helpful, so understanding, even, and still could scarcely believe it. 'Thank you. Thank you very much.'

Miss Bryce rose from her desk, her expression doubtful. 'Try not to be too starry-eyed about this,' she warned. 'Everything depends on your mother's friend, Mrs Hope. Are you sure she'll be able to take you in temporarily?'

'Oh, yes, she did before and she'll want to, I know she will. And she'll help me look for a job. I mean, she gets the paper with adverts and all.' Shona's heart was singing as she began to take in that things might really be changing for her, that she might really be going to get her way. 'It's my Saturday to see her this week; I can explain everything then.'

'Very well, but I'll also be writing to her, making sure she understands the situation.' At the door, Miss Bryce's face suddenly relaxed into a faint smile. 'My goodness, Shona, you're full of surprises, aren't you? But you're a bright girl and I'd like to see you succeed. I'll wish you the best of luck for your future.'

It was Miss Bryce herself who was full of surprises, Shona thought, as she managed to get out another thank you and left the office. Who'd have thought she would have been so helpful? Just wait till Cassie heard!

Hurrying along to find Cassie, she was waylaid by Archie Smith, who put a beefy hand on her arm and asked how she'd got on. 'Heard you were seeing Miss B today. What she find for you, then? Kitchen maid's job?'

'No fear!' Shona retorted. 'To tell you the truth, she was very helpful. I'm no' sure yet what I'm going to do, but it won't be domestic service, that's for sure.'

'Same for me.' Archie gave a wide grin. 'Know what she gave me? Choice o' two jobs as boot boy: one in Perthshire, one in Aberdour. Boot boy! Me? If you work hard and keep out o' trouble, you might move up to assistant footman if you're lucky. I told Miss B no, thanks, no damned boot boy job for me.'

'Bet you didn't say that exactly,' Shona said, laughing. 'You know what she's like about swearing.'

'Call what I said swearing? Wait till I get going in the navy!'

'You're joining the navy?'

'Sure – early entry.' Archie put his face close to Shona's. 'Think you might go out with me when I'm in my bellbottoms? All the nice girls love a sailor, you know!'

'Go on!' she said, pushing him away and laughing again. 'I'm going to find Cassie. It's nearly tea time.'

'Don't need to tell me,' he called after her as she sped away. 'I'm starving!'

But he was already far from her mind, which was occupied only with the changes that would be coming her way.

Fourteen

'I know the very place for you to get a room!' cried Mrs Hope, her face alight with excitement when Shona had finished talking the following Saturday afternoon.

They'd had an early cup of tea, just the two of them, as Jock was at the mill, Kitty at the bakery shop where she now worked, Biddy and Pat out with friends and Jamie and Dair playing football in the street.

'And you can tell Miss Bryce, who's going to write to me, that you can stay with me till we get things fixed up,' Addie Hope went on, refilling their teacups. 'Which'll no' take long because Mrs Gow is just up the street here, eh?'

'Mrs Gow who lives at the top, in the Row?' Shona was immediately interested. 'I remember her. Didn't I hear that Trissie Gow got married and moved away?'

'Aye, Joan's been on her own since then. George Gow died a while back, so it was a blow when Trissie wed an Aberdeen man, but there you are, lassies have to make their own lives, eh?' Mrs Hope sighed. 'I'll bet my girls don't stay long, either. Kitty's already got an admirer – one o' the bakers where she works.'

'I know, she told me,' Shona said with a smile. 'More than once.'

'Well, she's nearly sixteen, just the age to be noticing the boys. Listen, what I want to tell you is that Joan Gow's very keen to let Trissie's room, but scared in case she gets the wrong person. That's why she's never advertised – says you never know who'll you'll get. But you'd be perfect, Shona, eh?'

'Would I?'

''Course you would! Joan knew your ma, knows all about you. I say, if we go up and see her now, she'd take you on the spot!'

'Won't she be at work, though?'

'She's at the same bakery as Kitty, but doesn't work Saturdays.' Addie leaped to her feet. 'Come on, let's go.'

The way things went with Mrs Gow was Shona's second piece

of luck, the first being Miss Bryce's surprising cooperation. Would there be a third? Shona wondered, after it was arranged she should move into Trissie Gow's room as soon as she left Edina Lodge. Would it just so happen that the ideal job would fall into her lap? Probably not. Too unlikely. No harm in hoping, though.

Certainly, it looked as though she'd found a grand place to live, thanks to Mrs Hope, for Mrs Gow's house was neat as a pin and comfortable with it, and she herself was something of the same. Fair and on the large side, she had mild blue eyes and an easy manner, especially when she greeted Shona, exclaiming at her height, how she'd grown up and how it was so lovely to see her, before finally folding her into a warm embrace.

'I canna believe it's four years since this lassie went to the orphanage!' she cried to Addie. 'And now she's seeking a room and a job. Have you thought of anything, pet? There's always the bakery business here, or else a few women's jobs at the mills. But maybe you want something different, eh?'

'I've thought about it, Mrs Gow, and it may sound a wee bit odd, but I'm wondering if I could find some work to do with plants.'

'Plants?' The two older women exchanged dubious glances.

'You mean gardening?' asked Addie. 'Don't see many women gardeners, Shona.'

'Don't see any,' said Mrs Gow. 'Except ladies, maybe, gardening for a hobby. But then they have a man to do the heavy stuff, eh?'

'Well, it was just an idea,' Shona admitted. 'Because I love the gardens at the Lodge, and I've always liked flowers, too.'

'Fancy the orphanage having a garden!'

Mrs Gow at that point had waved a hand to her little staircase. 'But come and see the room, then, though you'll ken fine what it's like anyway, seeing as it's the same as all the second bedrooms in the Row.'

The same, yet not the same, thought Shona, looking round the delightful room that had been Trissie's. It was far removed in comfort from her own plain little room at Edina Lodge, or Addie's and Jock's, that was stuffed with everything they couldn't fit into the double room the girls had been given. It was clear that Mrs Gow was a true homemaker, with a talent for making pretty curtains and bedspreads, and the late Mr Gow had been something of an amateur carpenter, for he had made the chest of drawers and wardrobe and painted them, too.

'What do you think, then?' Mrs Gow had asked, and of course Shona and Addie had been quick to praise, as well as truthful.

'I love it,' Shona had declared, 'and I'd love to rent it, if you're willing, Mrs Gow. The only thing is, I'm no' sure how much I can pay until I find a job. I've a bit my mother left me and I can always use that to begin with.'

'No need for that, Shona. I'll no' be charging a fortune, and we can leave fixing a price till you get yourself a wage. I'll make you a nice bit o' breakfast and a good tea so you'll have no worries, eh?'

Fifteen

No worries. So it seemed, and Shona still couldn't believe how smoothly her plans were working out. Until, back at Mrs Hope's, when all the family had returned, the first scan of the advertisements in the evening paper showed nothing at all of interest. Plenty of jobs going for domestic servants, of course. Plenty for shop assistants, too, but as the Hopes took turns at calling out what was on offer, Shona only sighed and shook her head.

'Greengrocer's assistant!' cried Dair, looking at her with round brown eyes so like his mother's and Kitty's. 'Any good?'

Weighing carrots and potatoes, sorting out cauliflowers? Oh, no!

'Draper's in Lothian Road,' said Biddy, twelve years old and with features like those of her fair-haired father, not yet back from the mill. 'That'd no' be bad, eh? Working with materials?'

Measuring and cutting, selling curtaining and cushions? Shona looked mournful. She'd die of boredom doing that.

Even when Kitty found her a dress shop position, to 'suit young lady interested in fashion', she had to turn the suggestion down.

'No' exactly a young lady, am I? And I know nothing at all about fashion. They'd never want someone from an orphanage, anyway.'

There was a silence as they considered this, and it was only Mrs Hope, setting the table for tea, who called across that being an orphanage girl should make no difference at all. Shona would get a good reference from Miss Bryce and as soon as folk saw her, they'd know she'd do well.

'Got to get them to see me, though,' Shona said gloomily. 'And so far I've no' even seen a job I'd like. I want to learn something – maybe a craft, you know – for a career.'

A career? The Hopes fixed her with wondering eyes. They didn't know anyone who had what could be called a career.

'What was all that about wanting to work with plants?' Mrs Hope asked as she waved her family over to the table, seeing her Jock come through the door. 'That wouldn't be a career, would it?'

'Oh, I wasn't serious,' Shona murmured, taking her place next to Kitty. 'I know I couldn't have that sort of job.'

'Hello, Shona!' Jock Hope cried cheerfully as he washed his hands at the sink. 'Nearly ready to leave Edina Lodge, eh?'

'Looking for a job,' his wife told him, as Shona smiled and nodded. 'Nothing in the paper today but there'll be other days. It's never easy to find just the right thing.'

'If you don't want to be a housemaid,' said Kitty. 'And who does? How about a bakery, Shona? I love selling bread and cakes.'

'Well, there might be something for another lassie where I am,' said Jock, eyeing his wife's meat pie. 'Doing packaging and that sort o' thing. I could put in a word if you're interested.'

'Oh, Dad, Shona'd never want mill work!' Kitty cried. 'She's looking for something different from that.'

'That right? Well, it's probably no good, then, but I did see a notice on a shop in George Street. You remember, Addie, when we went up to town on my half day?'

'What notice?' asked Addie, busy organizing food on to her family's plates. 'What shop was it? That ironmongers?'

'No,' Jock answered, as he slowly cut into his portion of pie. 'It was a flower shop.'

A flower shop? As a great bell began ringing inside her head, Shona put down her knife and fork.

'No' Maybel's?' she asked tremulously. 'Maybel's Flowers?'

'That's it. That's the one. Big place, window full o' plants.'

'Plants?' cried Addie. 'Why, there you are, Shona! That's just what you were wanting – a place o' flowers and plants. Now, why did I no' see that notice?'

'You were too busy looking in the shoe shop next door,' Jock said with a laugh. 'But it was there, all right, on the window. "Junior Assistant Required. Apply Within." That's what it said.'

Shona was sitting very still, a look in her eyes that seemed to have removed her far from Addie's table and all those watching her.

'I remember seeing that shop with Ma,' she said in a whisper. 'It was one day when we'd gone up to the summer sales – over the bridges, no' in George Street, they'd have been too dear. We came back through the West End and Ma says, "let's have a look at the shops". And Maybel's was where we looked.' Shona gave a great sigh, and appeared suddenly to come back to her surroundings. 'Oh, you should have seen their flowers!' she went on. 'So beautiful! And so scented! I peeped into the shop and it was all cool and sort of shady inside, and there was a lady doing watering and she said, "Can I help you, dear?" But Ma came in and grabbed my arm and hurried me out.' Shona hesitated for a moment. 'I've never forgotten Maybel's,' she finished slowly, 'but I never thought there'd be a job there.'

'Sounds ideal!' Addie exclaimed. 'You'd best apply as soon as you can.'

'But have your pie first,' said Dair kindly.

'Of course she canna go now!' cried Kitty. 'You've to be back by six, eh, Shona? It's nearly that now.'

'I'm sorry, Mrs Hope, I don't feel very hungry,' said Shona, looking down at her filled plate. 'I'm just too excited. Supposing the job's already gone, though? Maybe I could just run up to George Street—'

'No, no, the shop'll have already closed and, like Kitty says, you've to be back by six.' Addie's voice was firm as she leaned across and tapped Shona's plate. 'You settle down, eat up, go back to the Lodge and ask Miss Bryce to help you apply to Maybel's. The job won't have gone yet; we only saw the notice on Thursday, so you'll be in with a chance.'

As Shona took a deep breath and began to eat, Addie smiled and sat back.

'Never turn down a meal if there is one,' she pronounced. 'You never know when you'll get another, eh?'

'Is there any more pie, then?' asked Dair and Jamie together, at which there were groans from the rest of the family, but their mother did find second helpings, causing Jock to ask was she a magician, then? Sure, she was just like that laddie in the fairy story who had a pocket that never emptied, eh?

'Well, the pie dish is empty now,' Addie said, laughing, and even Shona, lost in her thoughts as she was, joined in.

Sixteen

All the way home, however, she was consumed by anxiety that she would not be able to find Miss Bryce, or that even if she did find her and was helped to apply for the job, she would be too late and it would have already gone. What she would do then, she didn't know, for she was strangely certain in her mind that this was the job for her, that it was what she'd been looking for without knowing it.

Was it silly, she wondered, to be so keen on something she really knew nothing about? She'd talked of working with plants but she had no idea what it would be like to work in a flower shop, or train as a florist. All she knew was that she didn't want to miss the chance of it, and hurrying to Miss Bryce's office when she got back to the Lodge Shona hoped that luck would be with her and that Miss Bryce would be in and agree to help her. 'Apply within', Maybel's notice had said. Oh, if only she could have already done that!

But only Miss Ruddick, the dark-haired, pleasant-faced assistant to Miss Bryce, answered her knock on the office door. Seemed Miss Bryce was not there – it was her evening off and she'd already left for a concert at the Usher Hall.

'Oh,' said Shona, ready to turn away, her shoulders drooping, when Miss Ruddick surprised her by giving her a sympathetic smile.

'It's Shona Murray, isn't it? Perhaps I can help?'

'I don't think so – thanks all the same. I was going to ask Miss Bryce to help me apply for a job.'

'Oh? What sort of job is that, then?'

'It's in a flower shop in George Street. Maybel's, it's called. "Maybel's Flowers". Someone told me there was a notice in the window asking for a junior assistant.'

'Maybel's? That's a lovely shop, isn't it?' Miss Ruddick opened the office door more widely. 'If you'd like to come in, Shona, I could perhaps help you to write something out and show it to Miss Bryce tomorrow? Would that be any good?'

'Oh, yes! Yes, it would! Miss Ruddick, that would be grand!'

Shoulders up, her face all smiles, Shona took a seat while

Miss Ruddick provided paper and pencil and told her she should write out what she wanted to say first, then make a fair copy in pen and ink.

It sounded so easy, but faced with the blank sheet of paper Shona's eyes were huge with anxiety, and turning the pencil over and over seemed to bring no relief.

'Come on,' Miss Ruddick said patiently. 'What do you think should go at the top? Wouldn't it be "Application for the post of Junior Assistant at Maybel's Flowers"?'

'Oh, yes.' Shona, blushing, began to write. 'And then my name, and age?'

'And address, Edina Lodge.'

Shona hesitated. 'Think they'll mind I'm from an orphanage?'

'No, definitely not. Miss Bryce will make it clear when she gets in touch with them that you're a very bright, hard-working girl. Having been brought up in an orphanage should not matter at all. What you have to do is convince the employers that you're really keen to work with flowers.' Miss Ruddick smiled a little. 'You are, aren't you? Somehow, I can tell.'

'I'm keen,' Shona agreed, and as her pencil seemed to take on new fluency, she began to write of how she'd always liked plants and trees when she'd lived in the Dean Village, and of how she'd then learned to love flowers in the gardens of Edina Lodge. Though she had no experience of working in a florist's, she was very willing to learn and hoped very much that she would be considered for the post with Maybel's.

'There!' she cried, laying down her pencil. 'Think it's all right, Miss Ruddick?'

'I do, it's very good. Perhaps you might add that references will be provided? From Miss Bryce, of course, and maybe one of your teachers?'

'Oh, yes, the headmaster gives references if we need them.'

Some of her euphoria fading, Shona gazed at Miss Ruddick. 'I'm very grateful for your help,' she said quietly. 'But it might all be too late, eh? There might be no job to apply for.'

'We must look on the bright side,' Miss Ruddick answered briskly. 'I don't think myself that they will have appointed anybody yet. But now I'll get you pen and ink and another sheet of paper – I'm afraid you must write your application out all over again.'

The deed was done, the application carefully written in Shona's best handwriting and left for Miss Bryce to study tomorrow and then do what she thought best.

'Probably she'll telephone the shop and check that there is still a vacancy,' Miss Ruddick told Shona at the door of the office. 'If there is, she'll say something to recommend you and send off your application.'

'You think she'll do that?'

'I'm sure she will. It's part of her job to see that leavers are settled into work.' Miss Ruddick gave Shona's shoulder an encouraging pat. 'Off you go now – you must have missed most of the recreation period already.'

'How shall I know if Miss Bryce does what you say?'

'She'll tell you, of course. Next thing you know, you might be getting an interview.'

An interview? Shona, searching for Cassie, was delighted at the idea, but then was firm with herself. No thinking about that until it happened. And even if it did, an interview was just that, not a job offer.

'You'll get an interview,' Cassie said with the cheerfulness of one whose job had already been secured. 'Why shouldn't you?'

'Because there won't just be me wanting to work for Maybel's.'

'Still, you had Miss Ruddick to help you apply. She'd be good. Awfully bright, they say.'

'She's much nicer than I thought, Cassie. And I was just thinking, when I looked at her, that she's got a very kind face.'

'Must've been very helpful, for you to say that,' Cassie laughed. 'When she first came all you wanted was Miss MacLaren back again!'

'She was helpful,' Shona agreed seriously. 'And I was grateful. Now I've got to wait to see if Miss Bryce is helpful, too.'

And she was. As Miss Ruddick had said she might, Miss Bryce rang the shop, discovered that the job was not yet taken, recommended Shona and posted off her application. Three days later, a letter arrived from Maybel's Flowers, signed by Mrs May, the proprietor, inviting Shona to come for interview on the following Tuesday at 2 p.m.

'Told you!' cried Cassie.

Seventeen

All young persons leaving Edina Lodge to begin work were able to choose some clothes from the stores to replace their orphanage uniforms. Suits, or sports jackets and trousers for the boys; costumes in tweed or serge for the girls. Nothing exciting, the girls would complain, nothing fashionable! Still, with no families to provide anything else, they couldn't grumble, and most of them were going into service just as the boys were going into the army or navy, and would find themselves in other kinds of uniforms anyway.

Shona's costume, of a rather loose jacket and a longer skirt than she would have liked, was made in dark blue tweed. With it she wore a white blouse with a neat collar and pearl buttons, and a dark blue beret, and on the day of her interview thought she didn't look too bad. Quite smart, in fact, though rather pale; she was so very nervous.

'I know it's no use telling you not to worry,' said Miss Ruddick, accompanying her to Maybel's as the time approached two o'clock, 'but just try to relax and do your best. I've every confidence you will.'

'Thing is, there'll be plenty of others in for this job,' Shona pointed out. 'Maybe more suited than me.'

'You will be as good as anyone, I'm sure.'

'But I've got to be better.'

'Better, then.' Miss Ruddick placed an encouraging hand on Shona's arm. 'Remember that. But here we are – here's the shop. And we're just ten minutes early. Perfect.'

They halted at the door to Maybel's, open on that fine summer afternoon, though a striped awning shielded the windows from the sun. Miss Ruddick dropped her hand. 'I'll just take you in and introduce you before I leave you, Shona. Then I'll look round a bit and come back later.'

Strung up as though on wires, Shona could only nod, before following Miss Ruddick into the interior of the flower shop. Where, immediately, strangely, she felt calmed. It was all just as she remembered. Cool, shady, filled with plants and massed containers of flowers, the air moist and scented like no other air in George Street – how it took her back! Back over the years to the time when she'd left her mother and sneaked a look at the lovely shop and been so charmed. Of course, she'd had no right then to be there, whereas now she was expected. But only for an interview, which might or might not go well. Breathing fast, she stood very still, only her eyes moving everywhere.

As soon as she spotted Shona and Miss Ruddick, a young woman with light brown hair wearing a green blouse and skirt stepped forward to ask if she could help, while at the back of the shop a blonde girl, also wearing green, was looking only at Shona. Wondering if she was a candidate, no doubt. But where were all the other people hoping for the job?

Miss Ruddick was introducing herself, saying she was from Edina Lodge, then presenting Shona. 'This is Shona Murray; she's come for the interview at two o'clock.'

'Oh, yes, with Mrs May.' The brown-haired girl gave Shona a smile. Her face was square and freckled, her eyes brown and friendly. 'Would you like to come this way? Mrs May is in her office.'

'I'll leave you, then,' Miss Ruddick whispered. 'Good luck.'

Nodding briefly and holding herself very straight, Shona followed her guide through the front shop, passing the girl at the back, to enter a large office where a slender woman rose from behind a desk.

'Miss Murray for interview, Mrs May,' said the young woman, at which Shona's eyes widened. 'Miss Murray'? She'd never been called 'Miss Murray' in her life before.

'Thank you, Brigid.'

As Brigid withdrew, Mrs May sat down and motioned to Shona to take a chair opposite her desk. 'So, you're from Edina Lodge, Miss Murray?'

Her smile was pleasant, though not particularly warm, Shona thought. Mrs May's face was too narrow, her mouth too small. Her eyes, like her hair, were almost dark enough to be called black, and her brows, too, were black, though so thin they might have been only pencilled lines. Perhaps they were, for it was obvious that Mrs May, though not young, liked to use make-up, and was one of the few women Shona had met who wore not only bright lipstick but rouge as well.

Still, she was very smart in a grey dress and jacket. So smart, indeed, that Shona had to fight hard not to lose confidence, for she couldn't see herself appealing at all to anyone like Mrs May. This was not the time to give up, though. Remembering the lovely shop she'd just been through, she found the courage again to be calm.

'Yes, I'm from the orphanage,' she replied. 'They took me in there after my mother died four years ago. My father was killed in the war.'

'I'm so sorry.' Mrs May's voice had softened; so had her dark gaze. 'But I think the orphanage has done well for you. My husband and I, who run Maybel's, were quite impressed by your application.'

Good news? Good start, anyway. Not sure what to say, Shona gave a polite smile, as Mrs May went on: 'Although this post is just for a junior assistant, Miss Murray, it's very important that we get the right person. The successful candidate will be expected to want to train in all aspects of floristry, and Maybel's has a first-class reputation.'

'Oh, I know,' Shona said earnestly.

Mrs May raised her thin eyebrows and smiled. 'It's good that you know something about us. I'd like to tell you more. My husband and I founded the business some years ago. We now employ three assistants and a delivery man with a van. We do flowers for weddings, banquets, private parties, all sorts of occasions, as well as serving the public, who might come in to buy a little bouquet. So – as you can see – anyone who joins us will have to work hard, but will also have a wonderful profession.' Leaning forward, Mrs May fixed Shona with a long, searching gaze. 'Tell me, is that what you really want?'

'Yes,' Shona replied. 'It's just what I want.'

'There isn't time to go into all the details of what we do, but you'll realize, of course, that we have to know about what we sell. Everything about flowers and plants, how they grow, when they're ready, how to care for them, what goes with what, how to put together displays and bouquets, making everything look special. And that's still what you'd like to do?'

'Just what I want to do.'

'Well, then, let's have another look at your application.'

As Shona lowered her eyes to her clasped hands, Mrs May read quickly through her so carefully written letter. 'You say here that you learned to love the trees and plants of the Dean Valley, but also the flowers in the gardens of Edina Lodge – which was a well-known Edinburgh garden at one time, I believe. Can you tell me a little more about the flowers? Which ones did you like best, for instance?'

Flowers . . . Oh, Lordy, which ones? Which had she liked best?

Suddenly, Shona had a moment of panic. Everything seemed to be going out of her head, yet she knew she must remember, must say something; otherwise it would seem she'd been making everything up in her letter, just to get the job. 'Roses,' she gasped. 'The roses are beautiful.'

'Roses. Yes. Anything else?'

What else? Why couldn't she think? She knew the flowers, of course she did, she watched for them every year, blooming in their season . . .

'There were so many,' she stammered. 'It's – hard – to pick ones out –'

Mrs May said nothing. Just waited.

And then, like an answer to a prayer, an image came into Shona's mind. An image of a tree, covered in white flowers that were not exactly flowers, more like leaves, yet not only leaves, either. Sitting up in her chair her strength returned to her, and she knew what she must say. 'I think my real favourite in the garden does have flowers, but they're leaves as well, growing on a tree. It's called the Handkerchief Tree.'

A little spark seemed to flash in Mrs May's dark eyes, and up rose her eyebrows again in a kind of wonder. 'You know the Handkerchief Tree? That's very unusual; I didn't know they had one in that garden. Do you happen to know what those strange flowers are called?'

Yes, Shona knew. Mark had told her, on her very first day at Edina Lodge. She'd been eleven. Who'd have thought she'd need to know what he'd told her then all these years later? She almost smiled at the memory, but only said, quietly, 'They're called bracts. Leaves that bear flowers.'

And Mrs May for a moment or two seemed to have nothing to say. Then she nodded and rose, Shona with her, and looked at her watch. 'I think I've just time to tell you about the name of the shop before I show you the workroom. In case you've been wondering, it is of course made up from our surname, "May", plus the word "Bel", which my husband thought would sound like beautiful.' Mrs May gave a little laugh. 'We hope it describes our services. Oh, I should mention: you haven't asked, but we're offering a wage of eighteen shillings a week, with lunches provided. All right, Miss Murray?'

'Oh, yes, Mrs May.'

'Well, now, we'd better make haste if I'm to show you the

workroom. I have another candidate to see at a quarter to three. This way, please.'

Another candidate. Quarter to three. Oh, well, she'd always known she wouldn't be the only applicant. Yet Shona, following Mrs May, was still feeling a slight kick of dismay. As there hadn't been anyone else around, she'd rather hoped she might have been the only one in for the job. Now, here was definite news of at least one rival. Probably there were others, so what was the point of her seeing a workroom she might never work in? Once again, she had to dig deep for confidence. Who knew what would happen? She might be lucky, eh? Better look interested, then, she told herself, in seeing this workroom.

And it was worth seeing. A light, airy and spacious room with long windows, white walls and a tiled floor. There were fresh flowers standing in tall buckets, bunches of dried flowers hanging from the ceiling, baskets, jugs, metal containers and a wide trestle table covered with rolls of twine, pliers, scissors, wire – everything, Shona supposed, a florist might need. And where a florist was in fact sitting, for here was the blonde girl again, smiling as she trimmed leaves from long stemmed golden flowers.

'This is Willa, one of our senior assistants,' said Mrs May, putting a hand on the girl's shoulder. 'Willa, this is Miss Murray – Shona, perhaps I might say.'

'Oh, yes, please!' said Shona, feeling sudden hope of success at the use of her first name. But then, it might mean nothing at all. There was still this other candidate arriving, at a quarter to three . . .

'My husband's had to visit our supplier today,' Mrs May was saying. 'Usually he works here on our major displays, and has the most wonderful way with flowers. Willa, will you take Shona back to the front shop and, if the next candidate has arrived, show her into my office, please?'

As Willa leaped up, Mrs May shook Shona by the hand.

'Thank you for coming, my dear. We'll be in touch by letter within a few days.'

'Thank you,' said Shona. 'Thank you for seeing me.'

So, it was over, her interview. How had she done? She didn't want to think about it, and didn't want to see the rival either, but there she was: a pretty girl, dressed in a navy-blue outfit, being escorted away by Willa while Brigid attended to a lady customer, and Miss Ruddick was coming, smiling, through the door.

'How did it go?' she asked when she and Shona were out in the street. 'Not that you'll be able to tell.'

'I think it was OK, but you're right, I don't have any idea.' Shona looked gloomily down George Street, at all the carefree passers-by, none of whom would have to wait for a letter as she must do. 'Did you see that pretty lassie in the shop? Dressed in navy blue?'

'I can't say I noticed. What about her?'

'She was another one for the job. I thought she looked well to do. Why would she want to work in a shop?'

'Because it's a flower shop, Shona. It's not like a grocer's or a sweet shop – it has what you want, hasn't it? The promise of a career?'

'Yes, I do want that.'

'Well, let's hope that came across at your interview. But however things go, you have a great deal ahead of you, anyway. Your birthday. Your move to lodgings. Your farewell to the Lodge. How d'you feel about that?'

'Never thought I'd say this,' Shona answered, after a pause, 'but I'm going to miss it. Quite a lot.'

Eighteen

Everyone was having birthdays, or so it seemed. Cassie had hers, Mavis Maxwell had hers, Archie Smith and his cronies had theirs, which meant that celebratory iced buns – the Lodge didn't run to large cakes – were becoming a regular event at tea time. Only Shona's birthday – due in late June – was yet to come, and she wasn't interested in having buns or little presents, or anything. Just one letter from Maybel's Flowers would do. As long as it contained good news.

On the morning of her birthday, she was on wires again at breakfast waiting for the post, though she put on a good act of being perfectly happy with the cards she'd already been given. One from Cassie, of course, another from Mavis, several from other girls in her class, and one from Archie Smith, who waved and grinned when she looked over to thank him. There was also the usual card from Miss Bryce – she sent one to all leavers on their last birthdays at the Lodge – and one from Miss Ruddick, again wishing Shona good luck. If I am lucky, Shona thought, it'll be partly due to her.

There was no sign of any sort of luck, however, when the post finally came, for all it contained for Shona were cards from Mrs Hope, Kitty and Mrs Gow.

'Oh, what a shame!' Cassie commented as she and Shona set out for one of their last days at school. 'It would have been a grand present if you could've got good news on your birthday.'

'But if I'd got bad news, it would have spoiled my birthday,' Shona replied, trying to put a brave face on her disappointment. 'Might still, eh? If the letter comes by second post.'

'Don't think about it,' Cassie advised. 'Just remember, tomorrow we are leaving school. Can you believe it?'

'And the next day I'll probably be job hunting. I can believe that.'

But there was to be no more job hunting for Shona. When she returned from school that afternoon, Miss Donner informed her that there was a letter for her, come by second post.

'A letter?' whispered Shona. 'Where is it?'

'I have it here.' Miss Donner put the envelope into her hand with a sympathetic smile, for she, like most at the Lodge, knew what Shona had been waiting for. 'Come on, be brave. Open it!'

'Aye, open it,' said Cassie, almost as excited as Shona herself.

'Might no' be the one.' Shona was looking at the typewritten envelope. She knew it *was* the one.

'Want me to open it?' asked Miss Donner.

'No, no, I'll open it.'

Tearing open the envelope, Shona pulled out the typewritten sheet it contained. And turned pale.

'Oh, dear,' sighed Cassie.

'Bad news?' asked Miss Donner.

'Good news.' Shona's colour was rushing back. 'Oh, Cassie – Miss Donner – I've got it! I've got the job! They want me to start week after next. Oh, I must tell Miss Ruddick!'

'Miss Bryce first,' Miss Donner warned, then gave Shona a sudden hug. 'Well done, Shona! We're so pleased for you.'

'Aye, Shona, we are, we are,' Cassie cried, taking a turn at hugging her. 'You got your grand birthday present after all, eh?'

It was her best ever birthday, Shona decided, apart from those she'd had when she was a wee girl and both her parents had been alive. She remembered them well. There'd been little gifts – her toy rabbit had been one – and a cake her mother would have baked with icing and candles; other children invited in to play all the old games. She'd never wanted her birthday to end then, but of course things were different at the Lodge, where birthdays passed without any great celebration. There were the iced buns and cards from those who knew you best; otherwise the special days were much like any others.

Not this year, though. This year, Shona's fifteenth birthday was one she knew she would always remember as the day she'd heard she'd got the job at Maybel's. So many congratulations, so many good wishes, from Miss Bryce and all the staff, from the girls Shona knew and even some of the boys, Archie Smith being one, of course, because everybody realized that Shona had done something rather remarkable: turned down the idea of domestic service and found herself a job in a shop that was no ordinary shop but a business of prestige, where she could learn a craft that was just what she wanted. Lucky girl, then! But most knew luck was only a part of it.

'I couldn't have done it without you,' Shona told Miss Ruddick sincerely. 'You set me on the way, helping me with my letter and everything. And then you kept cheering me up and telling me to be confident. In the end, I was! Sort of.'

'No, no, Shona, you got that job on your own efforts,' Miss Ruddick told her. 'I couldn't be there for your interview and that's where you must have impressed Mrs May. I have the feeling that you're going to do really well – you'll be running the business before you know it!'

'I don't see Mrs May letting anybody else do that,' Shona said with a smile. 'I bet even Mr May doesn't get much of a say, but I don't really know what he's like. I won't meet him till next week.'

'When you'll be fully absorbed into your new job, but tomorrow it's your last day at school – you'll be feeling strange about that. Everyone remembers their last day at school.'

'Aye, it'll be strange.' Shona was looking thoughtful, picturing it. 'Even stranger when we all leave here, eh? Cassie to her new place, Archie to the navy, me to my lodgings. I hope we don't cry when we say goodbye!'

'If you do, you'll soon stop,' Miss Ruddick said dryly. 'You'll be too excited about your new life to think too much about the old.'

Nineteen

When the leaving day came, though, there were a few tears: mostly from the girls, though a few boys, too, were feeling sentimental about the place where they'd all at one time felt lost and had gradually come to know. They had settled, made friends, accepted the life it gave them, and if they were keen now to begin new lives, they couldn't just forget the Lodge, the nearest thing any of them had had to a home.

'We'll be all right,' Shona murmured to Cassie as they gathered in the hall for a last word from Miss Bryce. 'If you get sad, think about no' wearing orphanage uniform any more.'

'I'll still be wearing uniform,' Cassie murmured, 'but it'll be different. The print dresses are nice. I've seen 'em, and the black ones are really smart.'

'You'll keep in touch?' Shona just had time to ask before Miss Bryce arrived, accompanied by Miss Ruddick and other members of staff. 'We'll write to each other, eh?'

'Sure we will,' Cassie agreed, her blue eyes fixed on Miss Bryce, who was looking around her leavers with one of those smiles of hers that was neither warm nor cold. Imagine, some of them were thinking, after today she would no longer be a part of their lives. Someone else would be in charge, but Miss Bryce, whose very name had had such power, would be of no importance – at least, not to them. That took some believing, eh?

Perhaps, when she began to speak, they'd decided to wait to believe it tomorrow, for with her so-strong voice and definite manner, she could still hold their attention. Especially when she was saying quite nice things, praising them for their contribution to Edina Lodge and hoping that they'd remember all they'd been taught there about values and the right way to live in the world outside. Now it was time to say goodbye and they must go their separate ways. She and all the staff wished them the very best for the future, and if they ever wanted to come back, whether it be for advice or just to say hello, they'd be very welcome.

As she paused and stood back everyone clapped, including the staff, after which it was time for the shaking of hands and saying goodbye – to Mr Glegg, Miss Donner, Miss Anderson, Matron, Miss Ruddick and, of course, Miss Bryce herself, who had a special word for everyone.

For Shona, it was 'congratulations' again, which made her feel good, and then it was Cassie's turn, followed by the irrepressible Archie Smith's, while Shona moved away to speak again to Miss Ruddick. 'Will you come to the flower shop some time?' she asked quickly, for she had seen Mrs Hope, who'd come to meet her, bobbing on the steps outside.

'Of course I will,' Miss Ruddick said warmly. 'I'll look forward to following your progress. Now, have you got all your stuff, then?'

'Yes, thanks, there's no' much.'

Shona, buttoning on her orphanage raincoat, which she would need to wear until she could afford something new, picked up her small case and holdall and waved to Mrs Hope. 'I'll away, then,' she finished awkwardly. 'Don't forget to visit the shop, eh?'

'I won't!' cried Miss Ruddick and Shona, with Cassie at her side, joined the other leavers milling on the drive.

'There's just one thing I want to do, Mrs Hope,' Shona whispered. 'Would you mind waiting a few minutes?'

'Of course not, pet. Have you forgotten something?'

'I just want to say another goodbye.'

Away went Shona, as Mrs Hope and Cassie looked on, mystified, until a light of recognition shone in Cassie's face. 'I know where she's gone,' she told Mrs Hope. 'To see that tree she likes, eh? Och, she's going to miss it.'

Shona, gazing at the Handkerchief Tree, was thinking the same. Even without its load of mysterious flowers, which had now passed, it was still beautiful and meant so much to her that she really didn't want to say goodbye at all. Perhaps she wouldn't. She'd just come back from time to time, to visit the Lodge and her tree again. Yes, that was what she'd do. Having made her decision, it was easy enough to run back to Mrs Hope and Cassie, who had now been joined by Archie, sporting a great kitbag on his shoulder and whose eyes were fixed on Shona.

'I thought you'd disappeared!' he cried. 'I've been waiting to say goodbye.'

'Archie, that's nice. Sorry, I just had to have another look at the garden.'

'And that tree you like,' he said with a grin. 'What a crazy lassie you are, then! Listen, if I write, will you write back? I'll send you my address, eh?'

'You don't know mine.'

'I do.' He gave a last grin. 'This lady here gave it me.'

'That was all right, eh?' asked Mrs Hope, smiling, and Shona said it was. What else could she say?

'You going for a tram?' she asked.

Archie shook his head. 'I've got transport coming,' he said grandly. 'The navy's that keen to get me, they're sending a truck.' He laughed, then hesitated. 'You lassies take care, then?'

'Don't worry, they will,' said Mrs Hope, picking up Shona's canvas bag. 'Cassie, can I carry something for you?'

'No, thanks, I've just the one bag.'

'Let's away, then.'

Following others making their way down the drive, the three of them – Mrs Hope, Shona and Cassie – set off under Archie's watching eyes, though just for a moment the two girls paused and looked back at the Lodge. There it was then, the place that had been their home for so long. And yes, Shona thought, it had been a home to them in the end. Within its limits, it had been a good place to live, and they could say that on the whole they'd been lucky. Now it was a chapter that was closed, and they were on their own, to make of their lives what they could.

Turning back, they gave a last wave to Archie and began to step quickly down the drive that would lead to the road and the trams. As they reached the security gate, a Royal Navy truck came through and put on speed as it moved away. Archie's transport had arrived!

'Didn't know whether to believe him or not, did you?' Cassie whispered, and Shona and Mrs Hope smiled.

'Seemingly, he's going to be on his way, just like us,' said Shona.

Where to, though? They might think they knew, but none of them could be sure how would it be.

'I see our tram!' Mrs Hope cried when they'd almost reached the stop on the main road. 'Cassie, yours will be along soon, eh?'

'Yes, you go!' cried Cassie. 'Don't wait for me.'

And as their tram clanked to a stop, Mrs Hope and Shona ran fast and climbed aboard, waving back to Cassie until the tram had moved away and she was out of sight.

Twenty

'Now, take some bacon, Shona, please do,' begged Mrs Gow, standing at her stove with a frying pan at the ready and a paper of bacon rashers in her hand. 'All you've had is ma porridge and it'll no' see you through the morning, eh? Why no' try a bit o' bacon, then?'

'Honestly, Mrs Gow, I've had plenty,' Shona told her, rising from the kitchen table. 'And I'll have to go: I don't want to be late at the shop.'

'As though you'd ever be late!' Mrs Gow shook her fair head. 'Every morning since you started you've been dying to get to work. I've never seen any lassie so keen.'

'Why, this is only my fifth day!' Shona exclaimed, laughing. 'Being keen – might wear off, eh?'

'No' with you, pet. You've found what you wanted, seems to me.'

'And me. Thanks, Mrs Gow, that was grand. I'll just get my coat.'

Standing in front of the mirror by the front door, Shona, wearing the dark green blouse and skirt worn by the girls at the florist's, checked her appearance. Hair well brushed, face shining clean, skirt straight, blouse freshly ironed – yes, she looked all right. Had to make sure, Mrs May being so particular how her assistants appeared to the public. Even if it was a windy morning, you were expected to arrive without a hair out of place. That was how she was herself, of course – always immaculate, even wearing an apron and working so hard alongside her husband in the back room.

Oh, yes, the Mays worked hard and their staff were expected to work hard, too, as Shona had learned very quickly, but that was no trouble to her. She had never minded hard work and wanted to do her best in this job she already enjoyed.

True, it was early days yet but things could only get better, as far as she could see for, if up till now she'd only been allowed to water plants and keep everything tidy, very soon her real training would begin. Next week she'd heard there was to be a big wedding at St John's in Princes Street. Maybel's were doing the flowers and Willa had said cheerfully, 'Maybe you'll get to help with the buttonholes.' Buttonholes? Yes, please, thought Shona.

''Bye, Mrs Gow!' she called. 'See you tonight.'

''Bye, Shona. Got your penny for the tram fare?'

'Always have that, Mrs Gow!'

There was no wind, and the July morning was calm and warm as Shona arrived at Maybel's and went through a door at the side of the shop to the staffroom at the rear, where she found Willa and Brigid drinking tea. 'Morning, Willa, morning, Brigid,' she called, hanging up the raincoat she hadn't needed to wear. 'Mr and Mrs May no' down yet?'

The lucky Mays didn't have far to come to work, as they lived in what was known as a 'double-upper' flat over the shop.

'We wouldn't be having this tea if they were!' Brigid answered with a laugh. 'Mrs May likes us to start work as soon as we arrive.'

'Why, it isn't nine o'clock yet,' Willa, the attractive blonde, protested. 'I don't see why we should begin before then.'

'Och, you know what Mrs M is like.' Brigid shrugged. 'Thinks we should all love work as much as she does.'

'I do love my work,' said Willa. 'But my own time, too.' She glanced at Shona, who was slowly sitting down, looking worried, and gave a quick smile. 'Hey, don't look so glum, Shona! We shouldn't be giving you the wrong impression of Mrs May. She's a good boss, really. Here, have a cup of tea.'

'Thanks!' Shona's expression had lightened. 'I've no' been here very long but so far I think she's been very nice. Mr May, too, though he doesn't say much.'

'Daren't!' said Brigid, her brown eyes dancing. 'Oops, shouldn't have said that, eh? No, he's a happy man, is Mr May. As long as he's got his bouquets and displays to do, he doesn't want any more.'

'Wish I was as good as he is,' Willa remarked. 'Mrs May's good, but he's got something extra, don't ask me what. But then she handles all the business side of it and she's *very* good at that.'

Glancing at the clock on the wall, Brigid sighed and rose. 'Can't deny it's nine o'clock now. I'll go and open up.'

'And I'll do these tea things,' said Willa, moving cups and saucers to the small sink in the corner. 'Just in case Mrs M pops in.'

'Mind if I ask you something?' Shona said as she found a tea towel.

'Anything at all.'

'Well, Mrs May mentioned I'd got someone's job, and I was wondering who'd left. No one's said anything.'

'Oh, you mean Nesta. You want to know why she left?' Willa set cups to dry and rinsed out the tea pot. 'We've forgotten her already, I'm afraid. Truth is, she didn't like it here very much.'

'Didn't like it?' Shona was taken aback. 'Why not?'

Willa shrugged her elegant shoulders. 'She thought at first it would be something special, working in a flower shop, but then she found it was quite hard work and there was a lot to learn. So she put in her notice and got a job in Haberdashery at Logie's.'

'And that's no' hard work?'

'Well, she doesn't have to do anything herself, you see. She just sells what's there.'

'Just why I didn't want to work in an ordinary shop!' Shona cried, at which Willa's blue-grey eyes brightened and she put her hand on Shona's arm for a moment.

'I'm so glad you've come, Shona. I'm eighteen now but I was only your age when I started and felt like you – I wanted something different. I found it here. I've been very happy. You will be, too.'

'It's nice of you to say that,' Shona answered, flushing a little. 'I know I'll be happy working with you and Brigid.'

'Oh, yes, Brigid likes to complain, but it's just her way. She enjoys her work as much as anyone. And she's good at it.'

'Girls, girls, it's after nine o'clock!'

At the sound of the voice from the door, they looked up to see Mrs May staring in at them, her pencilled eyebrows raised. 'There's plenty to do, you know.'

'Sorry, Mrs May,' Willa said with smooth contrition. 'It was my fault – I didn't notice the time.'

'Well, never mind now, but I see some of the hydrangeas in the front are looking a little tired. See if you can tidy them up and if there are any we might spare for drying. Shona, please come to the workroom. I want to show you how to make a buttonhole.'

As Mrs May withdrew, Willa, on her way to the hydrangeas, looked back at Shona and gave an impish grin. 'Said you'd be helping to make buttonholes!' she whispered.

'Glad you were right,' Shona whispered back.

Twenty-One

The buttonhole Shona made that day was, of course, to be the first of many. She had been worried about it, afraid her fingers would be all thumbs, but after she'd been shown by Mrs May how to wire and bind a pretty pink rose, then frame it with leaves and a little maidenhair, her finished effort was not too bad.

In fact, Mr May, who had paused in his work on a spectacular bouquet to watch, declared it very good and described Shona as a 'natural', at which Mrs May had said it was too early to say that on the strength of one buttonhole. On the other hand, yes, it seemed Shona might have the touch for delicate work, not that she would be ready to use it for some time. First, she must learn the routines of the front shop.

'Not too difficult,' Mr May remarked, beginning to insert lilies and phlox into his frame of foliage and giving Shona an encouraging smile. Older than his wife, he was a tall, heavy-shouldered man, his hair thick and grey, his eyebrows to match, and seemed more as Shona imagined a lawyer or a businessman might be, rather than a flower arranger. Yet he had the delicate hands all right, and whenever she could, she liked to watch him at his work, wondering as Willa did, what could be his secret?

'Not difficult, maybe, but vital,' Mrs May retorted. 'The front shop is what people see first, it's how they judge us. That's why I want my staff to be always at their best, have the right manner towards customers, find what they want and present it beautifully.' She turned to Shona. 'Always remember, Shona, presentation is everything where flower-giving is concerned. Cellophane, ribbons, bows – all must be immaculate. To match the flowers themselves.'

'I understand,' said Shona.

'Of course you do,' Mr May agreed. 'Why, that's why my wife appointed you. Isn't that right, Phyllida? Because Shona really appreciates flowers?'

'You're talking about the Handkerchief Tree?' Shona asked.

Mrs May favoured Shona with a brief smile. 'Yes, I must admit, that swayed me. Very few people of your age, Shona, could have shown so much interest in a tree, however unusual.'

So that's why I got the job, thought Shona, and a reminder of Mark Lindsay flashed into her mind. She hadn't thought of him for some time, she realized, but just then she wished she could have told him how he'd set her on the road she wanted to take. Perhaps one day she'd see him again? But then his image vanished, as Mrs May told her to follow her into the front shop where Willa or Brigid would begin to instruct her in what she needed to know.

The weeks went by. With her keenness and ability to learn, as well as her striking looks, her height and her bright hair, Shona soon became an asset in the front shop. Both Willa and Brigid were excellent teachers, helping her to identify the flowers and indoor plants, standing by when she dealt with her first customers, showing her how to satisfy Mrs May's order that all purchases must be beautifully wrapped, tied with ribbon and finished with bows.

On the days when the flowers and plants arrived from the market garden outside Edinburgh and they had to open early to take in the cold, sweet smelling cargo, Shona was never happier than when unloading, helping to arrange the new arrivals. Ideally, she would have liked to visit the market garden to see what was available, but Willa said that that was strictly the province of Mr and Mrs May.

'How about the big weddings and functions, then?' Shona asked. 'When might I get to help at them? I still only make the buttonholes.'

'Sorry about that,' said Willa. 'I know Brigid and I take it in turns to go with Mrs and Mrs May, and you're always in the shop with one of us, but your time'll come, you'll see. I expect you'll be progressing soon to corsages, anyway.'

'Corsages?'

'For the mothers of the brides, mainly. There's more to them than buttonholes – you'll have fun making them.'

'But the big arrangements, for the church and that – they're always done by Mr and Mrs May?'

'We do get instructed in what to do, and we are allowed sometimes to help.' Willa smiled. 'Don't worry, Shona, you'll get your chance. They think very highly of you, the Mays.'

'You think so?'

'Oh, yes. It won't be long before you're doing as much as Brigid and me.'

Shona wasn't too sure of that, knowing Mrs May was never going to take risks letting inexperienced staff take on work before they were ready and believing she was right, anyway. She had to learn to walk before she could run, as Mrs Gow said comfortably when Shona occasionally discussed her work with her, and she had plenty still to learn.

The time came, however, when she did progress to making corsages from the prettiest flowers, moss, ivy and the thinnest wire, and enjoyed herself, producing something really exquisite for the unknown mothers of the unknown brides.

'Well done,' Mrs May would say, and 'Excellent', Mr May would chime, so that really it was no surprise when Shona was finally instructed in learning to create her first bouquet. Oh, it was tricky, getting the stems and leaves to do just what she wanted, never mind inserting the flowers, especially with Mrs May's dark eyes following her every move, calling at intervals 'Watch your shape! Remember your height!' Finally, however, the task was done and Shona was able to sigh with relief when Mrs May, after a cliffhanger moment, pronounced the bouquet satisfactory.

'That's not to say it's perfect – see, you have quite a gap here, you'll have to fill in with something that looks right – but for a first attempt I think it shows promise. One day I can see you contributing well to our outside functions. Not yet, of course.'

One day. Not yet. Ah, well. As Shona knew, as she'd told herself often enough, she had a long way to go before she could call herself a florist, but one day she'd get there. She knew that too.

'How'd you get on with your bouquet?' Brigid asked later, during a lull of custom in the front shop. 'Bit of an ordeal, eh?'

'It wasn't too bad,' Shona told her. 'Mrs May said it wasn't perfect, but she quite liked it. 'Course I'll no' be going with the Mays to any functions yet.'

'I shouldn't think so.' Brigid laughed. 'Why, you're still only a bairn! Lucky, really, to be making bouquets already. Poor old Nesta never got that far.'

'Nesta wasn't interested,' Willa put in, as she gathered up some containers for rinsing out. 'Mrs May knew that. She'd never have taken her along to weddings and such.'

'Well, I bet there's one wedding Shona might be able to attend.'

Brigid was looking coy. 'Now, Shona, say whose you think it might be.'

'I've no idea. Unless it's yours?'

'Mine? Definitely not. I've no plans of that sort. No, I mean Willa's. Now don't look like that, Willa. We've all seen that fellow come in here, pretending to look at flowers but only if you're around!'

'What fellow?' asked Shona quickly. 'Willa, you're no' really going to get wed?'

'Of course not!' Willa was quite unruffled. 'Brigid's just playing the fool again. There is a young man who comes in here and tries to talk to me, but he's not my young man and I don't want him to be. Satisfied, Brigid?'

'I'll wait and see, Willa. Wait and see!'

'I'm just so glad you're no' leaving,' Shona said sincerely. 'I mean, that'd be awful.'

'It's nice to think you'd miss me. But you needn't worry, I'm not going anywhere.'

'Nor am I,' put in Brigid. 'Though things are always changing. Nothing stays the same.'

'Don't say that!' cried Shona. 'I've just got used to this place as it is!'

Twenty-Two

On her way home, Shona decided that the day had been a good one and that she'd made some progress. And then there was the relief in knowing that Willa was not going to leave, which would have been a definite blow.

She'd been surprised, at first, that someone so poised and confident as Willa should have turned out to be so warm-hearted and helpful, but had soon come to rely on her, rather than Brigid, for advice and understanding. Brigid was all right, good at explaining things, but the thing about her was that you never knew where you were with her. She sometimes seemed to regard everything as a huge joke which wasn't always easy to accept, whereas Willa was more like Miss MacLaren and Miss Ruddick – steady, trustworthy, always the same. Who could imagine Miss Ruddick, for instance, springing any surprises?

Shona smiled to herself as she neared Mrs Gow's house, and thought again that she might pop back to Edina Lodge some time seeing as things were going so well, to tell them how she was doing. And call on Mrs Hope again, and see Kitty. No need to write to Archie, for he'd quite forgotten his promise to write to her, but she would write to Cassie. Maybe they could arrange to meet in their free time and have a grand talk together.

Yes, and there was one more thing Shona wanted to do, but the evenings were growing darker now and she'd have to wait till Sunday afternoon before she could do it. Sometimes she met Kitty on Sundays if she wasn't seeing her young man, and they'd go for walks by the Water of Leith, but she never went with Kitty to the Dean cemetery, her destination this time. For visits to her mother's grave, she always went alone.

There was no headstone, just a weathered wooden cross in a corner, but one day Shona hoped there would be a proper memorial, for even though everyone said she had to keep her small inheritance for a rainy day, she was already saving a little from her wages every week to buy a stone. If her father had to lie with his comrades in France, at least her mother would have her resting place marked in the right way. But, of course, even now, she could have flowers.

Carrying a small bunch of asters, bought at cost from the shop, Shona, on the following Sunday, made her way through the ranks of graves lining mossy paths to her mother's cross, marvelling as usual on how much some folk had been able to spend on their loved ones in this place.

See the great marble angels balancing over tombs and the sculpted figures looking down from tall columns, the marble books, the stone flowers, the gravelled stretches in front of graves, marked by railings and set with urns for flowers. Sadly, some of the older gravestones had lost a good part of their inscriptions, so that only odd letters still stuck out from crumbling masonry. At one time, all those names and dates would be read by grieving relatives; now there were no relatives left and no names to read.

Sadder still were the memorials to dead children, and Shona always hurried past those, not wishing to think about the young lives snatched away from what would have probably been comfortable homes and happy futures. Where were the memorials to those dead children who hadn't come from comfortable homes, though? Only in the hearts of those they'd left, and maybe that was saddest of all.

Here, at last, at the end of the cemetery was the marker for the grave of Emily Edith Murray, Born 1888, Died 1919, where Shona halted for a long moment before hurrying to fill a jar at the cemetery tap.

'No need to worry about height or shape with these, Ma,' she whispered as she arranged her flowers in the jar. 'But I'll make 'em look nice, anyway. There, they look just right; should last till I come again.'

For some time she pulled out weeds from before the cross and tidied away leaves that were beginning to blow as a December breeze rattled through the graves. It was growing colder and she knew she would have to go soon, for the cemetery closed early in winter. There was just time to stand in silence, hoping that her mother might somehow know that all was going well for her.

No need to worry, Ma, she would have liked to say, I'm happy, I think it'll work out all right. And if her mother couldn't hear, well, Shona felt the better for telling her, anyway.

'Gates closing!' she heard a man's voice calling and quickly scrambled up, dashing away a tear or two.

'Wait!' she cried. 'I'm just coming.'

And Shona ran down the paths and out of the gate, back into the world.

Twenty-Three

Five years on, Shona, the day after Willa's wedding, could still remember Brigid's unusually serious words: 'Things are always changing; nothing stays the same.' And thought how right she had been.

Having arrived early at work on a beautiful June morning in 1928, Shona was alone in the staffroom, dwelling on the changes she herself had seen since she'd left Edina Lodge. Why, even the fact that she was here, drinking tea and not worrying, was a wee change in itself, brought about when she had persuaded Mrs May to allow her staff to have a tea before they started work. After all, it was true enough that they were often too rushed to have anything later, and Mrs May had agreed.

But then, she often did agree with Shona these days, and maybe that was a change, too, to be compared with Shona's transformation from raw young junior to experienced and talented florist. Now twenty years old, confident and professional, she had become someone immensely valued by the Mays – even more than Brigid, who was still at the shop, and perhaps as much as Willa, who now, of course, was not.

Oh, Lord, how she was missed, even if her leaving would no longer be the blow it might once have been. Shona sighed a little, remembering how dependent she had been on Willa in the early days, and of how, as she began to equal her in experience, that dependency turned to pleasant friendship.

If only Willa hadn't had to go and marry that admirer of hers, that fellow who had haunted the shop until she agreed to go out with him! Next thing they were engaged, and though Grant Henderson had a good job in a George Street bank, the engagement had been a long one. Though not long enough, for here they were, married, and after a lovely wedding at Colinton Kirk, held on the shop's half day closing so that Shona and Brigid could be bridesmaids, and with flowers provided by the Mays as their personal present, they were away on honeymoon. Back at Maybel's, the day after the wedding, it was all an anticlimax.

'Hello, hello!' cried Brigid, bursting in, with the new assistant, a pale young girl named Isla Wardie in tow. 'Got the tea made, Shona?'

'I'll make some fresh,' said Shona rising, but Brigid was turning Isla in the direction of the gas ring and kettle.

'No, no, Isla can make it. You'd like to, wouldn't you, Isla?'

'Oh, yes,' the sixteen-year-old answered hastily. She was a pretty girl with large, apprehensive blue eyes and dark bobbed hair, and as she filled the kettle and stood uncertainly holding it Shona, with a sympathetic smile, lit the gas for her and pointed out the tea caddy.

'It's only your second week, eh? And last week was a bit hectic, with the wedding and all, so you didn't get to do much. It'll be different now.'

'Aye, more boring,' said Brigid, looking in their biscuit tin and taking out a ginger nut. 'Sorry, only joking. Don't want to put you off, Isla, when you'll be feeling pretty pleased with yourself, having got the job.'

'Of course she's pleased!' Shona cried quickly.

She knew, as Brigid knew, that Isla's mother was a friend of Mrs May's, which perhaps accounted for Isla's having been selected at interview. Maybe not, though, because Mrs May had said she was very 'artistic'. Perhaps she was in any case the best candidate, but Brigid was being grumpy about it and Shona didn't want trouble.

'Isla, don't take any notice of Brigid,' she continued smoothly. 'I expect she's just feeling a wee bit down because the wedding's over.'

'And thinking Willa's on honeymoon and I'm not!' Brigid said snappishly. 'You know, it's made me look at my Robbie in a new light. Maybe I'll be the next to go, eh? And then it'll be you, Shona, and that sailor laddie of yours. Looks like it'll be Isla running this place before she knows it! Here, is that kettle boiling yet? I'm desperate for my tea.'

As Isla, giving Brigid terrified glances, managed to make the tea, Shona said she'd open up and went out smiling. She knew that Brigid would never marry the young office worker she called 'her Robbie', as she had no intention, she often said, of ever becoming a housewife. And as for Shona's marrying Archie Smith, that was a piece of nonsense only Brigid could dream up. It was true, when he was on leave, that he always came straight to the shop to see if Shona would go out with him, and she usually did, but then there were one or two other young men who asked her out and she went out with them too. Never would she be walking up the aisle with any one of them. Not when she was so happy in her job.

'Nine o'clock, girls!' she heard Mrs May calling at the door of the staffroom.

'I'm opening up, Mrs May!' she called back, flinging open the shop door to the June sunlight, and as the sense of anticlimax began to fade, she felt her usual rush of excitement for a new day and her wonder for what it might bring.

Twenty-Four

While Isla toured the plants with her watering can under Brigid's watchful eye, Shona went into the workroom to start a dinner-party arrangement that was to be delivered that afternoon ready for the next day. As Mr May was to be doing flowers for the hall and drawing room at the same house in the New Town, Shona wanted to discuss her ideas with him and was surprised, therefore, to find him not already at work.

'Hugh's just coming,' Mrs May told her, seeing her questioning look. She laughed shortly. 'At least, I hope he is. I left him still having breakfast in his dressing gown.'

'Oh, well, I expect he'll be along soon,' Shona said, still surprised. The Mays usually came down from their flat together and she knew Mr May would be keen to get on with his hall arrangement which was, he'd already told her with a grin, going to be very 'dramatic'.

'Tall flowers for me, Shona, and low flowers for you, eh?'

'I know what you mean,' she'd answered, laughing. 'Guests want to see each other across the table. I'm using miniature roses, mainly, apricot coloured and cream, to match Mrs Lockyer's dining room curtains.'

'And I'm using dark red gladioli, to match the décor of the hall, with white lilies for the drawing room, exactly following Mrs L's instruction. You know what she's like – very sure of what she wants!'

Oh, yes, Shona knew. Mrs Lockyer had used Maybel's Flowers before and was a valued client – better get things right, then.

'Just make a start,' Mrs May advised. 'I'm sure Hugh will be down in a moment.'

It wasn't Hugh May who came into the workroom, however, but Miss Bonar, the Mays' housekeeper, a tall, grey-haired woman in her fifties. Always rather pale, she appeared quite white as she approached her employer.

'Why, Miss Bonar, what brings you down here?' Mrs May asked in surprise. Miss Bonar was very rarely seen out of the upstairs flat.

'Madam, I think you'd better come up to see Mr May – he's not looking at all well.'

'Not looking well?' Mrs May appeared transfixed, her own colour draining from her face so that the patches of her rouge showed up like theatrical make-up. 'What do you mean? He was all right when I left him.'

'If you'd just come, though, Madam.'

Mrs May turned her dark eyes on Shona. 'Come with me, Shona, will you?'

'Of course, Mrs May.'

Moving fast, the three women made their way from the workroom to the upstairs flat, where Mrs May called desperately, 'Hugh! Hugh! Where are you?'

'He's on your bed, Madam,' Miss Bonar told her breathlessly. 'He went there when he said he didn't feel well – left his breakfast – never ate a thing—'

'Oh, God!' Running into her beautiful all-blue bedroom, Mrs May knelt by the double bed where Mr May lay back against pillows, his face without colour, his eyes closed, his breathing ragged and erratic. 'Oh, God, Hugh, what's wrong?'

For a long moment the watchers thought he would not open his eyes, but at last the eyelids fluttered up and he was able to fix his wife with a panic-stricken gaze.

'I – don't know, Phyl,' he whispered. 'I just – don't feel so good.'

'Is it your heart, darling? Let me feel it!'

'No, no, I don't know what it is . . . I just feel . . . not myself.'

'Madam, shall I ring the doctor?' asked Miss Bonar.

'I'll do that,' said Shona. 'It's Doctor Dell, isn't it? Where can I find the number?'

'By the telephone in the living room,' Mrs May gasped as she held on to her husband's hand. 'Tell the operator to put you through straight away – it's urgent!'

'The doctor's ordering an ambulance,' Shona reported, hurrying back from the telephone. 'When I told him the symptoms, he said Mr May would need to go to hospital.'

'But is the doctor coming?' asked Mrs May. 'Is he coming?'

'Yes, right away. He's only in Charlotte Square, eh? He won't take long.'

'And I want Hugh to go to a nursing home, not the hospital. We know a good one – he went there with his appendix.'

Might be worse than he was with his appendix, Shona thought uneasily. She had never seen anyone look as ill as Mr May since she'd said goodbye to her mother in 1919.

'He'll be all right, Mrs May,' she murmured, suddenly daring to put an arm round her. 'The doctor will know what to do and the ambulance is coming as well.'

'That's right, Madam,' Miss Bonar put in. 'Doctor Dell's very good, he'll soon have Mr May better.'

But as Hugh May lay with his eyes closed again, Mrs May began to sob.

After that things began to happen, with Dr Dell, small and quick, arriving first, to be followed soon by the ambulance men with a stretcher, while Shona and Miss Bonar kept out of the way, exchanging bleak glances.

'I don't know what to do,' Miss Bonar suddenly wailed, twisting her hands together. 'Shona, I don't know what to do.'

'He's in good hands,' murmured Shona, trying to find words of comfort, but thinking how terrible it was that life could always catch you out, springing surprises you weren't prepared to face just when you might be feeling that everything was fine. Take what had happened to her mother: struck down, out of the blue, not like her dad who was in the war, where the worst might have been expected, but without warning, just as Mr and Mrs May had had no warning. How could folk cope with no warning?

'Maybe I should make some tea?' asked Miss Bonar, but Shona shook her head.

'I don't think anybody will have time to drink it. My guess is they'll be taking Mr May to the nursing home as soon as possible.'

'Oh, dear, oh dear,' sighed Miss Bonar, dabbing at her eyes with the corner of her apron, 'That sounds bad, eh?'

Shona, patting her shoulder, said again that he'd be all right and that he was in good hands.

'I'll go and tell the others,' she finished, and Miss Bonar nodded.

'Yes, go and tell them. They'll be wondering what's going on.'

Me, too, thought Shona.

Twenty-Five

'What are we going to do?' asked Brigid, her brown eyes huge on Shona's face while Isla stood close beside her, fearfully eyeing a lady customer examining peonies who might suddenly ask her something. Anyone could tell that something was wrong, anyway, from the looks on the faces of the two older assistants. Anyone could sense their anxiety that was beginning to hang over the front shop like a black cloud.

'What can we do?' Shona whispered. 'Try to carry on, d'you think? Till we know what Mrs May wants?'

'But she'll be going with Mr May to the nursing home; she won't even have time to speak to us.'

'Listen!' Shona cried. 'They're leaving; I can hear footsteps coming down from the flat! I'll see if I can catch Mrs May.'

But Mrs May herself suddenly appeared, looking as they'd never seen her before, wearing a brown jacket round her shoulders and a hat that didn't match, with her face so colourless it was as though her make-up had now faded away and a woman they didn't know was showing through.

'The ambulance is just off,' she said hoarsely, beckoning Shona and Brigid to come close. 'I'm to follow. The doctor says Mr May has abnormally high blood pressure and they're going to try to bring it down before he has a heart attack – or a stroke. I don't know when I'll be back.'

'What would you like us to do, Mrs May?' asked Shona.

'Do? What can we do? Close the shop. Put a notice on the door – "Closed, owing to illness".' Mrs May put a hand to her brow. 'I'll have to leave it to you. I must go.'

'What about Mrs Lockyer?' asked Shona. 'Shall I telephone her?'

'Mrs Lockyer? Oh, God, I don't know. Yes, yes, ring her. Tell her what's happened. She'll understand.'

'Mrs May, are you there?' came Dr Dell's voice. 'I'm ready to follow the ambulance now.'

'Just do as you think best – I must go!' Mrs May cried and ran wildly from the shop.

'Excuse me,' said the lady customer quietly after a moment or two, 'but I couldn't help overhearing. If you're closing the shop, would you like me to leave?'

Shona and Brigid exchanged glances. 'We're no' sure,' Shona said at last.

'Oh, but Mr May's ill, isn't he? Such a lovely man, and does such beautiful arrangements!' The customer gave a sympathetic sigh. 'Could I perhaps just take my peonies while I'm here?'

'Certainly,' said Brigid, rapidly taking on the transaction, choosing the flowers, wrapping them and ringing up the cost on the till while Isla held back, watching, and Shona stood in troubled thought. As soon as the customer had departed, saying she did so hope Mr May would be better soon, Brigid closed the door and looked at Shona.

'Shall I lock it, then? Shall I write the notice?'

'I don't know,' Shona answered slowly. 'I'm trying to think what Mr May would have wanted us to do.'

'Well, we know what Mrs May wanted.' Brigid shook her head. 'But did you ever see such a change in anyone? I thought she'd be the sort to keep calm in a crisis but she seemed to go to pieces, eh?'

'She's very close to Mr May. They've always been together.'

'But then to give up on the shop like she did – it's so out of character.'

'I know. That's why I'm wondering if we shouldn't think what's right to do. What Mr May would want us to do, I mean.'

'Keep the shop open and fix Mrs Lockyer's flowers?' Brigid whistled. 'Can we, do you think?'

'We can try. After all, if we don't do anything, we'll only be waiting for news and worrying. And Dan will be around with the van to pick the order up around two, anyway. If we shut up shop he won't know what's going on.'

'You're right. Let's get started, then. You do your table arrangement and I'll try to do Mr May's hall piece. Oh, my fingers are trembling already!'

'You're not going to leave me in the shop on my own?' Isla asked in alarm. 'I'll never be able to manage!'

'We can hear the shop bell from here; one of us will come if there's a customer,' Shona told her. 'Don't worry, you'll be fine.'

'Hope we are too,' murmured Brigid.

Twenty-Six

Silence descended over the workroom as the two young women settled to their tasks, breathing hard in their concentration as they selected their flowers, stripped leaves and shaped and cut, positioned them, stepped back to check, came forward and sighed. Did their work look all right? Would it do?

'Damn!' cried Brigid. 'There's the bell!'

'I'll go,' said Shona. 'I've nearly finished. What do you think of these roses? They're still in bud but they'll be open tomorrow, and then I've got the cream amaryllis.'

'Lovely,' said Brigid, frowning over her own tall, dark red

arrangement of June flowering gladioli. 'But you'd better go if you're going, before Isla has a nervous breakdown.'

Isla, in fact, was already at the workroom door.

'There's a gentleman in the shop,' she gasped. 'He says he has an appointment.'

'An appointment?' Shona stared. 'With Mrs May?'

'Yes, will you see him?'

'On my way,' said Shona, taking off her overall.

The man waiting in the front shop was large. A large, dominant figure Shona could see at a glance as she approached him, while in his presence, young Isla seemed almost to fade away. Tall and heavy-shouldered, with a broad, strong face made attractive by dimples as he smiled, he wore a lightweight summer suit and a grey trilby hat which he removed to reveal sandy hair. His eyes were green and narrow, his gaze on Shona keen.

'Fraser Kyle,' he declared, putting out a hand – large, of course. 'Here to see Mrs May at twelve o'clock.'

'I'm Shona Murray, one of her assistants,' Shona told him, shaking the great hand. 'I'm afraid Mrs May isn't here. Mr May was taken ill this morning and she's with him at the nursing home.'

'What, Hugh's ill? I'm sorry to hear that.' Mr Kyle shook his head in concern. 'He's always seemed so well.'

'I know. Is there anything I can do?'

He smiled. 'You don't know who I am, do you? I've taken over the nurseries – MacVicar's market garden.'

'Oh, I'm sorry.' Shona went pink. 'I remember now. Mrs May said some time ago that Mr MacVicar was retiring and someone new had bought the business. But we hardly ever go to the nurseries – Mr and Mrs May do all the buying.'

'Shame,' Fraser Kyle said pleasantly. 'You'd be very welcome if you ever came over. But, look, I'm really sorry about poor Hugh – if you see Mrs May, please tell her that for me, will you? And say I'll ring her later to find out how he is.'

'I'll give her the message as soon as I see her.'

'Fine. Thanks very much.' Touching the hat he had replaced, the large man smiled at Shona. 'Try to come over some time to see my stock.' He waved a hand around the shop. 'Before it arrives here, eh?'

'That'd be lovely,' Shona answered, meaning it, and walked with him to the door, which suddenly opened to admit two well-dressed women, sisters well known to Maybel's.

'Customers,' Fraser Kyle murmured. 'Never short of them here, eh? Well, good day, Miss Murray. It was very nice to meet you. I hope we'll meet again.'

'I hope so too.' As his eyes met hers Shona looked away, after which he opened the door and was gone. For a moment, she waited, her hand on the door latch, then moved to Isla who was anxiously watching the sisters.

'Ask if you can help,' Shona whispered.

'They're just looking at the carnations.'

'Well, see if it's carnations they want.'

Sighing a little, Shona guided Isla through the purchase of the sisters' choice of mixed carnations and sweet peas – 'something for the drawing room, dear' – helping her to wrap and tie, ring up the cost at the till, find change and see the smiling ladies out.

'Now that wasn't so bad, was it?' she asked, longing to return to the workroom. 'You're surely ready to do a sale on your own now, eh?'

'I suppose so,' Isla agreed, yet still called after Shona, 'but if you hear the bell, you'll come, won't you?'

'Yes, yes, don't worry.' As she returned to the workroom, however, Shona was looking worried herself. 'I don't know, Brigid, I'm wondering if Isla's ever going to get the hang of this job. She just gives me the impression that she can't wait for closing time.'

'Never mind Isla,' Brigid replied, still studying her hall arrangement and tweaking flowers into place. 'What about this fellow who wanted to see Mrs May? What was he like?'

After a moment's thought, Shona answered simply, 'Big.'

'Big?' Brigid laughed. 'Not much of a description.'

'Well, it sums him up. He's big enough to make sure he gets his own way, I should think. His name's Fraser Kyle. He's taken over MacVicar's.'

'Oh?' Brigid's eyes gleamed with interest. 'Fancy! I knew someone had bought the nurseries some time ago but never heard who it was. Looks like it'd be something about the plants, then, that he wants to see Mrs May. You told him what had happened?'

'Yes, he seemed quite upset. Said he'd ring her later.' Shona sank on to a stool at the worktable. 'We haven't heard anything yet, have we? I wonder how Mr May's getting on?'

'No news is good news, they say.' Brigid stood up. 'Tell you what, though, I think we should have a quick sandwich for lunch and then do that drawing room arrangement for Mrs Lockyer. Before we know it, the van'll be here, so we'd better crack on.'

'It shouldn't take too long. Mr May had the white flowers ready – lilies and phlox and so on. I've been thinking about it.'

Over her sandwich, however, Shona was surprised to find herself thinking not of the white flowers waiting for her but of Fraser Kyle and why he might have wanted to see Mrs May. He wasn't the sort to waste his time; it must have been something important that had brought him into Edinburgh. She couldn't explain why, but pondering on this made her feel very slightly uneasy.

On the other hand, she knew she was also remembering the look she'd seen in Fraser Kyle's green eyes when they'd rested on her. He had been attracted, she could tell, as women usually could, which was of no interest, really, as she was not attracted to him and was not likely to see him again. 'Try to come over some time,' he'd told her, but it was not possible for her to organize a visit to his market garden – that was up to Mrs May. And who knew what Mrs May would be doing in the future?

Twenty-Seven

Even by the time Dan Hardie, the delivery van driver, arrived at two o'clock, there'd still been no news on Mr May's condition. A lean-faced man with a short army-style haircut, the driver had had no morning deliveries and had not heard the worrying news until Brigid told him, at which he looked deeply distressed.

'Och, what a thing, eh? Such a grand boss, and always looked that well, I canna believe he's been took ill. And you've heard nothing?'

'Not so far, but we'll just have to get on. Shona, I'll go with Dan, eh? And explain why we've done Mr May's flowers?'

'Might be best,' said Shona. 'I'll look after things here.'

'Looks like you lassies have done a grand job,' Dan commented as he loaded the arrangements into his van. 'Mrs May'll be that grateful.'

'Don't know about that,' said Brigid. 'She was all for closing the shop today.'

'Closing the shop?' Dan shook his head. 'Now that shows how she was feeling, eh? She'd never be one to close the shop, even if there were bombs dropping on George Street!'

'Mr May's illness is worse than bombs to her,' Shona murmured. 'She's taken it very hard.'

'Well, let's just hope he's OK, eh?'

When Dan and Brigid had driven away Shona felt suddenly exhausted, as though the day's events had taken their toll. She would have given a great deal to sit down with a cup of tea, but the shop was busy and it wasn't until Brigid returned, reporting on Mrs Lockyer's shock over Mr May's illness, that there was a lull and they had time for a break. But it didn't last long, and they were just about to return to the front shop when the staffroom door opened and Mrs May swept in, looking, incredibly, almost her old self.

'Oh, girls!' she cried, her eyes alight. 'The news is good! Hugh hasn't had a heart attack and his blood pressure is being treated. They say he's stable, that he should be all right, but he will have to take great care. Oh, I'm so relieved, I can't tell you!'

Heavens, no wonder she was looking better! She'd powdered her nose and put on some lipstick, but it was clear to both Shona and Brigid that it was the good news about Hugh that had transformed her back into the woman they knew. And, of course, they felt better themselves, feeling a great weight lifting from their shoulders as Mrs May came in and sank into a chair.

'That's grand news!' Brigid cried. 'Really grand!'

'Oh, it is!' Shona chimed in. 'We've been thinking about Mr May all day.'

'I knew you would be.' Mrs May had taken off her hat and was putting back her dark hair from her brow. 'But what's been happening here, then? I thought you were going to close the shop?'

The girls exchanged glances.

'We thought, maybe, we could keep it going,' Shona answered. 'And maybe do the order for Mrs Lockyer, seeing as the van was coming anyway.'

'You did the flowers for Mrs Lockyer?' Mrs May's eyes widened. 'Why, that's wonderful! Oh, I'm so glad. It's been on Hugh's mind; he's been terribly upset, thinking he'd let her down, and I'm sure it was making him worse. But I'm going back to spend the night at the nursing home – I just came home to pack a few things – and if he's awake, I'll tell him there's no need to worry. I can't thank you girls enough.'

'Can we make you some tea?' Shona asked, but Mrs May was rising and shaking her head.

'I'm going upstairs now; Miss Bonar will make me a cup. Oh, dear, I should be exhausted but I'm so happy, I feel I could keep going for ever!'

'By the way, Mr Kyle from the nurseries called,' Shona told her. 'He said he had an appointment, but I told him what had happened.'

'Fraser Kyle?' Mrs May frowned. 'I remember now, he did ask to see me but didn't say why. Did he tell you?'

'No, just said he was very sorry to hear about Mr May and he'd phone you later.'

'Oh, well, I don't suppose it's very important. He's a good businessman, though. There've been a number of improvements since he took over from Mr MacVicar.' Mrs May put on her hat again and smiled. 'Can't think about that now. Look, you girls have done a grand job here – do you think you can keep going with things tomorrow? I'm not sure when I'll be back.'

'We can manage,' Shona said firmly. 'Don't worry about it.'

'And you've got young Isla to help out, too. How's she shaping up?'

'Fine.' Shona glanced at Brigid. 'A lot to learn, of course.'

'Everything,' added Brigid.

'Well, you'll look after her, won't you? Girls, I'll see you when I can, but thank you again for all you've done. So much appreciated!'

When Mrs May had left them, Shona and Brigid gave long relaxed sighs.

'Thank God, Mr May's OK,' said Brigid.

'Amen to that,' murmured Shona. 'I wonder when he'll be back?'

'If he comes back at all.'

They were silent for a moment, then Shona said there was no point in discussing it, they'd better just get back to the shop.

'Aye, rescue Isla, I suppose,' said Brigid.

It had been such a relief to hear about Mr May, to feel their anxiety rise and float away, that it was only when closing time came and Shona and Brigid could lock the door and end their long, long day that exhaustion again set in.

'I don't know about Mrs May, saying she feels she could go on for ever,' Brigid sighed, 'but I feel if I don't get home soon, I'll just drop where I stand.'

'Me, too,' said Shona. 'But thank the Lord we can get out into the fresh air at last!'

'And have something to eat and a gallon of tea.' Brigid was checking her purse for her tram fare to Marchmont, where she lived with her parents and younger brother. 'Ma'd better not suggest I do the washing up tonight, either. Why should I do it, when Rory sits about reading comics?'

Shona glanced at Isla. 'How about you, Isla? You got any lazy brothers?'

'No, I'm an only child.' Isla, looking happier than she'd looked all day now that she was going home, was putting on a light jacket. 'Wish I weren't, though.'

Snap, thought Shona, but she only smiled as she locked the shop door and they turned to go their different ways.

'So pleased about Mr May,' Isla ventured as she moved away.

'Best news ever,' said Brigid. 'See you tomorrow, then.'

'Tomorrow,' agreed Shona.

It was good to be walking home in the summer evening when the sky was still blue and the sunshine pleasantly warm on her face and hair, for she'd taken off her hat. At the Dean Bridge, she stopped to look down at the valley, at the houses she knew and where she was heading, and felt for a little while relaxed and at ease.

Soon, however, as she continued on her way, a certain nameless anxiety seemed to be working through her thoughts, and she quickened her step as though the feeling would leave her. What was she afraid of? Mr May was going to get better. There was no need to worry. Yet she had the feeling that change was on its way. *Everything changes, nothing stays the same* . . . What might be going to change at Maybel's? She didn't know. Perhaps nothing. Like a cold wind, the idea that that might not be true flowed round her all the way home, and it was only when she was back in Mrs Gow's unworried presence that she put the anxiety away and began to talk of the day she'd just lived through.

Twenty-Eight

Three weeks went by and Shona's unease remained with her, though she tried to put it to the back of her mind. Obviously there were changes in their routine at the shop, with Mr May still unable to work, even though out of the nursing home, and Mrs May too preoccupied to do her usual floristry. Not only was she frequently up in her flat, checking on Hugh, she also seemed to be spending more time in her office, often emerging with a deep frown etched between her dark brows. No doubt things would settle down soon when Hugh returned to duty, and he hadn't ruled it out when the girls visited him in the nursing home.

He'd looked frail then, his eyes larger than usual, his face thinner, and had admitted that he'd had a bit of a fright.

'When you reach the precipice and think you might have gone over, it gives you a funny feeling,' he'd told them, trying to laugh. 'You just have to get over that and keep reminding yourself you're still around.'

'I'm sure the doctors were very good,' Shona said, 'helping you to feel well again.'

'Och, yes, I suppose so.' He'd made a face. 'Pumped me full of God knows what – iodide of potassium, was it? I'm not sure, but they did a good job. Kept me from having a heart attack – or, worse, a seizure. Couldn't have stood that.'

'You're doing well,' Brigid told him robustly. 'Before you know it, you'll be back doing your arrangements again.'

'Maybe. But listen, I want to thank you girls for doing those flowers for Mrs Lockyer. Knowing you'd done that did me a world of good, I can tell you.'

'So you take care and come home soon,' Shona told him. 'We can't wait to have you back.'

'You can say that again,' Brigid had said when they were outside the nursing home. 'It may have escaped your notice but we're doing all the work at the moment, except for Isla's tidying up.'

'She did make some quite decent buttonholes for that wedding last week, don't forget.'

'Aye, but put her in the shop and she goes to pieces. Oh, well, things'll get back to normal one of these days, I expect.'

But then Mr May came home and didn't return to work, and Mrs May went around with that frown on her face, her earlier euphoria quite forgotten, while the extra work for Shona and Brigid showed no signs of easing.

'Guess what,' Brigid said one Wednesday, when Mrs May was away from the shop, 'I've been a bit naughty, but I've found out where she's gone today.'

'What's it matter?' asked Shona, setting out the flowers she needed for an order.

'Well, it's of interest, eh? I sneaked a look at her appointments diary on her desk and you know where she is, probably at this very moment?'

'Oh, just say. Don't be so irritating!'

'All right, she's at the Caledonian Hotel, having lunch with Mr Kyle.'

Shona laid down a long stemmed rose and stared. 'Mr Kyle?'

'That's right. Said in the book, "Lunch at the Caledonian, 12.30 p.m., with Fraser Kyle."'

'So he didn't come back here,' Shona said slowly. 'What's he want, I wonder?'

'Now that I don't know. Maybe we shall never be told, but it seems odd he'd spend so much money lunching Mrs May at the Caledonian.'

'Maybe she's paying?'

'Are you joking? No, I think it sounds as though he does want something from her.'

'And what's she got to give?' asked Shona, but she didn't answer her own question and neither did Brigid.

As soon as Dan had taken their flowers for delivery Shona left to meet Cassie, whose half day it was too.

Poor Cassie, Shona reflected as she toiled up the Mound to a café off George IV Bridge, she'd not had much luck since she left Edina Lodge. All she'd wanted was to be part of a household where she'd have friends and be valued, but nothing had worked out as she'd hoped.

In her first place, with the family in Hermitage Circle, the master, the rich businessman, had been a terrible one for 'wandering hands', as Cassie put it. None of the maids were safe and if they hadn't shared a bedroom and locked their door he'd have been in. No wonder, then, that there were always vacancies for female staff in his house, and his poor wife was used to writing 'characters' for departing servants.

In Cassie's second place, the home of another wealthy businessman, it wasn't the master who was at fault but his eldest son – only a schoolboy, but if anything worse than the father in the first house: always chasing the maids, pinching bottoms, stealing kisses, rattling bedroom doors, while his parents remained oblivious. It was not long before Cassie was asking for another 'character' and registering at an agency which seemed to think it eccentric she should want to work in a house where there were only women. In the end they found her the place where she was now, and so intensely miserable, she told Shona over lunch at the café, that she simply didn't know what to do.

'I thought they'd be all right, you see, the Misses Orde – two cousins, maiden ladies – that there'd be nothing to worry about. But they're so pernickety, Shona, and such skinflints! You wouldn't believe what they're like. Rolling in money, and have the lowest light bulbs, the smallest fires, the cheapest cuts o' meat. They drive Trudie – that's the cook – crazy, and me as well. Never off my bones, following me round to check I've swept into corners, dusted behind every picture, polished every fiddly bit o' furniture, and they've got plenty. And it isn't as though I'm no' thorough, you ken. I always do my best, but they never leave me alone. I don't know how I stick it!'

'Well, why do you?' Shona asked, finishing her poached egg on toast. 'You can move on; you've moved on before.'

'Aye, and I'll be getting a name for it, eh? But if I try to leave the Misses Orde, I bet they wouldn't give me a good character, and then I'd be stuck.'

'What you should do is find another kind of job altogether, Cassie. Give up service and get some independence.'

'I wish I could. I wish I'd been like you and gone into something different.'

'How about the dressmaking? You'd be good at that.'

'I'd never get taken on as an apprentice now, and I'd no' earn enough to live on even if I did. I've thought about shop work, but first I'd need the character, eh?' Cassie sighed, then gave a sudden grin. 'Maybe I'll marry the milkman. He has asked me.'

'The milkman? Cassie, you never said you had an admirer!'

'Och, we only went out together a couple o' times. I think all he wanted was somebody to run the dairy. Anyway, I said no. I'd never marry a man I didn't love.'

'Oh, no,' Shona agreed fervently. 'Neither would I!'

Later, as they strolled down Princes Street, looking at the shops, an idea came into Shona's mind. 'Listen, Cassie, if there was ever a vacancy where I am, would you be interested?'

'What, in your flower shop?' Cassie's eyes were large with surprise. 'Why, I know nothing about plants! And it'd be far too posh, eh? They'd never take me on.'

'What a piece of nonsense! They took me on, and I'm no different from you. And I think you'd be very good with the customers, as well as working with the flowers. Your fingers are as nimble as those of anyone I know.'

'I've no' got your talent, Shona.'

'I think you could learn the job and reach a high standard. If anything cropped up, you should definitely apply.'

'Well, is it likely?'

Thinking of Isla and whether or not she would stick it out, Shona shrugged. 'I don't know. I could tell you if there ever is a vacancy, anyway.'

'All right, tell me. It might be worth a try.'

'Of course it would.'

Feeling as though they'd settled something, though in fact they had no real promise of settling anything, the two girls moved into one of the department stores and enjoyed themselves immensely, trying on hats and pricing dresses they couldn't afford, until it was time to go for a cup of tea.

Walking home alone, though, after she'd seen Cassie on to her tram, all of Shona's doubts about the future returned. Maybe she shouldn't have said anything about possible vacancies at Maybel's to Cassie. Maybe there were things happening that would change everything. Or maybe she was just looking on the gloomy side?

She had the strongest feeling that she was going to find out very soon what the future might really hold, and not wanting to spend the evening thinking about it, decided to pop round to see Kitty, now married and living in Baxter Row only a few doors from her mother.

It would be nice, Shona thought, to see folk as happy as Kitty and her young baker husband. As long as they didn't consider her to be playing gooseberry.

Twenty-Nine

Next morning, though she'd half been expecting it, Shona could still scarcely believe it when the blow fell. So soon? Had she got second sight, or what? She could have laughed at herself for that, except she didn't feel like laughing and was as serious-faced as Brigid and Isla when Mrs May announced that she had some important news to tell them.

It was before nine o'clock and they were in the staffroom, drinking that early tea Shona had battled for, when Mrs May had appeared. Though her make-up was in place and her hair immaculate, she seemed strained, the frown between her brows still evident, as though it might have become a permanent feature. When they half rose from the table she waved them down and took a chair herself.

'Girls, I have something to tell you. It's very important – to you – to all of us.'

That was when Shona knew she'd been right to expect some sort of news and sat rigidly in her chair, Brigid and Isla beside her, her eyes and theirs fixed on Mrs May.

For a moment her lip had trembled, but she'd soon achieved control, and came out directly with her announcement. 'The fact is, girls, and I'm sorry to have to tell you, but Hugh and I are selling the shop.'

There was a stunned silence.

Brigid caught her breath and Isla sat with her mouth open, while Shona felt she'd taken a step that wasn't there, for though she'd expected something, she hadn't expected anything so final as this. The Mays were to sell Maybel's? Leaving their life's work? For a moment, that feeling of falling was so real she put her hand out as though to steady herself.

And then, all became clear. Yes, the shop was to be sold, she had to believe it, and she knew who was going to buy it. No wonder he'd been making appointments to see Mrs May, no wonder he'd been lunching her at the Caledonian! He'd wanted something from her and the shop was what she had to give. Or, at least, sell. Fraser Kyle was the new owner of Maybel's.

'As you know,' Mrs May was continuing, 'my husband has been quite ill and doesn't feel he can carry on working. For a time, I thought I might manage to keep going without him, and he was all for that.' She cleared her throat a little. 'After all, the shop has been our life for many years; it was hard to think of being without it. But then I realized things wouldn't be the same without Hugh, and that really I should be spending time with him and looking after him.'

Here, Mrs May paused and looked at the girls, but no one spoke and after a moment she resumed. 'By sheer coincidence, while we were thinking about this, more or less out of the blue we received a very generous offer to buy the business. It was from Mr Fraser Kyle, who has taken over MacVicar's.' Mrs May smiled briefly. 'We didn't wait long to accept. When the legal matters are completed, he will be the new owner of Maybel's.'

Another silence fell, then Shona spoke. 'Mrs May, I want to say we're very sorry you're having to give up Maybel's.'

'Aye, can't believe it,' put in Brigid. 'It doesn't seem possible – I mean, Maybel's without you and Mr May.'

'I haven't been here very long,' Isla said, surprising everyone by speaking up, 'but I feel the same as Shona and Brigid. Everyone knows Maybel's – they'll be really sad.'

'Ah, you're so good, you girls,' sighed Mrs May. 'So sweet, so sympathetic. I can't tell you how bad we feel, Hugh and I, leaving all of you, but there's one thing I can do and that's to put your minds at rest about your jobs. They're quite safe. Mr Kyle will be keeping everyone on, so you've no need to worry.'

'Thank you, Mrs May,' Shona murmured as she and Brigid exchanged quick glances. 'That's good to know.'

Mrs May rose, glancing at the clock. 'I see it's almost opening time. I think I've just time to tell you that though Mr Kyle will probably be making some changes, I'm sure they'll be good ones. He's an ambitious man, but shrewd. He won't rush into things, and he's done well so far, expanded his father's ironwear business and made money when he sold it.'

'How's he going to run the shop here if he has the market garden to look after as well?' asked Brigid. 'He can't be in two places at once.'

'He's dividing his time between the two. Mr MacVicar's right-hand man, Arthur Weir, can be relied upon to manage the garden very well, anyway, and Mr Kyle is taking over our flat to be on the spot here. He's planning to make offices of the first floor, keeping rooms for himself on the second.'

The girls looked at one another.

'But where are you going, Mrs May?' cried Shona. 'We never thought you'd be leaving the flat.'

Mrs May laughed. 'You wouldn't expect us to stay on, would you, breathing down poor Mr Kyle's neck? Anyway, we want to go by the sea for our retirement. We're going to look for a place in Anstruther in Fife.'

'Oh,' said the girls, and for the first time fully realized how final this break between the Mays and themselves was going to be. There seemed to be no more left to be said, however, and as Mrs May returned upstairs Brigid told Isla to unlock the shop door and turned to face Shona.

'Well,' she said shortly, 'what do you make of that?'

'I don't know. I don't know what to make of it.'

'One thing's for sure: it's going to be very different, working for Mr Kyle, isn't it?'

'We've no idea what he'll be like.'

'All I know is what you've told me. That he's big. We'll be working for a BIG man, Shona.'

Somehow, the idea struck them as funny and they began to laugh, but the laughter was close to tears and very soon they grew serious and moved out of the staffroom to begin work.

Thirty

Knowing nothing of lawyers and their ways, the girls had expected the new owner to be installed fairly soon, but it was October before the sale of the shop was completed and they were able to say goodbye to the Mays.

Of course, Mr Kyle came to the shop to introduce himself before that and, as Brigid said afterwards, flattened them all the minute he walked in. Not only was he a large man physically, he had a personality to match, which allowed him to dominate any space in which he found himself, and any people, too. Certainly, he filled the front shop as though it was altogether too small for him, though he quickly disclaimed any idea of that.

'This is perfect, eh?' he said genially, walking round, doffing his hat to the girls and the customers who were watching him in awe. 'I've always admired this shop. Used to come up from Leith with my folks and always look in the window. Wonderful!'

His light green eyes went to Isla's small, anxious face and he put his hand on her shoulder. 'Now, you're Isla, eh? And not been here long?'

'Not very long,' she answered hoarsely.

'But I bet you can take care of the shop for a while, can't you, Isla? Just while I have a word with these two young ladies next door? I'd like to include you, but of course someone has to see to the customers.'

Swallowing hard, Isla nodded. 'Yes, Mr Kyle, I'll look after the shop,' she said and he smiled, showing his dimples.

'They can tell you what I've said afterwards. Now, Shona and Brigid – you don't mind my using your first names? I'm not one for formality. Shall we go into your workroom?'

At the long table he took a stool and motioned to the girls to do the same. 'No one here today,' he remarked, looking round. 'I understand the Mays are out house hunting, but Mrs May told me that this is the hub of the shop, where all those wonderful bouquets are made up. It never ceases to amaze me what can be done with the flowers I grow.'

'Amazes us too, sometimes,' Brigid told him with a smile.

'No, no, you people know how it's done – I don't.' He looked from one to the other of them. 'But can I take it that you both want to stay on?'

'Oh, yes, Mr Kyle, I do,' Shona said at once.

'Me, too,' said Brigid.

'That's good. I'm glad. Because you two are my experts, of course. As I say, I know nothing about flower arranging.' Fraser took out a silver cigarette case, then smiled at the looks on the girls' faces and put it back. 'Sorry, no smoking here, of course.'

'Only in the workroom, really,' Shona told him.

'I won't forget. Now, I just want to talk to you about my plans. I feel you're entitled to know what's in my mind.'

They waited, saying nothing.

'I'm ambitious, I'll admit,' he went on, 'but what I'm hoping is that this flower shop will not be the first I'll be running. I'd like to see a chain of shops in the main cities of Scotland – and maybe over the border too, one day – all of 'em with the same standards as this one, all providing the style of flowers people want. And I've done my homework. Since the war, people want some beauty and colour in their lives. Where better to find it than in flowers?'

The girls, now staring at his large enthusiastic face, mesmerized by the light shining in his eyes, were speechless. What on earth was he talking about? A chain of shops, all like Maybel's? Had he not realized that Maybel's was unique? You couldn't expect to find its like all over Scotland!

He was watching them, gauging their reaction, not surprised perhaps by their astonishment. 'I know all this may sound unusual to you, but it's the way money is made, you see. Someone gets on to a good thing and decides to try it somewhere else, finds success and carries on. I did it in a small way with my ironmongery shops, and you can see the same sort of thing with Lipton's the Grocer's, can't you? When someone shops at a Lipton's, they know just what they're getting. It'll be the same with Maybel's Flowers.'

'You're keeping the name?' asked Shona quickly.

'Of course! It's a good name. I've bought it with the shop, to the Mays' full agreement.'

'They know what you'd like to do?'

'Ah, well, not really. I haven't gone into details. They know I've got plans, as with my market garden, but we'll leave those for the moment. All I need to know is that if I begin to develop things, you'll be happy?'

'I expect it'll all take some time,' Shona said cautiously.

'Oh, sure. Rome wasn't built in a day.' Fraser stood up. 'But even to begin with, I'll probably take on more staff. Build up the outside ordering. And then there'll be alterations to be made to the upstairs flat for my admin department. Might also turn Mrs May's office into an indoor plant room.' He grinned. 'Think you'll find this place whizzing pretty soon, eh?'

'Sounds like it,' said Brigid.

They made their way back to the front shop where Isla, amazingly, was at the till, ringing up a price for a lady's mixed flowers. As Brigid stepped forward to serve a new customer, Fraser touched Shona's arm.

'You looked a bit stunned back there,' he said in a low voice. 'Haven't alarmed you too much, have I?'

'No, of course not. I'm sure it's a good thing to expand.'

'That's true. Even if you don't really believe it now, I bet I can make you see it eventually. Tell me, when are you coming over to the garden?'

She looked at him in surprise. 'Why, I suppose when the sale is completed. Mrs May is still ordering the flowers.'

'So she is, and I'll be taking over that job in the future. Doesn't mean you can't come to the gardens, does it?'

'No, suppose not.' In spite of herself, Shona was showing her disappointment; she had been hoping that the job of selecting the flowers might come to her.

'So, when the signatures are on the dotted line you'll be along, won't you?' Fraser went on, disregarding her look. 'Don't forget, you said you'd like to come and I'll hold you to that.'

He put on his hat and shook hands, first with Shona, then Brigid and Isla, saying how glad he'd been to meet them and how much he was looking forward to working with them. Not long now! With customers around, there wasn't much the girls could say until they'd gone, but as soon as there was a lull, Brigid jogged Shona's arm.

'Honestly, have you ever heard such a piece of nonsense? Opening a chain of flower shops? I mean, they're not grocery stores, eh?'

'I can't see it working out,' Shona replied. 'He doesn't seem to realize that flower shops have their own character.'

'Just hope he doesn't find out the hard way and go bankrupt.'

'Mrs May did say he was a shrewd businessman, remember.'

Brigid, her usual cheerfulness seeming to have deserted her, shook her head.

'I just wish Mrs May was staying, and Mr May as well. This place isn't going to be the same.'

'At least we're keeping our jobs.'

'If we want them,' Brigid said darkly.

Some weeks later the news came that the formalities had been completed. Maybel's Flowers was officially owned by Mr Fraser Kyle, and Mr and Mrs May were making their goodbyes. A house had been found at Anstruther, and though they would be staying at a hotel until it was ready, as soon as they moved in the girls were told they must come and visit. Standing in the street, ready to get into their car, the Mays told the girls any Sunday would be perfect.

They could have lunch, stroll around the harbour – now they did promise to come?

'Try keeping us away,' said Brigid, giving a signal to Shona, who dived back into the shop to bring out the exquisite bouquet they had made for the Mays, and handed it to Isla to present.

'They couldn't decide which of 'em should give it to you,' Isla said with an unusually confident smile, 'so they said it should be me. We just want to thank you both – for everything.'

'All you've done for us,' said Brigid.

'And to say we're going to miss you so much,' murmured Shona. 'Take care, eh?'

'We don't know what to say, do we, Hugh?' Mrs May whispered. 'You've been such good girls. We do hope all goes well for you.'

'Aye, with everything,' Hugh muttered. 'Things are going to be different, but you'll be fine – everything'll work out.' He gave a smile that for a moment made him look well again. 'And you know, I'd say we're the ones who are going to miss you.'

There were hugs and sniffs and final waves as Mrs May, having carefully placed her flowers on the back seat, took her place in the driving seat and, with Mr May beside her, slowly moved into the traffic of George Street and away to their new life.

For some moments the girls were silent, reflecting on their own new life still to come, before returning to the shop and, for a little while, the life they knew.

Thirty-One

Even before work had begun on his alterations to the upstairs flat, even before he'd been able to do anything at all, Fraser told Shona that the time had come for her to visit his market garden. He would drive her over the following morning. 'No time like the present,' he told her cheerfully. 'Even if it's tomorrow.'

She looked at him doubtfully. 'What about Brigid?'

'What about her?'

'Well, she is senior to me. I think you should take her first.'

His eyes flashed a little but his smile didn't waver. 'Shona, I'm taking you. No arguments. Brigid can go some other time, so warn her that she'll be in charge tomorrow. She'll have Isla to help out – I understand she's doing quite well these days.'

'That's true. It just seemed to click with her, that time you told her to look after the shop.' Shona smiled. 'And she did. But I'm really worrying how Brigid will cope if there are any orders to prepare.'

'There aren't, I've checked.' Fraser's tone was pleasantly triumphant. 'Ready to come tomorrow, then?'

'Yes, Mr Kyle.'

With some reluctance, Shona found Brigid and told her about the arrangements for the next day, showing no surprise when Brigid's look hardened.

'You're going out to the garden tomorrow? First I've heard of it.'

'It's only just been arranged.'

'And I'm supposed to hold the fort? Our dear Mr Kyle might have told me himself.'

'I think he's on the phone to the people coming to do the work upstairs.'

Brigid shrugged. 'Oh, well, it doesn't matter to me. But you know why he's taking you, don't you?'

'Looks like you're going to tell me.'

'Obvious, isn't it? It's his way of getting time alone with you. That's what he wants. This has nothing to do with work so don't be fooled, Shona. I'd watch my step if I were you.'

'Brigid, I don't know what you're talking about!' Shona's cheeks were burning. 'I've never heard such nonsense! Mr Kyle's no' interested in me. I don't know why you should say such a thing.'

'Doesn't have to be spelled out when somebody's sweet on somebody else. His eyes follow you wherever you go. I noticed it from the beginning.'

'Well, even if that's true, I'm sure there won't be any reason for me to watch my step, as you put it. Mr Kyle isn't the sort you have to worry about. But if it's of any interest to you, I've no interest in him.'

'Big enough to make sure he gets his own way – isn't that what you told me once?' Brigid smiled coldly. 'Better make sure you know what his way is, then.'

Such warnings would have been quite enough to ruin Shona's little trip into the country had it not been for Brigid's repenting of her ill humour the following morning, when she waved goodbye as cheerfully as though she'd never said a word against Mr Kyle.

What a relief, thought Shona, sitting in the passenger seat of his large old Vauxhall and enjoying the drive to the garden centre. The winding road was lovely, so quiet and countrified, with only grazing sheep for company and, in the distance, a view of the Moorfoot Hills rising into the clear sky. Really, she now felt quite grateful to Mr Kyle for inviting her, and even to Brigid for obviously regretting her remarks.

'Hey, why so silent?' Mr Kyle cried as he drove smoothly down the quiet road. 'It's a beautiful October morning with sunshine on the hills. Even the sheep look happy. Not still worrying about Brigid, are you? I've told you she'll have her turn.'

'Yes, you did. Sorry. To tell the truth, I'm just enjoying the scenery. You forget what the country's like, living in a city.'

'That's why I'm lucky: I've a foot in both places. A flat in Peebles and now another in Edinburgh. What more could a man ask? Where do you live, Shona?'

'I've got lodgings in the Dean Village.'

'Below Telford's bridge? Ah, now I don't know that at all well, but I believe it's got quite a history. Full of bakers and flour mills, eh?'

'That's right. But there used to be two villages at one time. One called the Village of Dean, near where the cemetery is now, and the other the Water of Leith village below the bridge. Now there's just the one – under the bridge – and that's called the Dean Village.'

'Complicated! But you say you're in lodgings. Don't live with your parents, then?'

Shona was staring fixedly at the road ahead. 'My folks are dead. My dad died in the Great War and my mother died of the Spanish flu. I was brought up in Edina Lodge – the orphanage.'

For some moments Mr Kyle was silent, and when she stole a look at his face she saw it had darkened, as though a shadow had covered his smiles.

'You're an orphan?' he murmured at last. 'I didn't know, I'm sorry. Must have been difficult for you. But, here we are. MacVicar's Nurseries. Haven't decided yet whether to change the name or not. In we go, then.'

Long white gates were open, letting them through into an open space before a one-storey stone building. On their right was a place to park cars. On their left was a bank of trees, from which two large black cats came out to inspect them, while beyond the building came the glint of the sun on glass houses. Though she couldn't yet plainly see them, Shona guessed that past the glass houses would be the plantings. Yes, acres and acres of plants, shrubs, trees, flowers and, as she stepped out of the car, Shona knew that whatever her misgivings, she was indeed going to enjoy this day.

Thirty-Two

'Come and meet my chaps,' Mr Kyle said to Shona when he'd parked his car. 'My guess is that they'll have got the kettle on!'

He pushed open the door of the one-storey building and ushered her into a small room where four men in working clothes were seated round a table drinking tea. A tin of biscuits was open to hand and all four of the men, two middle-aged, two young, were smoking.

'Morning all!' Mr Kyle called, at which they looked up and grinned. 'Got any tea in that pot?'

'Morning, Mr Kyle,' said one of the older men, rising to his feet. 'Come on in. Terry, put the kettle on again. Dickie, fetch the chairs.'

As the two young men rose to obey orders, Mr Kyle brought Shona forward. 'This is Miss Murray from Maybel's; it's her first visit to the garden. Shona, this is my right-hand man, Arthur Weir – we call him Art. Next to him is his main assistant, George Wilson. Young Terry MacPhail is making the tea and Dickie Logan is bringing us chairs.'

Feeling the full battery of curious eyes on her, Shona managed a smile and a word of thanks as Dickie placed a chair for her, and said how much she was looking forward to seeing the source of the shop's flowers.

'No Mrs May now, of course,' said Art Weir, thin and weather-beaten, with greying hair and long-sighted grey eyes. 'My word, it'll be strange no' seeing her again, eh?'

'Always knew what she wanted,' commented George, taller and plumper than Art, but equally weather-beaten. 'Never took second best.'

'Sounds exactly like me!' Fraser Kyle exclaimed, at which the men exchanged looks and grins.

'Aye, Mr Kyle, you're right enough there,' Art agreed. 'Terry, where's that tea?'

'Coming, Mr Weir – just getting the cups.'

It was an awkward tea break, Shona thought, aware that she was still a focus of interest, mainly for the younger men who made no conversation but watched closely as she took a biscuit and sipped her tea. Meanwhile, of course, Mr Kyle was quite at ease, sitting back, lighting a cigarette, chatting to Art and George but eventually, to Shona's relief, rising and saying they must get on.

'I just want to give Miss Murray a quick guided tour, then we'll maybe have a bit of lunch in Peebles and get back to the shop. All right, Art?'

'All right, Mr Kyle. We're getting back to work now, anyway. Come on, lads, clear away, then. There's a load o' weeds out there just waiting for your attention!'

'Keeps everyone on their toes,' Fraser Kyle commented, putting his hand for a moment on the older man's shoulder. 'But couldn't manage without him, and that's the truth.'

'Well, sounds like you're giving yourself plenty to do over at Maybel's,' Art remarked. 'Knocking doors out o' windows is what I hear.'

'No, no, it'll all work out for the best, Art. I've got a very good fellow to draw up plans for the alterations and I've got very good staff to look after the shop. Miss Murray, for instance.

'But no Mrs May.'

'No Mrs May. But let's face it, if Mrs May was there I wouldn't be, so can't have everything, eh?' As Art shrugged, Fraser grinned, then moved to the door. 'Thanks for the tea, lads. Shona, do you want to come with me?'

Outside in the fresh autumn air she took some grateful breaths, adjusting her hat over her bright hair while Fraser watched.

'Too much cigarette smoke for you, was there? But, look, I've put mine out.' He laughed a little. 'I hope you didn't mind being a centre of interest? The lads don't see many stunning young ladies over from Edinburgh, remember.'

'They see Mrs May,' she answered, flushing.

'Very attractive, too, but – well – not exactly young. Not like you.'

'Mr Kyle—'

'I know, I know, I shouldn't be making personal remarks. I apologize. Let's go and look at the glass houses.'

Seeing flowers again, this time ranked in beautiful masses under their glass protection quickly soothed Shona's faint worry that

Mr Kyle was going to turn out as Brigid had prophesied, for here she was on home ground and at ease again. Mr Kyle himself was being very polite and, for him, subdued as she went around exclaiming over the amazing choice of flowers, sometimes turning back to smile at him over what she was finding.

'So lovely to see so many blooms like this, Mr Kyle!'

'Even chrysanthemums?' he asked wryly. 'Some gardeners are a wee bit snobby about them.'

'And dahlias, I know. But I think that's wrong, I think there's a place somewhere for every flower. In gardens and in flower arranging, too. And when it's winter, the mums can be a godsend.'

'You're a real enthusiast, aren't you, Shona? When did you begin to like flowers?'

'I think I'd always liked plants, but maybe it was when I first went to the orphanage and I saw the Handkerchief Tree that I really got interested.'

'The Handkerchief Tree?' He raised his eyebrows. 'A bit exotic for an orphanage, isn't it?'

'We were lucky, I was at Edina Lodge – it used to belong to a wealthy man and we still had his garden. That's where I saw the tree.'

'And somebody told you about it?'

'Yes, he's now the orphanage doctor. His father, the doctor there at the time, had one, so he explained about its flowers that were sort of leaves.'

'Strange story,' commented Fraser, his eyes very attentive on her face. 'And do you still see this doctor?'

'Oh, no. I've been back to the orphanage but he's never been there.'

'Pity. Well, shall we move on?'

Shona felt she had never spent a happier morning, moving round the few acres of the garden, studying the amazingly neat planting of the vegetables that made up a good part of the income, admiring the varieties of plants, from hardy flowers to those grown for foliage, finally returning to peep into a smaller glass house where late tomatoes were ripening.

'It's amazing,' she told Fraser. 'So well taken care of and thought out. It's no wonder Mrs May used it for the shop.'

'I believe she had one or two other sources, didn't she? Told me she also tried the local market.'

'Sometimes, but mainly she relied on MacVicar's. Or Kyle's, as it might be.'

'I'll have to make up my mind on that, won't I? Look, if you've seen enough, shall we make our way to Peebles? I'm feeling peckish.'

'Would you mind if I just had something light? My landlady always likes to make a hot meal in the evening.'

'Sure, you can have anything you like. Maybe we'll both have something light. I could do with losing weight. I'll just have a quick word with Art and then we can be on our way.'

So far, so good, thought Shona, as they made their farewells to Art and his workers and took to the road again. After the tricky tea break, she'd really enjoyed her visit to the garden. Now all she had to get through was the lunch. Maybe it wouldn't take long; she really didn't want to spend too much time alone with Mr Kyle.

Thirty-Three

Seemed he knew just the place to go for a light lunch in Peebles, an ancient royal burgh that was the county town of the area, and was soon parking near a small main street café that specialized in soups, salads and anything with eggs.

'Nice,' commented Shona when they were seated at a window table. 'Just the sort of place I like.'

'Been to Peebles before?'

'Once or twice. A long time ago with my mother.'

Again, a shadow seemed to cross Mr Kyle's brow. Or had Shona imagined it?

'Here comes the waitress,' he said, putting on his cheerful voice. 'What would you like? Soup of the day and a cheese omelette?'

'That'd be grand. Thank you very much, Mr Kyle.'

'I wish you'd call me Fraser,' he murmured when he'd given the waitress their order, at which Shona caught her breath sharply.

'Why, I couldn't! It wouldn't be right.'

'Not at work. But we're not at work now.'

She hesitated. 'I'm still no' sure I can.'

'Well, give it a try, eh?' He sat back, taking out his cigarettes, then shook his head and put the packet back in his pocket. 'Better not. Don't want to spoil your lunch.'

After a moment, he leaned forward, his look quite serious. 'You know, Shona, I was very sorry to hear about your parents. I mean, first your dad being killed in the war, and then your mother dying with the flu. A real tragedy. For me, too.'

'For you?'

'Well, I mean, something similar happened to me. I went right through the war without a scratch. Seemed to lead a charmed life, folk said, but when I came home I lost my girl. To the Spanish flu, just like your mother.'

'Oh, I'm so sorry!' Shona cried. 'Oh, that must have been terrible for you!'

'Aye, it was. And ironic. There I was, perfectly all right after a war that had killed millions, and there was my Meggie, safe at home, dead after two days.' Fraser put a hand to his brow. 'I thought I'd never get over it. But you do eventually, of course. The pain lessens bit by bit. You were only a child, though, when your mother died. Must have been bad for you.'

'It was, but I suppose, like you, the pain went after a time. Most of us at the orphanage were in the same boat. We'd all been through it.'

'Two soups,' said the young waitress, setting down bowls of celery soup. 'All right?'

'Fine,' said Fraser, taking up his spoon. 'This looks good, eh?' But his look was still serious.

They said no more until the omelettes came, when they discussed what Shona had seen at the garden for a time, and Fraser said again what a grand fellow Art was, a real rock, and how he couldn't do without him. It was only when the coffee came that Fraser leaned forward again to look into Shona's eyes.

'The thing is, Shona,' he said softly, 'you remind me of her, of Meggie. You've the same colouring exactly. Not quite the same features, but so much like her, I couldn't believe it when I first saw you. You must have noticed how I keep looking at you, haven't you?'

His eyes follow you, wherever you go. Brigid's words. Seemingly true. Shona, coffee cup in hand, sat, stricken. To look like a dead girl – Mr Kyle's dead girl – oh, God, no. No, she didn't want that. How could she? How could she want to look like someone dead, who'd been loved by this man sitting so close, now gazing at herself so very intently?

'I'm – I'm sure I don't really look like her,' she said, stumbling over the words. 'I mean, you said my face wasn't the same, eh? It's just my hair, then, and lots of girls have my colour hair.'

His look now was calm. Understanding. 'I've upset you,' he said quietly. 'I'm sorry. Of course you don't want to look like someone dead. I shouldn't have said anything.'

'It's all right.' She lowered her eyes. 'I understand.'

'No, I was wrong to mention it. Particularly because I've something I want to say to you and I don't want you to think—' Fraser ran his hand over his sandy hair. 'Well, I don't want you to think I'm saying it because I've a special interest, or anything of that sort.'

'What is it, then? That you want to say?'

'Well, as you know, I have to divide my time between the garden and the shop, so what I need is someone to stand in for me at the shop when I'm not there.' He smiled quickly. 'In other words, a manageress. I'd like you to take that on.'

'Me?' Shona's eyes, now raised, were wide with shock; colour was flooding her face. 'Mr Kyle, you can't mean what you're saying. I'm too young, I haven't the experience. Brigid is the person you should be talking to, no' me!'

'I knew you'd say that. You're always worrying about Brigid, but I have my answer ready. I'm used to sizing people up; I can recognize potential, and I know that you'd make an excellent manageress. You've got the knowledge, you've got flair, you've had a tough beginning but you've done well. That tells me a lot.' He waved his hands. 'All I need.'

'Brigid's older, she's been at the shop longer, she's the obvious choice. You can't pass her over!'

'I don't agree, and I'll tell you why. Brigid is a good worker but she thinks mainly of herself, whereas you think of the shop, the business, and that's what I want to see. And look at your interest in flowers! Look how you made the case for the chrysanthemum and the dahlia! Why, I bet you'd agree with me and say we ought to be thinking about using wild flowers for particular occasions – isn't that right?'

'That is right. I've often thought we should think about wild flowers. They're so beautiful and when you don't need an arrangement to last a long time they'd be perfect. Bluebells, cowslips – oh, I could think of all sorts to use, if we could only get them accepted . . .'

Shona was relaxing, her eyes growing dreamy, when suddenly she caught a certain look on Fraser's face that brought her up short. 'Oh, Mr Kyle, you're clever!' she whispered. 'Talking about wild flowers – getting me sidetracked – making me forget Brigid!'

'I thought you were going to call me Fraser,' he said, laughing and waving to the waitress for their bill. 'And I'm admitting nothing.'

'I didn't say I'd call you Fraser, and I didn't say I'd be manageress.'

'But you will. Come on, let's go.'

'Thank you very much for giving me lunch,' she murmured when they were walking to the car. 'It was very kind of you,' she stopped, then added hastily, 'Fraser.'

'My pleasure.'

As he assisted her into the car, she knew without looking that his smile would have that hint of triumph she had noted before. But then he must be used to his little triumphs. Hadn't she said that he was big enough to make sure he got his own way? But maybe, if she took the job, she might get her way too and persuade him to give Cassie a job?

As they drove swiftly back to Edinburgh, she cleared her throat and spoke. 'Did you say we'd be needing more staff?'

'I did say that, yes. Especially if I convert the old office into a plant room.'

'Well, I wonder if you'd mind considering somebody I know would do very well. She was my friend at the orphanage but then she ended up in service because that's what they wanted all the girls to do. I was the only one who wanted something else.'

'I bet you were!' Fraser gave her a quick glance. 'But if this lassie's in service and has had no experience, how do you know she'll do well as a florist?'

'Because she's very good with her hands. I'm sure she could learn the techniques very quickly, but she'd be very good with the public as well. She has a lovely personality.'

'And a good friend in you. Oh, well, I suppose I could give her an interview and see how she did. Leave her address with me and I'll suggest a time to see her.'

'She could only come on a Wednesday afternoon. That's her afternoon off.'

'Only come on Wednesday afternoon?' Fraser stared at the road ahead for moment then gave a great burst of laughter. 'Honestly, Shona, you thought you weren't suitable to be manageress – seems you're managing me already! I'd better take care, or you'll be running the whole place, eh?'

After a little hesitation, she laughed with him and continued her drive with him feeling more at ease than she'd thought possible.

Thirty-Four

After all the misgivings, as the weeks went by and the roof didn't fall in over Maybel's because Fraser Kyle had taken it over, gradually the girls had to admit that things were going well. Perhaps it was easiest for Shona to do that, for she worked more closely with Fraser and had gained confidence in him more quickly, but as time moved on the same confidence came to Isla and even to Brigid – though she had been for a time understandably hostile to all that was new. Particularly Shona's promotion.

'I knew you'd feel bad, Brigid,' Shona had groaned, 'but you don't feel half as bad as me.'

'Still took the job though, eh? But what did I expect? You're the blue-eyed girl with his Nibs, all right, even if your eyes do happen to be hazel. I've a good mind to put in my notice.'

'Oh, don't do that, Brigid! We couldn't do without you.'

'Wait till Mrs May hears about this, and Willa and all. They'll be astounded.'

'Well, we can find out when we see them, can't we?' Shona said with an unhappy sigh. She was still feeling guilty, but what could she do? Maybe she should see Mr Kyle and tell him she'd changed her mind?

'Och, let's forget it,' Brigid said suddenly, and turned aside. 'It's not worth falling out over, is it? I'd probably have done the same as you if I'd been in your shoes. And I don't really want to leave.'

'And I don't want you to!' Shona had insisted. 'I just want things to be the same as always between us.'

But as Brigid had once remarked, things were always changing, nothing stayed the same, and changes were coming so thick and fast to Maybel's it was hard to keep up with them.

First, there were the promised alterations to the upstairs flat, when Mrs May's rooms were turned into offices and a Mr Stuart MacNay – tall, thin and thirty years old – was appointed to look after the accounts. Quite an expense, that, which Mrs May had not taken on as she had always done her own accounts and her own typing, too – but then she was keen to save money and had had some training before she married. Though Mr Kyle might have done his own accounts, he certainly would never be seen doing his own typing, the girls said with a laugh and, sure enough, he soon arranged for Miss Elrick, his middle-aged typist from Peebles, to come over twice a week to do his secretarial work. Bit of a battleaxe, the girls thought her, but at least she was only part time.

'Next there'll be another assistant coming, I suppose,' said Isla. 'We'll need somebody when the new plant room's opened.

And that was the next new thing: Mrs May's old office undergoing transformation into a place specially organized for house and small bedding plants, which led Shona to ask Fraser when she could arrange for Cassie to come in for an interview.

'We're going to need another pair of hands pretty soon,' she told him. 'You did say you'd see Cassie on a Wednesday afternoon.'

'I know, I know, but I've been snowed under.' He smiled ruefully. 'Fix it up, then. Next Wednesday afternoon all right?'

'Fine. I'll send her a postcard this very day.'

'Can't wait to see this wonderful friend of yours, Shona. Is she anything like you?'

'Nothing like me, but a very good worker and very skilful. I think you'll be pleased with her.'

'Maybe,' was all he would say.

In the event, he was quite pleasantly surprised, for Cassie, desperately nervous as she was, acquitted herself well in the interview, coming over as a personable and helpful young woman who would be good with the public and quick to learn. If she might lack Shona's innate flair and natural affinity with plants, she could still develop into a useful member of staff, Fraser decided, and at the end of the interview he told her he was willing to offer her a job with a six-month trial.

'Now scoot off and tell your friend, Shona,' he said with a smile, as Cassie rose, speechless, from her chair. 'She'll give you all the details you need to know and I hope you'll be able to start work as soon as you've completed your notice.'

'Oh, thank you, Mr Kyle, I'm so grateful.'

'Off you go.' He held open the door of his new office and away she went, down the staircase, looking for Shona to share her relief and happiness.

'Oh, Shona, I can't believe it! I mean, me getting the job! Working with you at Maybel's!'

The two of them were hugging in the workroom, almost in tears at the thought of Cassie's being able to leave her tyrant employers, though Shona, who'd come in on her afternoon off, said they really must calm down – she had all sorts of official things to tell Cassie. And then they must work out where she was going to live.

'Oh, my, I'd never even got that far,' Cassie cried. 'Didn't dare to think of it in case I didn't get the job. But now I have – Shona, where will I go?'

Though Cassie was suddenly looking anxious, Shona said she must come through to meet Brigid and Isla in the front shop, then have a cup of tea.

'And don't worry about finding somewhere to live; I have an idea about it. If it works out, I'll let you know as soon as I can.'

'Shona, you're my guardian angel.' Cassie sighed. 'But I'd like to meet the other girls. I just hope they'll approve of me.'

'Of course they will. Why shouldn't they?'

'Well, I've no' got the right experience. I've only been in service.'

'That was in the past. Your future's with us now and you'll be fine. Come on, let's go to the shop.'

'She's nice,' was Brigid's verdict when Cassie had departed for her tram, all starry-eyed again about her good luck. 'I think she'll fit in and be quick to learn.'

'Quicker than me,' sighed Isla. 'But, yes, she's nice. I like her. Can you really find her somewhere to live, Shona?'

'I think so. I'm going round this evening to see my old friend, Mrs Hope, in the Dean Village. She's got no room to take Cassie in, but I think she'll know somebody who has.'

So it proved, with Addie being only too pleased to give her advice on helping out a sweet girl like Cassie, and approving of Shona's idea to ask Kitty to let her a room. Of course Kitty'd be glad to help Cassie out, too, and have the chance of earning a bit of extra money! After all, she did have two bedrooms, eh? And only needed one, seeing as there was no baby on the way yet.

'Let you and me go round and see her now,' Addie urged Shona. 'Then you can tell Cassie and set her mind at rest.'

'I thought of Kitty straight away, but I didn't like to ask her without seeing you first, in case you felt she'd rather no' have a stranger in the house when she's a newly-wed.'

'A bit of cash will sweeten that along, and I'm sure Cassie will be no trouble. What a nice thing it is, her getting a job with you, then, eh? After all her troubles in service!'

As Mrs Hope had said, Kitty was quite willing to let her spare room to Cassie, saying she remembered meeting her very well when she'd come over for tea sometimes with Shona from the orphanage. As for what Johnny, the young husband thought, that wasn't clear, for he was so much under Kitty's spell that anything she said seemed to be all right with him, which made Shona and Mrs Hope exchange glances and smile.

'I'll tell Cassie then,' said Shona, 'and she'll come round when she can to see the room and make arrangements. Thanks so much, Kitty – and Johnny, too. Cassie will be so happy. I'm sure she'll be a very good lodger and no' be too much in the way.'

'Nae bother,' Kitty told her. 'We're just glad she's getting out o' that service job. What a life, eh? No' for me!'

The following morning, having sent off a letter to Cassie, Shona was in the workroom, preparing flame-coloured gladioli for an order, when Fraser put his head round the door.

'Morning, Shona. I just popped in to ask – are you pleased with me?'

'Pleased?'

'For giving your friend a job, of course. That was what you wanted, wasn't it?'

'Oh, yes, and it was good of you to give her an interview, but I know very well you didn't give her the job because of me.'

'And how do you work that out?'

He came to the table where she was working and, perching his large bulk on a stool, fixed her with his light green stare.

'Well, because you're a businessman. You wouldn't take on a person who wasn't going to be right just to please somebody else.'

He raised his eyebrows, still keeping his gaze on her. 'Well put, Shona, and very shrewd. I can see I've no chance of fooling you into gratitude. Cassie did do well and I wanted to give her the job. I think, eventually, she'll be an asset.'

'It's nice of you to say that.' Shona's smile was wide and genuine. 'Maybe I'll show some gratitude, after all,' she said jokingly.

'Enough to come out with me one evening?'

Her smile faded. 'Go out with you? Where?'

'I was thinking, if you haven't seen it, we could go to the cinema. They're doing a repeat showing of that new "talkie", as they call it. Al Jolson in *The Jazz Singer*. What do you think?'

He had taken her so completely by surprise that she had no answer ready. Fiddling with the leaves she had been forming into a frame, she tried to think what best to say, what excuse she could make – or did she in fact want to go? It was true she was not really attracted to Fraser but she was impressed by him and couldn't help feeling flattered and excited at the idea of going out with him. He was someone who'd had so much success, who might help her to do well and maybe help others, too.

'I would like to see the picture,' she said at last. 'People have been talking about it.'

'Raving, you mean. Well, that's fine, that's lovely. If you'd like to see it, we'll go. How about tomorrow night? I'll call for you at your lodgings.'

'No, no, there's no need to do that. I'll meet you at the cinema. Which one is it?'

'The Picture House. The second showing of the evening is eight o'clock.' He grinned and rose from his stool. 'You can see I've done my homework. Better let you get on, then. Don't forget to turn up, will you? Eight o'clock tomorrow evening.'

'I won't forget.'

When he had left her she sat for some moments before picking up a flower and deciding where to put it. Her fingers, she was annoyed to find, were trembling.

Thirty-Five

When Shona was going out for the evening, she always told Mrs Gow, who affected not to be 'nosy' but always took an interest, gently probing until Shona gave her details. When she heard the following day at teatime that Shona had arranged to see the new talking picture, she did cry, 'Fancy! How'd they do the voices, then?', but soon began to wonder whether Shona was going out on her own? Or with one of her admirers, one of those young men who came to the shop? Or that nice young sailor laddie?

'Archie? Oh, no, I haven't seen him for some time,' Shona told her. 'I think he's given me up. And I haven't seen what you call my admirers, either. They soon realized I wasn't interested.'

'I see.' Mrs Gow had the look of a hopeful puppy waiting for a titbit. 'You're never going on your own, dear? You never know who you might be sitting next to in the cinema!'

Shona waited a moment, deciding whether to be honest or tell a little lie. In the end she admitted she was going with Mr Kyle.

'He asked me if I'd seen the picture and if I hadn't, would I like to go with him. I thought I might as well.'

'Mr Kyle? Your boss?' Mrs Gow's face took on a concerned expression. 'Shona, is that a good idea? He's a lot older than you, eh?'

Shona rose and gathered together their dishes. 'Yes, but what's that got to do with me seeing him?'

'Well, an older man, and your boss . . .' Mrs Gow pursed her lips. 'Who knows what he'll expect?'

'Expect? He won't be expecting anything. We're only going to the pictures.'

'He might be married, eh?'

'Of course he isn't married!' Shona's tone was exasperated. 'Look, mind if I don't help with the washing up tonight? I'd better be getting ready.'

'That's all right, pet, I'll soon rattle through the dishes. You go and get ready.'

When Shona came down, wearing the dark blue coat and brimmed hat she'd recently bought with her savings, Mrs Gow said how nice she looked and she hoped Shona hadn't minded if she'd spoken out of turn, she hadn't meant to interfere.

'That's all right, Mrs Gow,' Shona answered, taking a last look in the kitchen mirror. It was true, she had been irritated by Mrs Gow's warnings, probably because she had her own misgivings about her evening out, but she was happy enough to give her landlady a hug and tell her not to worry, she hadn't minded anything she'd said. The last thing she would ever want was to quarrel with Mrs Gow, who had been so kind, and when she ran out for her tram, was relieved they'd parted on good terms.

As she was shaken along through lighted streets, she felt at first as though she were facing some kind of ordeal, then tried to laugh at herself. She'd agreed to go, so why shouldn't she enjoy it? No reason at all. But when she arrived at the Princes Street Picture House, she was still half hoping Fraser wouldn't be there.

Of course, there he was. Pacing up and down outside the cinema in a huge camel coat with a trilby hat over his sandy hair. And looking out for her. He heaved a long sigh when he saw her and took her hand, just for a moment, in his own heavy clasp to lead her inside.

'There you are, then! You came. I wondered if you would.'

'I said I would.'

'Ah, but things can happen. Never mind, you're here now and we're all set. Just have to get the tickets.'

'Mr Kyle – I mean, Fraser – I think there's a queue.'

'Not for the Circle,' he said kindly. 'Wait there a second.'

The Circle? Shona felt her jaw drop. She had never in her life been in the Circle at the cinema. Why, that would cost . . . She wasn't sure how much it would cost, but more than anyone she knew had ever paid. *Who knows what he'll expect*, Mrs Gow had said. So how much might he expect, then, in return for tickets to the Circle? Shona was beginning to feel her misgivings were turn into real anxiety, until Fraser came back with the tickets, his face was so open and his smile so much as usual, she felt herself relaxing. Just a little.

'This way,' he murmured. 'Up the staircase. Should have a really good view of Al Jolson's tonsils, eh?'

The view of the screen from the Circle was certainly splendid, and even though there were only advertisements showing, Shona's eyes were riveted. The pianist below was strumming away, and Fraser murmured as they took their excellent seats, 'Poor chap. He'll soon be out of a job, won't he?'

'What do you mean?'

'Well, who's going to need a pianist to accompany the pictures when we have the actors telling us what's going on?'

'Why, this is just a single picture, isn't it? They won't make all the films with sound.'

'Want to bet?'

They could say no more as the advertisements had ended, the lights were going down and the 'big picture' – the unique picture, as it happened – was about to begin.

At first, it was all just as usual, with Al Jolson playing the part of a young Jewish singer in Manhattan who runs away from home when his father, a religious singer at the synagogue, punishes him for singing jazz. It was only when the actor had finished singing a song on stage that the big moment came, and the words that were to change film-making for ever boomed into the cinema and the ears of those watching. Such ordinary, everyday words, the sort you'd hardly notice, 'Wait a minute, wait a minute, you ain't heard nothing yet!' Al Jolson cried to his film audience.

Wait a minute, wait a minute, you ain't heard nothing yet!

Was this the beginning of a revolution? Well, certainly when the Edinburgh audience heard them, the words were enough to rock them in their seats. Enough to make Shona give an involuntary cry and stare almost in fright at the screen. It was as though the actor was speaking directly to her, looking at her, making her feel she was drawn somehow into the picture, and though she knew that that was absurd, when Fraser reached over for her hand she took his gladly.

'Not scared, are you?' he whispered, and she saw the flash of his teeth and his eyes shining in the light from the screen. 'Don't think Al's coming out from the picture somehow?'

'No, no, 'course not!'

As the actor continued to talk and the effect began to fade, she relaxed and let go Fraser's hand. 'I was just being silly. But it was such a shock.'

'A shock wave round the world,' he murmured. 'At least, the cinema world.'

They were both silent then, Shona suddenly becoming more aware of Fraser's closeness, his great shoulder next to hers, realizing afresh that they were together, she and her boss, not quite believing it yet all the same excited.

It was calming to watch the story unfold, with Al Jolson visiting his mother, talking and singing to her, and eventually making his peace with his father, singing for him in the synagogue as he lay dying, and bringing the film to a tearful close. The credits rolled, the curtains closed for the intermission while the stunned audience began to chatter, and Shona, giving a long, exhausted sigh, turned to meet Fraser's eyes fixed on her.

'There's another feature if you want to stay,' he told her, 'but maybe you've had enough?'

'I think I have. I don't know why, but I feel sort of tired.'

'The result of a new experience, eh? But something tells me we're going to be so used to sound at the pictures, we won't even notice it.'

Thirty-Six

Outside the night air was cold and reviving, and walking to the car made Shona feel better, except when Fraser put her arm in his and then she was too conscious of him again.

'How about a quick drink before I take you home?' he asked as they took their seats in the car. 'I know a nice quiet hotel just round the corner from here.'

'I don't think so, thanks,' she said quickly. 'I'd best get back.'

'Next time, then.'

Next time? He was assuming there would be other times? As he drove her home, her thoughts were spinning, questions tumbling in her brain. What was happening? Where were they going? He was attracted to her, she knew, she could tell, and not just because she resembled his dead sweetheart. But how serious would he be, and did she want him to be serious, anyway? No, the answer was clear enough.

She felt something when she was with him, some great pull, but she knew she wasn't in love. She wasn't being carried along, as she would expect to be with someone she liked in that way, though to be honest she hadn't had much experience. There'd only been that time when she was young, a child, really, and had had thoughts of Mark Lindsay always in her mind. But that was long ago and no longer real, whereas the big man driving her home was all *too* real. Quite at ease, of course, and talking of the effect sound was going to have on the cinema industry, just as though that was all she might have on her mind.

'You think it's going to matter?' she asked. 'I mean, folk like the silent pictures well enough.'

'Come on, you saw the effect that fellow had tonight – imagine how all the film-makers will want to create that sort of excitement! And all the actors will have to be taking voice lessons and maybe lose their jobs if they're not good enough, just like the pianists. Because there'll be real sound effects from now on, much better than a poor guy can bring out on the old joanna!'

'All comes down to change, then?'

'Sure it does. It's a changing world, eh? And with this new development, we're in at the start. You'll always be able to say you heard the first talkie. Aren't you excited?'

'Maybe. I don't know that I always like change.'

'Can be good, you know, as well as bad. But which is the house where you're staying?'

As she pointed out Mrs Gow's number, he slowed down and stopped the car, giving her only a quick look before getting out to open her door. What now? she wondered. How do we get though the goodnights, then?

But he was looking up at the bridge, so tall, so dominant above them, and whistling.

'Good God! What's it like to live in the shadow of that, then?'

'We like it. We've always known it.' Shona stared up, too. 'And think what it would have been like before it came. Folk had to go right round by the village and the way down was awful steep, then up the Dean Path at the other side to go north. The bridge was a godsend.'

'You've convinced me,' he said, laughing, and drawing her from the car. 'Someday you must take me all round the village, show me the mills and the houses, and the Water of Leith. Will you do that?'

'If you want me to.'

Was this just another way of telling her he wanted to see her again? Shona, staring at him in the light of a street lamp, was still wondering what was coming next. The goodnight kiss? Most young men tried for that, but Fraser Kyle was no ordinary young man and this was their first evening out together. Of course, she didn't know whether he wanted to kiss her, anyway, but if he did, she guessed he'd go carefully – it wouldn't happen then. See how he was looking round at the street, the houses, the lighted windows. He wouldn't, of course, want an audience.

'Nice to see where you live,' he said, suddenly reaching for her hand.

'And where I used to live, before my folks died,' she responded, staring down at his hand in hers.

'Ah, where you were happy.'

'Yes, very happy.'

'You'll be happy again, Shona.'

'Hope so. In fact, I've had some happy times already.'

'That's good. As we were saying, people get over things.' He pressed her hand and let it go. 'You will come out with me again sometime? Maybe for a meal?'

Sometime. Not yet, then. Shona wasn't sure whether to be relieved or excited. Then, 'Yes, I'd like to,' she heard herself reply.

'That's good, that's wonderful. We'll fix it up.' He touched the brim of his trilby. 'Goodnight, Shona. See you tomorrow.'

'Goodnight, Fraser. And thanks for a lovely evening.'

'Exciting one, eh?'

He grinned and took his seat in the car, hesitated, then reversed quickly and drove away.

Mrs Gow was still up when Shona let herself in, and bustled about putting on the kettle and setting out biscuits.

'Had a good time, dear? What was it like, the picture, then? Could you hear the voices?'

'Oh, yes, they were loud! Seemed loud, anyway, and so strange.'

Shona took off her coat and hat and sat down at the kitchen table, aware that another question was trembling on Mrs Gow's lips.

'And Mr Kyle was fine,' Shona told her. 'Was the perfect gentleman the whole time.'

'Oh, well, that's good, then.'

Mrs Gow stirred the teapot and poured the tea. 'I was that worried, you know – couldn't help it.'

She gave Shona a sideways glance. 'You seeing him again, dear?'

'Perhaps. Nothing's arranged.' Shona drank her tea and rose. 'Think I'll away to my bed, Mrs Gow. That picture quite tired me out.'

'Yes, you go on up. I'll tidy away. Goodnight, Shona.'

'Goodnight, Mrs Gow.'

In her room, however, Shona sat for some time before getting ready for bed. Talk with Fraser of her parents had unsettled her, reminding her of the old days and of how she had always been able to talk things over with her mother and would have liked to talk with her then. Oh, yes, you could get over loss, but then there came times when you just wished you could see a person again, ask advice, express your worries. Not possible. Not ever possible. She was on her own, Shona knew, as she had been for a long time, and must work things out for herself. For now, better just go to bed.

Perchance to dream, as the play said, but when Shona finally did sleep and did dream, the dreams were not of Fraser Kyle, but of Al Jolson, singing in his amplified voice and staring straight at her, drawing her inwards into his strange world until, with a start, she woke up and then lay awake for the rest of the night.

Thirty-Seven

A week went by during which Shona was on edge, wondering if Fraser would make his move and how she should respond if he did, but then tension eased when Cassie arrived, all eager to start work, though feeling, she said, all a-tremble.

'Had one great almighty row with those two old biddies,' she confessed to Shona, when she came down to Mrs Gow's house after settling in at Kitty's on her first evening. 'That's why I'm early starting at Maybel's. When I said I would be leaving and working out my notice, they told me if I didn't want to work for them, I could leave right there and then without a character. Oh, they were so cross!'

'As though they've any right be!' Shona cried. 'And they can't deny you a reference just because you're leaving!'

'The very idea!' chimed Mrs Gow. 'I hope you told 'em what's what, Cassie!'

'Well, I didn't. I was just so glad to be leaving early, I told 'em to forget the character, I didn't need it. I mean, I've got two others from my previous employers and they were enough for Mr Kyle. I packed my bag and got the tram to Kitty's because she said I could move in any time.' Cassie turned her eyes on Shona. 'So, here I am, Shona, dying to start work but that terrified you wouldn't believe.'

'I certainly wouldn't,' Shona said robustly. 'You'll fit in, nae bother, you'll see. I'll call for you tomorrow morning and we'll take the tram together. Don't be worrying.'

'Easier said than done,' sighed Cassie.

In fact, she had no need to worry. Within a few days it was clear that she was quick to learn and would present no problems. Which was just as well, as Brigid remarked, for already the Christmas rush was beginning, with orders flooding in for wreaths, house flowers and potted plants as presents, so that everyone was working at full stretch.

While Cassie could not yet help in the workroom, she very soon picked up the routine of the front shop, working with whichever assistant was free to serve the public, taking orders, preparing simple bunches of flowers and managing the till, which made Isla's eyes widen.

'Och, you're quick, eh?' she whispered to Cassie. 'It took me ages to work out the till, and I was so scared of the customers, I sometimes thought I'd have to leave. But you're not scared at all.'

'Wouldn't say that,' Cassie responded cheerfully. 'I'm worried about doing the flowers, but when you've worked for folk like the Misses Orde, you don't mind the customers.'

'You're doing really well, I'm proud of you,' Shona told her later. 'And Mr Kyle's pleased with you, too. He said so.'

'Still so much to learn, though. I don't think I'll ever be as good as you at making up bouquets and all of that. And then it's been grand getting to know the girls here, but I never know what to say to that long drink o' water who works on the accounts, or the lady who does the typing. As for Mr Kyle, he's so big and confident, I feel sort o' squashed when he's around.'

As she gazed at Shona, Cassie's eyes glinted a little and she gave a little smile.

'You manage all right, though, eh? Because anybody can see he's sweet on you.'

'He's what?' Shona cried, putting on as good an act as possible. 'That's news to me.'

'Shona, you don't need to pretend with me. We're friends, remember? It's just the way he looks at you gives it all away. What's the harm in talking about it?'

'He thinks I look like a girl he knew, that's all. She died, of the Spanish flu.'

'A girl he knew who died? And you're taking her place?'

'No, no, that's as far as it goes. He knows I'm different from that poor girl.'

'And you've never been out with him?'

Shona looked away. 'Only once. We went to see *The Jazz Singer*.'

'Do you like him?' Cassie asked softly.

'I'm – I'm no' sure.'

'Be careful, then.'

'Why does everyone tell me that? He's no' going to hurt me!'

'I was thinking of you hurting him,' Cassie said quietly, at which Shona was silent.

'Must get on,' she murmured at last. 'Back to the Christmas wreath pipeline.' Where she was able to work very hard and very fast and give herself no time for thought at all.

It was a day or two later that Fraser caught her as she was leaving the workroom, and asked her how things were going.

'Very well indeed, Mr Kyle.'

'There's no one around; you can call me Fraser.'

'You know our rule. When at work, it's Mr Kyle.'

He shrugged. 'No matter. Nice to know we're doing so well. As a matter of fact, Stuart MacNay has already told me takings are up from the same time last year.'

'Because of the plant room, I expect.'

'Maybe so.' He looked down at her, his gaze direct as always. 'But that's enough of work talk. How about coming out for dinner tomorrow evening? Not singing carols or something, are you?'

She laughed and shook her head.

'Well, then? Are you interested?'

She hesitated, Cassie's words echoing in her mind. The last thing she wanted was to hurt Fraser, but then she might not. One dinner out – she wouldn't mind going. She still felt that pull he could exert, because of his huge personality, of who he was. It was hard to say no. 'I – yes – I'd like to come,' she heard herself say. 'As long as it's somewhere ordinary.'

'Ordinary? Look, I like to eat somewhere good. Why ordinary?'

'I don't want you to be spending a lot of money.'

He relaxed, smiling, and squeezed her hand.

'Don't worry about that. But if you insist, we can go to a nice little place in Frederick Street that doesn't charge the earth. And no nonsense this time about meeting me in town. I'll pick you up at seven. That all right?'

'Fine,' said Shona.

Thirty-Eight

When she followed Fraser into the restaurant he had chosen, Shona felt surprisingly touched. Checked tablecloths, waitresses instead of waiters, a handwritten menu pinned to the wall – this was more a café than a restaurant, and had been Fraser's choice solely to please her. Left to himself, she was sure he'd have gone for one of those places she'd have found so nerve-racking, all white linen tablecloths, snooty waiters and menus in French, and then would have enjoyed showing her how well he could handle it all. But he'd brought her here instead, somewhere she'd find just right, and she appreciated his thought.

'This do?' he asked as they were settled into a corner table.

'It's perfect. Thank you, Fraser.'

'Only aim to please. Now, what shall we have? Shame, there's no wine here. We could have toasted each other in a good red, eh?'

'You'll guess I don't know much about wine.' Shona laughed. 'Never taught that at Edina Lodge.'

'I could teach you,' he said seriously. 'One of the pleasures of life is drinking wine. Maybe next time we go out, you'll let me introduce you to it.'

There it was again, she noted, this willingness of his to talk about other times to be together, as though they already had a future. Better not go into that now, thought Shona and concentrated on the menu, choosing a mushroom first course and a chicken dish, while Fraser ordered the mushrooms and a steak, with pudding a later option.

'Excellent!' cried Fraser. 'Now we've got that out of the way, we can get down to the serious business of talking about each other. That's what folk do, eh, when they first go out together?'

'I don't know about that,' Shona replied, thinking back to evenings with the young men she'd known.

Neil Boath, who worked at the same bank as Willa's husband, Joey MacGibbon, from the Post Office, Archie Smith, now a fully fledged sailor. Not one of them had talked about her, all, even Archie, being too preoccupied with their own affairs. Sometimes she'd tried to get a word in and they'd been polite, but what, after all, could she talk about that would be interesting to them? The orphanage? The flower shop? Fixing her hazel eyes on Fraser, she wondered – would he be any different? Well, he certainly wouldn't need to be told about the flower shop!

'What are you thinking?' he asked softly. 'About all the young men you've been out with? I can't believe they didn't want to know everything about you.' As their first course arrived, he paused for a moment, then continued casually, 'I suppose there have been a number of young men, have there?'

'Only three.'

'Three. That's not counting the doctor chap?'

'The doctor?' Shona raised her eyebrows. 'Fraser, he's not really anything to do with me. He can't be counted.'

'If you say so. Just have the feeling he was someone important in your life.'

'Well, that was true once, but I haven't seen him for years.'

'Seen those three, though. They weren't important?'

'They were not! Look, Fraser, why don't we talk about you instead of me? You know everything about me. I lost my folks, I went to the orphanage, I got the job at Maybel's. That's all. So, tell me about yourself. About your family, for instance.'

He shrugged. 'Nothing out of the ordinary about us. There was Mum and Dad, my sister and me. My dad had a good business and we were happy enough. Then Mum died a couple of years before the war. I was sixteen, Heather twenty. Hit us hard, as you can imagine.'

'Fraser, I'm sorry.' Shona put her hand over his. 'Nobody knows better than me what that's like.'

'I know.' With his free hand, he covered hers, but then the waitress came to remove their empty plates and Shona took her hand away. It was some moments before Fraser continued. 'I found my consolation a year or so later when I met Meggie. We were both very young but we knew it was serious. I asked her to marry me when we'd saved a bit, but then the war came and I joined up. Never thought she wouldn't be there for me when I got back. But you already know about that.'

'You've had a bad time,' Shona said quietly. 'No one would know.'

'I don't usually talk about it.'

Their main course arrived and for a time they ate in silence, until

Fraser finished and put his knife and fork together. 'What saved me next was work,' he told Shona. 'Expanding Dad's business, making money. He wasn't keen, wanted me to keep things the same – until I became successful, when he gave me a free hand. Then he went to join Mum, had a heart attack completely out of the blue, and I decided that if life was as short as that, I might as well do what I wanted to do. I'd always been interested in plants, thought working with them would be a good prospect for me and took a risk. Sold my dad's shops, bought MacVicar's, bought Maybel's, met you.' He smiled. 'There you are, Shona, you know it all.'

It was hard to know what to say. Meeting her – that was hardly on the same level as everything else he'd told her, but the more Shona listened to him, the more she felt that their meeting had taken on a significance for him that was hard to believe. If only she could have been thrilled about it. If only she had wanted it to happen as much as he had . . .

'I think you did the right thing,' she said at last. 'I mean, switching to do what you wanted to do. And then doing so well.'

'Maybe.' He grinned. 'I could still fall flat on my face, you know. But let's think about a pudding. Do you want to see the menu – or just have coffee?'

'Coffee would be nice. Thank you, Fraser.'

'No need to thank me. I'm grateful to you for coming. But after coffee, maybe I'd better get you home. I have a feeling it might snow tonight. Think we'll have a white Christmas?'

Outside the café there was indeed a distinct feeling of snow in the air, though as yet there was no sign of it. Just time, they thought, to run to the car and beat the fall, but they were in fact too late, for as they reached the West End the snow flakes were already whirling around and settling on the road.

'It's not far; here's the bridge,' Fraser said cheerfully. 'Gently does it, down the hill, then, to your Mrs Gow's door.'

'I hope you'll be all right getting back,' Shona said worriedly.

'What, to George Street? I think I'll manage to get through a bit of snow as far as that!'

'As long as you don't skid.'

He looked at her in the darkness of the car, for he had carefully avoided the street lamp, and reached out to touch her hand. 'You'd really care if I did?'

'Wish you wouldn't talk like that,' Shona said, suddenly flustered.

Look, I think you'd better go before it gets too thick to get up the hill.'

'I'm on my way. Just want to say, Shona, that it's been a grand evening with you.'

'I'm the one to say that. It was grand, it was lovely. Thank you very much.'

He was still holding her hand, still watching her face. 'There's something else I want to say. I know I'm a good bit older than you and you might prefer to be with someone younger – no, don't say anything – but I would like it if we could go out together occasionally. I swear I won't make a nuisance of myself, but you must have realized I'm very attracted to you.' Suddenly he let her hand go. 'You can't blame me for wanting to be with you.'

As she sat very still, watching the snowflakes dancing on his windscreen, he leaned towards her, took her in his arms and kissed her gently. 'What's it to be?' he whispered, releasing her. 'Going to give me a little hope?'

'I – well, we could go out sometimes,' she said slowly.

'You'd like to?'

'Yes. All right, I'd like to.'

He gave a short sigh, then leaped from the car to open her door.

'Better run in,' he said hoarsely. 'Take care now!'

'Goodnight!' she called from Mrs Gow's door.

'Goodnight, Shona. See you in the morning.'

She was not surprised, when she went into the house, to find Mrs Hope sitting with Mrs Gow beside the range, empty teacups to hand, aware that they often called on each other to have a 'wee chat'. Still, she would rather not have had two pairs of eyes fixed on her so expectantly as she shook the snow from her coat and hat in the doorway.

'Shona!' cried Mrs Hope. 'Nice to see you!'

'Had a good time?' asked Mrs Gow. 'I've got the kettle ready if you'd like a cup of tea.'

'I had a lovely time, thanks.' Shona came nearer to the range to warm herself. 'But I won't have any tea – I've just had coffee.'

'No' snowing, is it?' asked Mrs Hope. 'Oh, that's me, then, Joan, I'd best get home.' She rose, pushing her chair towards Shona. 'Come on, pet, come and get warm. Which young man was it tonight, then? I always knew you'd never be short of admirers!'

'Her boss tonight,' Mrs Gow put in. 'This is the second time he's taken her out.'

'Oh, fancy!' Mrs Hope's round brown eyes widened. 'The boss, eh?'

'It's no' what you think,' Shona said quickly. 'We're just friends.'

The older women exchanged smiles.

'He'll be a lot older than you, eh?' asked Mrs Hope. 'And never married?'

'He was engaged, but his girl died of the Spanish flu.'

Again, the other women exchanged glances, but now without smiles.

'Very sad,' sighed Mrs Gow. 'But he must be ready now to look for someone else. Could be you, Shona.'

'Aye, and he'd be a good catch,' Mrs Hope said eagerly. 'A man like him, with his own business!'

'I don't want a good catch!' Shona cried, aware that she didn't really know what she wanted, and moved towards the door. 'Think I'll be going to bed now, Mrs Gow. Mrs Hope, it was grand to see you. Wrap up well for the snow.'

'Goodnight, pet,' Mrs Hope responded, hurrying to the door to give Shona a quick hug. 'Sorry if I upset you, talking of your boss. I ken fine, it's none o' my business.'

'Aye, we'd best leave the lassie to know what's best for her,' said Mrs Gow. 'Shona, you could do your hot bottle, seeing as the kettle's ready. Addie, do you want an umbrella?'

'No, no, it's no distance home. I'm away, then. See you soon!'

While the two women were fussing at the door, Shona found her stone-cast hot water bottle and began filling it from the kettle, mulling over what had been said. None of her business, Mrs Hope had declared, meaning what happened between Shona and her boss, and that was true. It was Shona's business, only hers. And she didn't know what to do about it.

If she'd said she didn't want to see him again, that would have been the end of it, so why hadn't she? Just because he was her boss, had she thought it unwise? No, no, more that she didn't want to hurt him, as Cassie had said she might. For he had let her see, unknowingly, she was sure, that under all his outer strength and confidence, there lay a vulnerable man.

Thirty-Nine

In Mrs May's time, after Maybel's had closed on its last day before Christmas, she had always invited the staff up to her flat for ginger wine and mince pies. That first year under new management, no one was sure if Mr Kyle would continue the tradition, but he said he'd be glad to, as long as they didn't mind shop-bought mince pies. Oh, and no ginger wine. A decent red, a pleasant white, would be what he was offering. Any takers? Everyone accepted.

As soon as Brigid had locked the shop door on Christmas Eve there was a rush to the staffroom for the girls to change from their green outfits into their best dresses, while upstairs Stuart MacNay solemnly combed his hair and Miss Elrick put on a red cardigan over her black working jumper and skirt.

'Everyone ready?' asked Brigid, preparing to lead the way to Mr Kyle's flat, but a knock at the shop door made her halt. 'That'll be Willa!' she cried, running to let her in.

'Who's Willa?' asked Cassie and Isla.

'She used to work here before she married,' Shona explained. 'We still miss her. Wonder if she's brought Grant?'

Yes, Willa, looking as attractive as ever, had brought her husband, tall, fair-haired Grant, and there were pleasant moments of hugs and introductions before they all made their way up to Mr Kyle's flat.

'I can't believe all the changes here,' Willa was murmuring to Shona. 'Mrs May's office a plant shop and her lovely room for an accountant now? But things are going well, eh?'

'Very well. We're really prospering.'

'Don't tell her that,' murmured Grant. 'She misses this place quite enough already.'

'Come on, I'll introduce you to the boss,' said Shona as they moved up to the top floor of the building, which Fraser had converted into a comfortable living room and bedroom, and took pleasure in seeing his eyes widen when he met the blonde Willa.

'So, you're the one that got away,' he said, smiling as he shook her hand. 'I've heard you were a great loss.'

'Don't know about that, Mr Kyle, but it was very kind of you to invite me – and my husband, Grant Henderson.'

Fraser, shaking hands with Grant, said it had been his pleasure to follow Mrs May's precedent in inviting her and her husband to the Christmas get-together. Now, how about joining everyone in a glass of wine and trying all the stuff he'd put together? Sausage rolls, ham rolls, cheese straws, mince pies? Who'd help to pass round?

'No ginger wine?' asked Grant, as he and Dan Hardie drank deeply of Fraser's 'good' red. 'This is a change, eh?'

'Aye, he's a generous man, Mr Kyle, and knows what's what. Ambitious, too. Planning to expand soon as he sees how things go.'

'Might be coming to us for a loan, then,' Grant said with a laugh, at which Stuart, joining them, raised his eyebrows.

'What's this about a bank loan?' Dan asked.

'Oh, I'm just thinking aloud,' Grant answered pleasantly. 'Nothing's been said.'

'I should hope not, seeing as I'd be the one to advise on it,' Stuart said a little coolly, and jumped as Fraser suddenly appeared, clapping him and Dan on the back.

'What are you men doing, all standing together?' he cried. 'Come on, circulate! Stuart, why aren't you eating? There's a ton of stuff here to get through, remember.'

'You know my stomach, Mr Kyle.'

'Thank God I don't!'

'What I mean is, I have to be very careful.'

'Just move about a bit, there's a good chap. I have to speak to someone now.'

The someone was Shona, who had been standing a little apart, dubiously trying the white wine she'd been given.

'All right?' Fraser asked when he joined her. 'You liking that?'

'It's a wee bit sharp.'

'Sharp? Never! It's a dessert wine – quite sweet.'

'If you say so.'

She saw his eyes following Willa and gave a wry smile when he murmured, 'Attractive girl, that.'

'I knew you'd think so.'

At once he turned back to her, his gaze now fixed on her delicate features, her parted lips, her bright, springing hair. 'Not to be compared with you, Shona.'

'No need to say that. Willa was always our beauty.'

He shook his head. 'Not to me. If I'm interested in her it's not for her looks, but for what I think I see in her. Rather the same as I see in you. She'd make a good manageress, in my view.'

'That's true, but she's no' working now, she's married.'

'Damned waste, eh? Why shouldn't married women work if they want to?'

'I ask the same thing, but there are the bairns, you see. Who takes care of them?'

'Has Willa any children?'

'She's hoping.'

'I see.' He shrugged. 'Have to see what happens, then.' He touched her glass. 'Like a top up?'

'No, thanks, I think we'll all be going soon. And you've your train to catch.'

He had already told her that he was taking the London train to spend Christmas with his sister, while she and Cassie would not be going far afield, having been invited to Mrs Hope's along with Mrs Gow.

'My train's not till late,' Fraser said easily. 'No need to worry.'

'Still, I think we should make a move.' Her smile on him was sweet. 'But it's been lovely, Fraser. We're all so glad you wanted to keep the tradition going.'

'Of course I did. I'm a great one for tradition, as long as it means something.' He bent his head towards her. 'Listen, don't worry about getting home. I'm giving you and Cassie a lift. Seems Brigid and Isla are going back with Mr and Mrs Henderson, Miss Elrick's meeting cousins in George Street and Dan and Stuart can fend for themselves.'

'You have it all worked out?' she asked, laughing.

'Sure I have. That's me, eh?' He laughed with her. 'I reckon they could put that on my tombstone. *He had it all worked out . . .*'

'I'll find Cassie,' said Shona, still laughing a little.

There were cheerful farewells all round, not only fuelled by the wine, as people collected their coats and exchanged hugs and promises to meet, before giving earnest thanks to Mr Kyle.

'Can we not wash these glasses?' Isla asked worriedly, but Fraser told her all the clearing up was taken care of. Mrs Yarrow, who cleaned the shop and his flat, was already in the kitchen and would be putting her magic touch on the place even before he got back from taking Shona and Cassie home.

'So, let's away!' he cried. 'Happy Christmas to you all. Mr and Mrs Henderson, nice to meet you, thank you for coming.'

'Thank you again for asking us, Mr Kyle,' said Willa. 'And all the best to you and everyone. Have a lovely Christmas!'

'I second that,' put in Stuart. 'Go easy on the Christmas pudding, eh? I'll have to be careful as usual.'

'Oh, God,' murmured Fraser, 'who cares about being careful?'

Forty

The night air was bitter on their faces as Shona and Cassie followed Fraser to his car, and the pavements so packed with freezing snow it was hard not to slip.

'Should've put my other shoes on,' Cassie groaned. 'These high heels are useless!'

'You know you have to suffer to be beautiful!' Fraser called, opening the car doors. 'Now, who's coming in the front next to me?'

'Go on, Cassie,' Shona urged, but Cassie was already settling herself in the back.

'I'm all right. You sit next to Mr Kyle.'

Trust Cassie, pairing me off with Fraser, thought Shona, taking her seat at the front, and saw him smile as he closed her door.

'Nice to get out of the cold,' she said politely.

'It's a killer, eh? Can't expect anything else this time of year.'

'Just as long as we don't all get snowed in,' said Cassie. 'Remember last winter? They even had blizzards in the south!'

'We might be lucky this time,' said Fraser. 'But it won't take me long to get you girls home. Just have to take it gently.'

Driving carefully on the short journey from the West End, especially on the descent into the Dean Village, he gave a sigh of relief as he drew up outside Kitty's house in Baxter Row. 'There you are, Cassie, got you back safe and sound. Wait till I open the door for you.'

'I could get out here, too,' Shona offered quickly, but Fraser shook his head.

'I'll drive on to Mrs Gow's, nae bother. Want me to help you across the pavement, Cassie?'

'No, thanks, Mr Kyle, I can manage. Thanks very much for the party and lift home. Shona, I'll see you tomorrow at Mrs Hope's, eh?'

Having reached Kitty's door without mishap, Cassie waved and let herself in, while Fraser gently eased his car down the street to Mrs Gow's, where he stopped.

'Home for you, Shona,' he said quietly, switching off the engine. 'Were you really going to get out with Cassie?'

'Well, it was no' far for me to walk on. I didn't want to trouble you to drive me.'

'You knew I'd want to say goodnight to you.'

'Yes, but Cassie might have expected me to get out with her.'

'I'd never have let it happen. I've been looking forward all evening to this little time alone with you.'

She twisted in her seat, looking out at the empty street where the snow was a white blur in the darkness, except for where light fell from the curtained windows and the street lamp. But Fraser had again carefully not parked close to the street lamp.

'We'd better no' be long,' she whispered. 'Folk can hear cars. Sometimes, they look out.'

'What will they see?' He took her hand in his and removed its glove. 'Very little, I'd say. Two people saying goodnight, maybe, if they open their curtains – but then we'd see them do that.'

Her hand still in his, she was feeling uneasy, as though she were in a goldfish bowl with the neighbours looking in, which was foolish, really, as so far no one's curtains had twitched. Still, she felt she'd better go and was beginning to withdraw her hand when he tightened his grip.

'No, no, Shona, you're not leaving me yet. Remember, I'm not coming back till after New Year. I have to make this meeting last.'

'Fraser, I think I'd better—'

'No, don't say any more.' He gave a long sigh. 'Truth is, I'm going to let the side down. I said I wouldn't make a nuisance of myself, yet here I am, doing just that. But I can't help it, that's the thing. I have to say what's in my mind, whatever you think, and I'm just hoping you'll understand. First, though—' He gave a subdued laugh. 'It's Christmas, eh? Can I have my Christmas kiss?'

Without waiting for her to speak he dropped her hand, drew her towards him and kissed her on the lips with the sort of strength and passion she'd read about but never experienced, and which sent her own feelings whirling like the snow that was once again beginning to fall.

'Fraser!' she cried, as he let her go. 'Fraser!'

'What?' he asked, his face close to hers. 'What do you want to say to me? Haven't you ever been kissed like that before?'

'No' quite like that.'

'Didn't you enjoy it? You did, didn't you? I wasn't the only one kissing, was I?'

'Fraser, it's getting late. You'd better go; you've a train to catch—'

'Plenty of time. I haven't said what I want to say yet.' He took her hand again. 'Maybe you can guess what it is, anyway?'

She shook her head, trying to come to terms with his kiss and beginning to remember the neighbours, as he stroked her fingers.

'I love you, Shona,' he said softly. 'I want us to be married. Not immediately. I'll give you time; I don't want to rush you. But I'd like you to think how it could be for us. I know I'm not the one, the special one, for you at the moment, as you are for me, but you needn't worry, that would come, I promise you. And when we were married, I'd want you to be a partner in every sense of the word. I mean, you'd have the chance to develop ideas, make your own mark. We'd be man and wife and business partners as well, making money, making a success of things.' He was pressing her hand until it hurt. 'Shona, don't you see what I could give you?'

'Fraser, I – don't know. It's all been – well – so quick –'

'I know, I know.' He released her hand, ran his own down her face, then kissed her again, very gently this time, very sweetly. 'But you can take all the time in the world to think about it. Starting with next week. No need to give me an answer, even when I come back after Hogmanay. I want you to be sure, you see. Absolutely sure. Then we can be happy. In the meantime –' He drew a small package from his pocket.

'In the meantime, I'd like to give you this.'

'Oh, Fraser, it's no' a Christmas present? And I haven't got you anything!'

'That doesn't matter.' He pressed the package into her hand. 'Hope you'll think of me when you open it.'

'I'm going to open it now. It's nearly Christmas anyway.'

He laughed as he watched her struggling with the wrapping which she eventually tore off to reveal a small jeweller's box. Not a ring, she thought wildly, it wouldn't be a ring, would it? It was a silver bangle.

A perfect gift, not too elaborate, not too important, just a very pretty thing to wear, which made her reach over to kiss him as sweetly as he had kissed her.

'Thank you, Fraser. It's beautiful. I love it.'

'I'm glad. You will wear it?'

'When I'm with you.'

'That's all I want.'

Smiling, he left the car and moved round, through the driving snow, to open her door.

'Goodnight,' he whispered. 'Goodnight, dear Shona, and Merry Christmas.'

Her hand was holding tightly to her present, her face damp with snowflakes as she let him help her to Mrs Gow's door.

'All right?' he asked gently. 'Got your key?'

'No need. The door's no' locked.'

'In you go, then. Get out of this weather.'

But she waited, as he touched his cap and returned to his car.

'Fraser!' she called. 'Safe journey!'

Only when he'd driven away, swallowed up in the darkness and fast falling snow, did she brace herself, putting her hands to her cheeks, to go into the house to face Mrs Gow.

Supposing she would be able to tell that Shona had just been kissed? Not in the usual goodnight way by an inexperienced boy, but hard and passionately by a man who knew what he wanted? Would she be able to see some sign? Some colour, or mark, of his shaved chin against Shona's face? Mrs Gow had been married: she must know all about passion, about making love that was so much more than kissing. What hope would there be of hiding Fraser Kyle's effect on her young lodger?

Why am I worrying, anyway? Shona asked herself, rubbing her cheeks as though to remove evidence. She had a perfect right to go out with a man who kissed her, hadn't she? Yet, as she sang out loudly, 'Hello, Mrs Gow! I'm back!' she knew she was worried. She didn't want Mrs Gow to know what was happening between her and Fraser when she didn't exactly know herself.

In fact, it was all right. Mrs Gow had fallen asleep in her chair by the range, hadn't heard the car and was still too sleepy to take in what Shona looked like. Oh, there was good luck for you! Shona even had time to put her new present into her bag.

'Shall I make some tea?' she asked cheerfully, but Mrs Gow was struggling up, rubbing her eyes and murmuring something about macaroni cheese keeping warm.

'No, no, pet, I'll get the tea. Why, you're all snow! You sit down and warm yourself. Did you have a good time at the party?'

'Oh, yes, thanks, it was grand. Mr Kyle had taken a lot of trouble. We even had proper wine.'

'Wine? Oh, my!' Mrs Gow was taking a dish from the warming oven on the range. 'But is wine suitable for you lassies? I've heard it gets you tipsy in no time.'

'Well, there were some men there, too – they liked it. I didn't drink much, anyway, but I did have a lot of the snacks. I'm no' sure I want any macaroni cheese.'

'Nonsense! Snacks will no' keep you going this weather. I'll just dish up, then we'll wrap our wee presents for the Hopes. It's that good of Addie to have us, eh?'

'It is, but I'm sorry your Trissie couldn't make it from Aberdeen. I mean, I'm quite happy to move out of her room whenever she wants it.'

'Och, there'll be no need for that. She can stay with my cousin, or one o' the neighbours.' Mrs Gow sighed. 'But with this weather and her expecting, I never thought she'd come. We'll have a good time, anyway, with the Hopes and your nice friend, Cassie.'

'We will,' Shona said firmly, thinking however noisy or busy it was at Mrs Hope's, it would be less stressful than being with Fraser Kyle.

How long did she have before she need give him an answer? All the time in the world, he'd said, but of course that wasn't true. He wanted an answer and he deserved an answer. What would it be? As she began to eat the macaroni cheese she didn't really want, Shona felt she was a long way from knowing.

Fraser had said, rightly, that he knew he wasn't 'the one' for her, meaning the special one who stood out from all the rest, and there was no way she could pretend that he was. On the other hand, to be married to him would give her a wonderful new life, one she'd always wanted, where she could realize her ambitions and have money and status thrown in as a bonus. What could she do with money? Help people, she decided. Help orphans. How? That would have to be worked out, but it could happen. If she decided to marry Fraser Kyle, who wasn't 'the one'.

'All right, dear?' asked Mrs Gow. 'You look a thousand miles away.'

'Not as far as that,' Shona answered with a smile.

'How about a nice cup of tea? And a piece of my Christmas cake? I can cut it today, seeing as we'll be having Addie's tomorrow.'

'Thanks, but just tea will be grand. Let's keep the cake to look forward to, eh?'

And drinking the tea with Mrs Gow, switching her thoughts to the little presents she still had to wrap, and that other present in her bag, Shona felt strangely at peace. There was, after all, lots of time before she need give her answer to Fraser Kyle.

Forty-One

It was the day before New Year's Eve. Shona was alone in the front shop, while Isla and Cassie were in the workroom and Brigid had gone with Dan to deliver an arrangement for a private house dinner.

No great light had shone into Shona's mind since Fraser's proposal. She still wasn't sure just how she would answer him, but there had been a gradual strengthening of feeling that she might – well, that she might accept him.

All right, he wasn't a knight in shining armour, someone to take her breath away, an answer to a dream, but what he'd said made sense. With time, he might well become 'the one' for her. He might make her very happy, because that was what he wanted to do, and she'd have all the advantages of being his wife. *If* she married him. But then, of course, she hadn't actually decided that she would.

The doorbell pinged and she looked up. Stared. Then took a deep breath. Was it—? She knew it was.

'Shona?' came a man's pleasant voice. 'Is it really you? Have I hit the right shop?'

The man standing at the shop desk was tall and slim. Not quite as thin as he used to be, perhaps because he was older. His hair was the same, as she could see from a lock straying from his hat brim – dark, glossy brown, probably just as unruly. And his eyes – she'd have known those vivid blue eyes anywhere, for they were Mark Lindsay's, and this man smiling down at her was Mark Lindsay himself.

'Doctor Lindsay,' she heard herself say quite calmly. 'This is a surprise.'

'Doctor? What's all this doctor stuff? Surely, after all this time, you can call me Mark? Especially when I've made such an effort to find you.'

'Find me?'

'Well, I knew you worked in a flower shop but I didn't know which one, and when I wanted to send some flowers, I thought, now I'll really find where Shona works, and here I am.'

She came round the counter, pushing back her hair, her manner so composed she felt like an actress playing a part. 'So, you're a customer?'

'I suppose I am. But I've often thought about you, you know. Wondered how you were getting on.'

'I never knew that. And every time I went back to the Lodge I never saw you.'

'For quite a lot of the time I wasn't there.' For a moment his smile died, his eyes lost their brightness. 'I don't know if you heard, but my dad died and I – well, for a while I sort of found it too difficult to carry on in the same place. I left my practice partner to look after things and went out to Australia. I found a job as a doctor, did all types of work.' His smile returned, his eyes shone. 'But, as you can see, I came back. And now I'm one of your customers.'

'I'm very sorry about your father,' Shona told him seriously. 'He would have been a great loss.'

'He was. But I'm reconciled to being without him now. Australia helped. As I say, I did a bit of everything – it was tremendous experience.'

'But now you're back in Edinburgh. Do you still go to the Lodge?'

'Oh, yes, I'm keen on doing all I can there.' He touched her hand. 'How about the Handkerchief Tree – do you see that when you go back?'

'I haven't been back for a while. But I don't need to see the Handkerchief Tree – I can remember it.'

'Ah, that's good.' He let go of her hand. 'But you haven't told me anything about yourself. How's life been treating you?'

'Very well, I'm enjoying it here. In fact, I'm sort of the manageress. But you remember Cassie Culloch? She's here, too.'

'Cassie is? Why, that's wonderful. She got away from service, then?'

The shop bell pinged again and a woman, well wrapped up against the cold, came in, breathing quickly.

'Last-minute New Year gift!' she cried. 'Don't worry, dear, I can see you're busy. I'll just look around.'

'I'll have to take your order, Doctor Lindsay – Mark, I mean,' Shona said hastily. 'What sort of thing are you looking for?'

'Help! I don't know. I can see I'll be spoiled for choice here.'

'Well, who are the flowers for?'

'A friend. A lady.'

'I see.' It had only been what she'd expected, but she felt a tiny pang all the same, and moved to the banks of flowers at the side of the shop. 'We do have a standard sort of bouquet that folk like. Mainly carnations and roses, with gypsophila and so on. Would you like to see a picture?'

'I don't think so, thanks – it sounds ideal. Could you have it sent round tomorrow? Ready for New Year?'

'Certainly, we could send it round tomorrow. If you just come to the desk, I'll take the details.'

As she busied herself, setting out her order book and pen, she looked up to catch a wry smile on Mark Lindsay's face as his eyes rested on her.

'Something funny?' she asked, frowning.

'No, no. I mean, nothing to laugh at. I was just thinking how you've – grown up.'

'Grown up? Well, I should think so! I'm no' eleven years old any more!'

'Grown up in the nicest, most efficient way.'

Mark's smile changed, becoming as wide and friendly as Shona had always remembered and, relaxing, she smiled herself, her small frown quite vanishing.

'You'll want the addresses,' he murmured. 'Mine's just The Surgery, Foster Road.'

'And the lady's name and address?'

'Miss Jane Ruddick. C/O Clare House, North Berwick.'

Shona's pen stopped and a blot formed on her page.

'Miss – Ruddick?' she repeated.

'Yes, that's correct.' Mark's eyes were puzzled, then light shone. 'Oh, of course, you know Jay, don't you? She was Miss Bryce's assistant.'

'She was – very helpful.'

'I know, that's Jay for you. She likes to be called Jay, says Jane makes her feel too prim, or something. But you couldn't meet a kinder person.'

'But has she left the Lodge, then?'

'Yes, not long ago. She got promoted: she's running an orphanage herself now. I've a devil of a job to tear her away to go to a concert or something.'

'Oh, yes?' Shona was beginning to feel a strange emptiness inside. 'Well, we'll have these flowers delivered for you tomorrow afternoon. What would you like to be put on the card?

'Oh, let's see – maybe just "Happy Hogmanay, Jay, All best, Mark". Thanks so much, Shona. How much do I owe you?'

When he had paid and she'd put his cash in the till, she said he must excuse her, she had to attend to the lady who was waiting so patiently.

'Don't worry about me, I'm still looking!' called the customer. But Cassie was already coming in, giving a squeak of excitement when she saw Mark, who shook her hand and said how nice it was to see her again, looking so well too.

'Oh, and so good to see you, Doctor Lindsay! Sorry I can't stop, I've just got to see to this lady.'

'Have a good New Year, then.' He turned to Shona, who was standing near the door, and put his hand on her arm. 'Look, can't we meet again? For a cup of tea or something?'

Her eyes were widening. 'A cup of tea?'

'Why not? It would be nice to talk. You must have an afternoon off some time?'

'We're opening the day after New Year, but I've got the afternoon free.'

'Perfect. I can take a bit of free time then too. How about that new place at the end of George Street? The Tea Box, it's called.'

'Oh, yes, I've seen it.'

'Shall we say we'll meet at three o'clock?'

'All right. Yes, three o'clock would be fine.'

For a fleeting moment she met his blue gaze, then looked away as he straightened his hat and with a last smile, opened the door and left.

Aware that Cassie was sending her interested glances while still serving her customer, Shona returned to the desk and looked down at the order book. There it was – his order for Miss Ruddick's flowers, and his message: 'Happy Hogmanay, Jay. All best, Mark.'

Well, he hadn't said 'Love', but that didn't mean anything. Any more than his invitation to Shona to have tea with him meant anything. Neither stopped Shona thinking, with a long, inward sigh, that when Fraser came back home, she might just as well say 'Yes'.

Forty-Two

Fraser had been due back on the Wednesday after New Year, but sent Shona a telegram to say he'd been delayed by bad weather and hoped to be back by Thursday. Heavens, what a relief! She'd been worrying about the meeting with Mark on Wednesday and what she would say if Fraser wanted to see her on her afternoon off. Well, of course, she'd decided, she would tell him the truth – she was meeting an old friend for tea.

An old friend? The doctor from the orphanage. Oh, Lord, he'd been interested in the doctor when he'd heard about him before. How could she explain? Luckily, it seemed she wouldn't need to – Fraser had been delayed. He'd never need to know about her little teashop rendezvous. As though it was important, anyway!

Cassie thought it was important, though, after she'd almost asked outright what the doctor and Shona had been talking about at the door and Shona, in exasperation, had told her.

'He's asked you to meet him?' Cassie exclaimed. 'Well, that's a surprise, eh?'

'It's just for a cup of tea,' Shona said irritably. 'To have a chat.'

'Never asked me to have a cup of tea and a chat!'

'Look, you needn't think there's anything in it. The only reason he was in the shop was to send flowers to Miss Ruddick.'

'Miss Ruddick?' Cassie was fascinated. 'That old maid? Well, she's no' so old, but I always thought she'd be like Miss Bryce and never marry.'

'Seemingly, she's isn't like Miss Bryce.'

'I'll say, if Doctor Mark's sending her flowers.' Cassie gave Shona a considering look. 'But then why's he asked you out for a cup of tea?'

'I told you. For a talk, a wee chat about old times.'

'H'm. So, what's Mr Kyle going to say about it?' Cassie shook her head at Shona's flashing eyes. 'Och, no need to put on the act, Shona, I told you that before. There's something going on between you two, anyone can see, so why don't you admit it?'

Shona, swallowing her annoyance, began to move away. 'We've work to do, Cassie.'

'And you don't want to talk about Mr Kyle? OK, let's leave it, then.'

'Let's,' Shona agreed with feeling.

Mark was already waiting when she arrived at the 'Tea Box' at three o'clock on Wednesday, as arranged. There had been fresh snow and the pavements were as treacherous as ever, but Shona, in sensible boots, had managed to stay upright and was in fact looking her best, her colour bright with the cold, her eyes sparkling.

'You made it,' Mark said admiringly as they entered the little tearoom together. 'I was half thinking of ringing you up to cancel – thought you might not want to venture out.'

'I have to venture out every day to go to work, Mark.'

'Of course you do. Silly of me. Now, let me hang up our coats and find a table.'

In spite of the weather, the tearoom was quite full, but they found a table at the back where it was warm, and were soon covertly studying each other from behind their menus.

'Scones or teacake?' Mark asked. 'Or black bun, Scotch pancakes or soda bread?'

'Oh, my, I think a Scotch pancake, please. With butter.'

'Of course. Can't eat much in Scotland without butter, which may or not be good for you.'

'Yes, Doctor,' said Shona, suddenly relaxing and feeling at her ease, and Mark laughed.

'Sorry, can't resist a bit of preaching. I like butter, anyway, especially on the scones they have here. Here comes the waitress.'

When he'd given their order, they faced each other more openly and Mark, sweeping back his thick, dark brown hair, sighed.

'You know, I can't get over how you've grown up, Shona. You don't look so very different – I'd always have known you – but, you're right, you're not eleven any more.'

'You haven't changed at all.'

'Except to put on a bit of weight.' He smiled. 'Better get to the squash courts, eh? No, I was already set in my mould when we first met, that's the difference between us. I've just grown older, not more grown up.'

And what's Miss Ruddick like now? wondered Shona as their order came and she poured the tea. In the early days of her time at Maybel's, Miss Ruddick had looked in a few times, but it was some time now since Shona had seen her. She found herself thinking of her, even longing to speak of her, but Mark was already asking about Shona's own work, what sort of prospects she had, where was she living and so on, and seemed so interested, Shona was willing enough to fill him in.

She even found herself talking of the new boss who'd taken over from Mr and Mrs May, though she hadn't intended to mention Fraser at all. Still, he had so many plans, she felt she should talk of them, and again Mark listened attentively.

'What's he like to work for, then, this boss of yours? Not a slave-driver, I hope?'

'Oh, no!' Shona, blushing, passed Mark the plate of scones and buttered herself another Scotch pancake. 'No, Mr Kyle's very nice, really. A good businessman, everyone says, but kind.'

'Like Jay,' Mark murmured, his eyes on Shona thoughtful. 'You get on well with Mr Kyle, then? Somehow, I get the feeling that you do.'

'We all get on well with him,' she stammered.

'But you're special? Didn't you say you were manageress now? He must have confidence in you.'

'Look, why are we talking all the time about me? What are your plans, Mark? You haven't said any more about yourself.'

'Oh, I've no plans. At least as regards work, which I love. I suppose I've other ideas – of what I might do with my life.'

'Tell me about Miss Ruddick,' Shona said boldly. 'What's her new job like?'

'Tough, I'd say. Her orphanage is not like the Lodge, it's much more old fashioned, more like a fortress, and her predecessor had old-fashioned ideas, too. Now, Jay's busy changing all that, and fighting for more money for improvements – you know the story.' He shook his head. 'She's doing a wonderful job – everyone's hoping she'll stay.'

Shona raised her eyebrows. 'Why shouldn't she? She's no' been there long.'

He shrugged. 'She's another who might have plans. Like some cakes?'

Plans. What was the betting Miss Ruddick's plans were the same as Mark's? Just accept that that was so, Shona told herself, gazing at the assorted cakes the waitress had left. After all, there was nothing new about Mark Lindsay being far away from her. What was new was that they were actually having tea together.

'I'll just have more tea, I think,' she said aloud. 'Then I should be going. It's getting dark already.'

'Don't worry about that. I've got my motor parked near here. I'll run you home.'

Another lift back with a different man? Just as well the darkness was descending, so that the neighbours couldn't see her arrival home, or what would they think? As she took her seat in Mark's car, Shona decided she was getting rather tired of worrying over what the neighbours might think. What a world of watchers she seemed to inhabit! From Fraser and Cassie at work to Mrs Gow and the folk next door. How pleasant it would be to come and go and not be noticed. But it wasn't possible even to imagine living like that – at least, not in Maybel's, not in Baxter Row.

'So, this is where you found lodgings?' Mark was remarking as he drew up outside Mrs Gow's. 'Is this near your old home?'

'It is. I know everyone around here.'

'You've done well,' he said quietly. 'Finding a job that suits you, finding lodgings, building your own life. I have to admire you, Shona.'

'Most orphans have to do the same.'

'They haven't all got the same goals. And though you've grown up, you're still very young, you know.' He laughed. 'Make me feel my age.'

'You're no' old, Mark!'

'No, just older.' He glanced at his wristwatch. 'Well, I'd better go. I've an early surgery this evening. Shall we meet again? We're friends, aren't we? Friends should meet.'

Took him a while to remember that, she thought, and though she couldn't really see the point of meeting again, agreed that they should.

'Maybe you'll come into the shop again?' she suggested. 'When you want flowers?'

'I might at that. I'll get in touch, anyway. So nice to see you, Shona.'

'You, too. And thank you very much for the lovely tea. Remember me to Miss Ruddick, eh?'

'Sure I will. I'm seeing her at the weekend; we're going to a concert at the Usher Hall.'

'That'll be nice.'

He came round to open her door, told her to take care on the treacherous pavements, watched her into Mrs Gow's house and with a jaunty wave, drove away.

'Goodbye, Mark,' Shona said softly from the doorway. Would she see him again? Probably not. Unless he did want to buy more flowers for Miss Ruddick. Which would not mean that he wanted to see Shona.

She was glad she was able to accept that he was not for her, even if seeing him again had brought old feelings back. It made life easier. All the same, she discovered, as she worked through all the little jobs she saved for her afternoon off – mending, ironing, tidying up – that she'd changed her mind about marrying Fraser. It mattered too much, after all, that he was not 'the one'. Seeing Mark again had made her sure of that. All that remained now was to tell him.

Forty-Three

As soon as she saw Fraser again, she felt bad. Guilty. He looked so happy that first morning of his return, freshly shaved and bathed after his journey by sleeper, wearing his sister's Christmas presents of a new shirt and tie, his green eyes alight as he looked for Shona in the front shop.

'Happy New Year everybody!' he cried. 'All had a good Christmas?'

'Yes, thank you, Mr Kyle,' they chorused.

'Did you, Mr Kyle?' asked Brigid smartly. 'You're looking very well.'

'Ate too much,' he answered with a grin. 'But how've things been here? No problems, Shona?'

'No problems, Mr Kyle. It's been quiet since we got back after Christmas, but that's usual.'

'Maybe, but I don't like things quiet.' He thought a moment. 'Maybe we should try making some New Year offers. See what you can mark down on the indoor plants and put a notice in the window.

Oh, and I'll send an advert to the papers. Shona, can you come into my office for a minute? We can draft something out.'

Ignoring the looks passing between Brigid and Cassie, Shona followed Fraser up to his office, her heart thudding heavily in her chest. It didn't surprise her that when they were alone together he took her in his arms and kissed her hard before releasing her with a gasping sigh. 'Oh, God, Shona, you don't know how much I've missed you! Being down there in the south so far away nearly drove me crazy.'

'But it was nice for you to be with your sister.'

'Oh, yes, and I don't see her very often, which is why I agreed to visit when she asked me. But that was before you and I got to know each other.'

He stood back a little, fixing her with his intense gaze while she, not meeting it, stood still, looking round his office as though it were of some interest.

'Are we going to write that advert?' she asked at last.

'Write the advert?' He laughed. 'Do you think I asked you to come up here to do that? I can write it myself in two minutes. No, I was hoping, since I've been away some time, you might have reached a decision. About my proposal.'

'You said I needn't give you an answer even when you came back from London.'

'I know, but I was hoping you would, all the same.' He hesitated, some of his radiance deserting him. 'You really couldn't decide yes, or no?'

She could. She had. But as she finally met his eyes, read their dismay, saw him change from happy expectation to crestfallen disappointment, she couldn't find the words to say her answer was 'No'. Sometime soon she must tell him, but not now. She'd ask for a little more time – that wouldn't be unreasonable, would it? After all, he'd said she could if she liked take all the time in the world.

'It's a big decision,' she said in a low voice. 'As I said before, it's all happened so quickly. We hardly know each other.'

'When you fall in love, you know all there is to know. It hits you like a bolt from the blue.' He smiled uneasily. 'That's why you see pictures of Cupid with his little bow and arrow.'

'And he can't see, can he?'

'You're saying you need to know me more, Shona? I told you, you're the one for me. I don't need any more time to be sure, if that's what you're wanting.'

'It is,' she said quickly. 'I need more time. You did say I could have all the time in the world.'

'I didn't think you'd need it,' he said quietly. 'But . . . well . . . it's true . . . I said I'd wait.' He smiled, showing his dimples. 'So, I'll wait.'

'Thank you, Fraser.'

He touched her arm. 'But don't make me wait too long, will you?'

'I won't. And I do appreciate that you've – you know – asked me. I mean, anybody'd feel . . . proud.'

'Would they?' He removed his hand from her arm and opened the door. 'Better tell them downstairs that we've got the advert done. And go through the plants with Brigid – decide which we can reduce in price.'

'I'll do that, Mr Kyle.'

Clattering back to the front shop, she called to Brigid and led the way to the plant room for the marking down, hoping that Brigid wouldn't make any comment on her trip upstairs. In fact, she did make a comment, but it was only to say that Shona was looking a bit down in the dumps.

'Everything all right?' she asked, inspecting a rather tired-looking poinsettia.

'Fine,' Shona answered sharply. 'Why shouldn't it be?'

'Well, as I say, you seem kind of low. Didn't get ticked off for anything, did you?'

'No, I didn't get ticked off.' Wish I had been, thought Shona, for a telling off would have been easier to accept than Fraser's sad gaze. 'Look, let's just decide which of these to reduce, then I'll write out a sale notice.'

'Mr Kyle can't bear failure, can he?' Brigid murmured as she began to sort out the house plants. 'Even if it gets quiet here for perfectly understandable reasons, he feels he's got to rush around trying to fix things. There's always a lull after Christmas, but he can't accept it.'

'He's a businessman. He has to keep up sales.'

True enough of Fraser, thought Shona, but also true was Brigid's shrewd assessment of his unwillingness to face failure. And was Shona going to be one of his failures? On her way to write out the sale notice in the workroom, when they had put aside a selection of plants to go on offer, she felt more depressed than ever.

It was in the workroom that Isla found her, sitting with Cassie who was completing an order, a few minutes later. 'Shona, there's someone to see you,' she told her. 'A young man.'

Archie Smith? Neil Boath? Joey MacGibbon? 'Who is it?' Shona asked, not feeling in the mood to see any of the young men she knew.

'He didn't say. But he's ever so nice looking.'

Nice looking? Shona glanced at Cassie, who was staring with interest. She couldn't imagine that any of her three admirers could be described that way. No' bad looking, maybe. But 'ever so nice'? This fellow, whoever he was, she must see.

'Aren't you the lucky one?' Cassie called after her with a mischievous grin as she hurried to the front shop.

He was standing by the flowers, a damp hat in his hands. A tall, slender young man in a thick plaid jacket with a fine head of thick black hair. His nose was straight, his mouth well shaped and firm, his eyes, turned on Shona, were what some might call 'fine' – large and lustrous, very dark.

Oh, yes, thought Shona, slightly taken aback, this man was 'ever so nice looking'. But who was he? Why had he asked for her? It came to her that he was probably trying to sell something, though he had no briefcase. Sometimes, commercial travellers tried to get a foot in the door by visiting the shop staff first before seeing the boss and peddling their garden equipment, tools and so on. But as soon as the idea came she dismissed it. She didn't want this handsome man to be someone she would have to disappoint. And flushed a little, wondering why.

'I'm Shona Murray,' she told him as he moved towards her. 'Did you wish to see me?'

'That's right. I hope you won't mind me coming to the shop like this, but I don't have your address.'

His voice was strange. American, perhaps. Or, a wild thought – Canadian? Shona was staring, trying to see some sort of likeness, but maybe she was wrong, anyway. She wasn't wrong.

'My name's Brett Webster,' he said, extending his hand. 'I'm your cousin from Toronto.'

From bright pink, Shona's face was now quite pale and she kept thinking, as she shook his hand, that this must be some sort of dream. After all, she'd had daydreams often enough when she was younger, when she'd wished so hard to see someone of her own family seeking her. Not usually dreams of the boy cousins she knew she had, but Aunt Mona herself, come to take her back to a real home again. Of course, it had never happened. No one came and as she lost hope, the daydreams faded. Was she daydreaming now, all over again? Or was this a real live cousin standing in front of her? The trouble was, she didn't know what to say.

Dimly, she was now aware of Isla, dealing with a customer yet casting glances her way, but the dark eyes of the Canadian cousin were all she wanted to concentrate on as she tried to make sense of this dream that seemed to be reality.

'I'm sorry, this has been a shock for you,' he murmured, letting her hand go. 'Maybe I should have written, but as I say I didn't have your address.'

'No, it's all right,' she said quickly. 'It is a bit of a shock, but I'm so happy to meet you. I mean, from Canada and everything. Look, we have a wee staffroom – can I get you a cup of tea?'

'Why, that'd be very kind, thank you.'

'Isla,' Shona whispered, 'could you tell Cassie and Brigid that I have a visitor in the staffroom? I'm just going to get him tea.'

'Oh, right,' Isla breathed, all agog, her eyes going to Brett Webster. 'We'll keep out, eh?'

'Just for a wee while.' Shona turned to her cousin. 'Would you like to come this way, Brett?'

'Thank you, Shona.'

Forty-Four

'I do hope I'm not being a nuisance,' Brett said courteously as Shona took his jacket and asked him to sit down and lit the gas for the kettle. 'I mean, this is your room for recess, I guess?'

'Don't worry, it's no' time for our break yet.'

She glanced back at him, noting with a smile that he was wearing what looked like a brand-new sweater in Royal Stuart tartan. 'Only thing is, you might prefer coffee to tea and I'm afraid we haven't got any.'

'You forget, my Mom is Scottish and so was my Dad.' He smiled. 'We were brought up on tea as much as coffee.'

'That's a relief. But tell me, how did you find me?'

'I called Edina Lodge. That was the only address we had. They wouldn't give me your home address, but they said I could ask for you at this shop. And here you are.'

'It's a bit like a miracle, meeting you. I never thought I'd see anyone from my family.'

He lowered his eyes. 'I'm sorry about that. Guess we've been at fault, eh? I mean, Mom ought to have written you more. She said so to me – that she felt bad.'

'I understand. Don't worry about it. I know she couldn't afford to come to Scotland.'

'That was it,' he said eagerly. 'We hadn't a dollar to bless ourselves with. Things were really tight after Dad died. Mom wasn't trained; she just earned enough to keep us going by doing house cleaning and so on. But she used to say about you that the more she got involved, the worse she'd feel about not seeing you, or taking you. So, she let it go.'

The kettle shrieked and Shona made the tea. 'What happened to you boys, then? You and . . . Sorry, what's your brother's name?'

'Andrew. We did pretty well, as a matter of fact. Got bursaries and both worked our way through college, Andrew becoming a chemist and me an accountant. He's older than me and married, settled. I thought I'd like to come to the old country, fixed up a visa – I've got dual nationality – and ended up in Edinburgh.'

He drank the tea she'd poured for him – black with no sugar – and he said it was fine. A shortbread biscuit, too? Great. Now he really felt he was in Scotland!

'So, what are your plans?' Shona asked.

'Hope to get a temporary job. Stay for a while. Know anyone who needs an accountant?'

'No' off hand.' She smiled. 'But I'm sure you'll find something.'

He was looking at her, she noticed, with a certain softness in his dark eyes.

'How about you, Shona? How's life been for you? Must have been so hard on you, a young kid, left an orphan? Andrew and me, we used to wonder about you, you know. How you looked. Whether you were like Mom, which we aren't, being the image of Dad, they say. She'd some old photos, so we knew what your parents looked like, but the only ones she had of you were some your mum sent when you were a baby.'

'I was always said to be like my mother,' she told him. 'Yes, it was hard when I lost her, after my dad died in the war, but I was lucky. The orphanage was well run and I managed to find a job I liked at the end of it. Things could have been worse.'

'Seems to me you were a very brave lassie.' He laughed as he rose from the table. 'See, I'm learning Scots words already. But I've taken enough of your time; I think I'd better depart.'

'Where are you staying?'

'Oh, at the YMCA for now. Might find myself lodgings when I get a job.' He hesitated. 'Look, is there any chance we could meet some time? Have something to eat, maybe?'

'Of course!' Shona was thinking furiously. What could she suggest? She had Fraser to consider – he'd be sure to want to see her that evening . . .

'How about tomorrow? We could go for a fish supper,' she said at last and his face lit up.

'A fish supper? That sounds wonderful! Where shall I see you?'

'Here. I finish work at half past five. Say, a quarter to six?'

'I'm looking forward to it already.'

'Now to run the gauntlet of the shop,' she warned, opening the door. 'You'll have guessed that everyone's dying to meet my mystery visitor?'

'Oh, no!'

But of course he passed through the ordeal of meeting three stunned girls with complete confidence, while a couple of customers in the background stood looking on with interest. When Brigid called him Shona's long-lost cousin, he smiled, and when Cassie breathed that it was like something from a story, he said he felt that too.

After Shona finally showed him out there was a definite sense of anticlimax, with the girls reluctantly turning back to their customers, until Brigid declared it was time for a tea break.

'No' for me, I've had mine,' Shona said cheerfully, knowing what Brigid was thinking. No gloom for her now, eh? No feeling of depression? It was some time, she herself realized, since she'd thought of Fraser Kyle. Back came the guilt.

Forty-Five

That same afternoon Shona told Fraser about her new cousin. He would have to know, for something told her that Brett Webster was going to be a part of her life for a while.

'Something strange has happened!' she cried when Fraser answered her knock on his door. 'I thought you'd like to know.'

'Tell me, then.' Waving her to a seat near his desk, he lit a cigarette.

'Well, it's amazing, really. You know I have this aunt in Canada I never hear from? Today, out of the blue, a young man walked into the front shop and said he was Aunt Mona's son, my cousin!'

Fraser raised his eyebrows and drew deeply on his cigarette. 'Amazing, as you say. Or, maybe not. A lot of folk come over from the dominions, want to see the old country.'

'But don't you think it's wonderful? That he wanted to look me up?'

'It's the first thing these people do. They always search out relatives who'll give 'em hospitality and show 'em round. How did he find you, anyway?'

She sat back, feeling rather nettled by his attitude. 'He rang the orphanage – it was where his mother last wrote to me. They told him where I worked, but no' my address.'

'Very wise. Can't be sure about strangers who just ring up.'

'Well, there's nothing to worry about where Brett Webster's concerned!' Shona declared. 'He knew all about my family and the orphanage and everything, and he told me about Aunt Mona and how upset she was that she couldn't have given me a home.'

Fraser shrugged. 'What's he like, then? This cousin?'

She hesitated. 'Well, I suppose you'd call him handsome.'

'Would I? More to the point, would you?'

'Yes. He's nice looking.'

'And your age?'

'No, a bit older. Late twenties, maybe. He's an accountant.'

'Good for him. He plans to work here?'

'If he can find something.' Shona's look was hopeful. 'You don't know of anything?'

'I've got an accountant.'

'Yes, but you might know some firm or other, where he might find a temporary job?'

Fraser shook his head. 'Sorry. Tell him to look in the evening paper small ads.' He stubbed out his cigarette. 'Well, thanks for giving me your interesting news, Shona. Now, I've things to do.'

'I'm just going.' Her tone was frosty and as she moved to the door he followed and held it for her, suddenly softening his own manner.

'Look, I'm sorry if I was a bit tetchy just then. I'm not too keen about handsome young men suddenly appearing in your life. You can understand that, eh?'

'He's only my cousin, Fraser.'

'A cousin you don't know. He can be attractive to you in two ways: as someone from your family, and as a new admirer. I don't stand a chance.'

She managed to laugh, easily and naturally. 'I am interested in him as someone from my family, because I've never had any family since my Ma died, but he's no' my admirer. We've only just met!'

'I expect you're going to see him, though, aren't you? What have you fixed up?'

'I could hardly refuse to see him some time, Fraser. A cousin arrived from Canada!'

'OK. When are you seeing him?'

She looked at him with stormy eyes. 'Tomorrow evening for a fish supper.'

'And when are you fitting me in?'

'Tonight. If that's what you want.'

Instantly his coldness melted. He drew her into his arms and held her tightly.

'Oh, Shona, and I thought you'd forgotten me!'

'That would be very difficult,' she murmured, her face close to his.

'Because I'm too big?'

'Because you're you. Look, I can't stay here . . .'

'Just one kiss.'

The one kiss turned into several, after which the now genial Fraser held Shona close again, only releasing her when they'd decided that he would pick her up from Mrs Gow's at seven and they would go to the cinema.

As she returned to the workroom she felt a little better, even though she knew that all she'd done was postpone the storm. Never mind, she'd gained a little time. She must make the true break with Fraser soon; it was only fair, but not yet. Not while there was so much excitement over the new cousin carrying her forward, as though on the crest of a wave.

Cassie was at the work table, hammering the stems of white chrysanthemums for an order.

'Good job that's what these folk want,' she murmured. 'There's no' much choice at this time of year, eh?'

'Oh, come on, there's lots of choice!' Shona retorted. 'All the early spring flowers, viburnum, almond blossom, forsythia!'

'Well, this guy only wants chrysanthemums, so I just need to find some foliage.' Cassie's blue eyes were suddenly sparkling as she turned to Shona.

'Listen, just want to say: isn't that cousin of yours gorgeous? I never knew you had such a handsome bloke in the family.'

'Neither did I. Hardly knew I'd any cousins at all. They were so far away they might have been on the moon.'

'But now this one's here and come to seek you out. You must be thrilled. Are you going to show him the sights?'

'Haven't much time for that, but we're having a fish supper tomorrow evening.' Shona paused, then on some impulse, added recklessly, 'And tonight I'm going to the pictures with Mr Kyle. How about that?'

Cassie, open-mouthed, stared.

'Oh, Shona, what's happening? Tea with Doctor Mark, a fish supper with your cousin, the pictures with Mr Kyle – you're so lucky, eh?

But Shona was already regretting her impulse. 'Don't say that,' she said quickly. 'Don't say I'm lucky. None of these things mean anything.'

Forty-Six

Everything about Edinburgh seemed to charm Brett, even though he was seeing the city at its most dreary, with chill air, snow turned to slush, and the people in the streets looking glum because Hogmanay was over, so was Christmas and spring was a long way away.

'I've given myself a little tour,' he told Shona on Friday evening when she took him up the Mound by tram. 'Saw the Castle and the New Town, and two museums and your Princes Street. So, now I'm going up the Mound, and that was made when they dug out the old loch, eh?'

'Yes, and began to lay out the New Town you saw today. All fine straight streets and lovely crescents. Bit different from the Old Town, where there's no sort of pattern, but plenty of history. If you like history.'

'Oh, I do. I want to see it all. Holyrood and Arthur's Seat and the High Street – the lot. I've got a stack of postcards I'm going to send back home.'

'Aunt Mona will be pleased. When did she last see Edinburgh?'

'1896, I guess. That was when she was married and she told me once that she and Dad emigrated that same year. She was only eighteen.'

'Here's our stop,' said Shona, as they reached the end of George IV Bridge, and as they left the tram and faced the wind she wondered what it would have been like to be Mona, marrying so young and leaving behind all she knew for a life in a strange country. Emmie, her sister, Shona's mother, had been only a child then, for there was a gap of ten years and three dead siblings between them. Perhaps it wasn't so surprising that Mona had never made much effort to take on Shona. She'd never really known her mother, never mind Shona herself.

'Not far to the café,' she said cheerfully. 'Just along Forrest Road here. I'm sorry it's so cold for you at the moment. This is our worst time of year.'

'Cold?' Brett laughed, showing splendid white teeth. 'This is summer compared with Canada. You have to be born there to stand the winters.'

'I want to hear all about it,' Shona cried, 'but here's our café. Oh, and it's lovely and warm! Quick, let's find a table and order our fish suppers. I'm starving, don't know about you.'

'I'm always starving,' Brett said, laughing again.

He was wearing a dark jacket that evening, with shirt and tie, and as he studied the menu it soon became obvious to Shona that everyone in the café was watching him, not her, though she knew she was looking pretty in a green woollen dress that Cassie had helped her make on Mrs Gow's sewing machine. No, just him. She supposed he must be used to attracting attention. Did his brother look the same?

'Have you any photos of your family?' she asked when they'd ordered.

'Why, yes. I brought a couple to show you. Want to see them?'

'Yes, please, before the fish comes and we get them all greasy.'

He took an envelope from his breast pocket and removed two or three small snapshots, which he passed to Shona.

'That's one of my parents together, that's my mother on her own, Andrew on graduation day, and Valerie, his wife.'

She studied them eagerly. Her family! How long she'd waited to see something like these wee photos. Oh, yes, there was Brett's father – you could see the likeness at once – a very handsome man. Standing beside him, Aunt Mona looked pleasant enough, with a broad, heavy face and fairish hair, while taken on her own she looked older and was unsmiling. Obviously her difficult life had taken its toll, and though Shona searched her face carefully, she could see no resemblance to her own mother. Finally, there was Andrew, smiling for the camera in graduation gown. Another Brett? Yes, though perhaps not quite as good looking. Were his eyes a little smaller? But he was still very handsome, and his young wife, Valerie, blonde and slim, was pretty, too.

Shona passed the photographs back to Brett and thanked him. 'I loved seeing them. It meant a lot.'

'You can keep them. I brought them for you.'

'For me?' She flushed with pleasure. 'Oh, that's so kind, Brett! I'll put them in my bag. I'm really thrilled.'

'Do you have some to show me?'

'Just two, of my folks. I never thought to bring them.'

'How about yourself?'

'Oh, no, I never have my photograph taken. Don't know anyone with a camera.'

'I have a camera.' He leaned forward, his eyes intent on her face. 'I'll take your picture. I'd like to very much.'

Her flush had deepened. She looked down, busying herself putting the photographs away, but when she looked up his eyes were still on her face.

'Hope you don't mind if I say –' He paused. 'If I tell you, Shona, that I never expected to find my Scottish cousin to be so beautiful.'

'Oh, now that's what we call a piece of nonsense. I'm no' beautiful, don't try to be.'

'Yes, you are. You're beautiful and different – I mean, quite different from us Websters. Yet we have the family link, which is good.'

They said no more, for the waitress had brought their plates of bread and butter, their tomato ketchup, and finally their fish and chips. And would they like tea to follow? She looked dubiously at Brett. Or coffee?

'Tea will be fine,' he told her, and when she'd gone he said in a whisper, 'No disrespect, but I've tried the coffee in town already. I think I'll be safer with tea.'

'Cheek!' cried Shona, and the slight awkwardness of his compliment-making melted.

'That was so good,' he commented when their plates had been removed and they were drinking their tea. 'Scotland's the place for fish suppers, no doubt about it. Next up, I have to try haggis. What is it, exactly?'

'Don't ask,' she answered, smiling. 'What you'll have to go to is a Burns Night supper, always at the end of January. There'll be haggis and neeps and tatties – turnips and potatoes – and a toast to the lassies. Och, you'll love it!'

'I know about Burns Suppers. We have them at home but I never went to one. I was told that the speeches went on for ever – not for me, I decided.'

'All part of the evening. You have to remember that Scots take their pleasures seriously. If they have plenty to eat and drink, they have to put in a few speeches, too. Only fair.'

Neither wanted to make a move, but eventually rose and found their coats before arguing over the bill.

'I'm the hostess tonight,' Shona said firmly. 'I'm paying.'

'Aw, now I can't let you do that, Shona. This is on me – my pleasure.'

'Next time, not tonight.' Before he could say more, Shona had advanced on the cash desk and paid. 'There you are, done. Let's go.'

'Will there be a next time?' he asked, as they set off against the wind for the tram stop. 'I hope so.'

'Well, if you're going to be here some time, I expect we'll meet again, eh? For a start, I want to show you the Dean Village, where I'm in lodgings and where I was brought up.'

'You live in a village? I'd love to see it.'

'It was a village. It's part of the city now but it's still got character. Look, here's my tram – no need for you to come with me, Brett, I'll be all right.'

'Are you joking? I want to come with you. Just try and stop me!'

Forty-Seven

In the shadows of the tram they sat close, with Brett's gaze once again intent on Shona instead of the lights of the city moving by.

'I hope I'm not treading on anyone's toes,' he said suddenly. 'I mean, expecting to see you. I daresay there's a string of fellows wanting to go out with you.'

A string of fellows?

Her thoughts went to Fraser and their trip to the cinema the previous evening. It had been very pleasant, she had to admit, with both of them enjoying *Wings*, a war film, and afterwards Fraser talking at length about his new plans to expand. True, he had meant to see how his present outlets performed first, but now he'd decided to take out a bank loan and set up another florist's on the south side. He'd already seen the very place – a retiring florist was selling up very reasonably, which meant that Fraser's offer should be accepted and he might have the new shop ready to open by the spring.

'Might please you, too, by putting in Brigid as manageress,' he'd finished. 'Had thought of asking Mrs Henderson but you're right, it's time Brigid had her chance.'

'Why, that's a grand idea!' Shona had cried warmly. 'Brigid will do well, I'm sure of it. And if Willa hasn't had any luck with a baby, maybe she'd like to come back to George Street?'

'Good thinking. We'll see how it works out, then.'

The evening had ended with friendly kisses in the car and Shona's going into Mrs Gow's. Fraser hadn't wanted her to meet him on Sunday as he had been asked over to see friends in Peebles, which was a relief to Shona, who had it in mind to take Brett round the Dean Village. If only her meetings with Fraser could always be so serene!

'I don't know about a string of fellows,' she answered now, and hoped not to say more.

'But there's one, is there?' Brett asked, not to be put off. 'Someone special?'

'I think perhaps I'd rather no' say.'

'Of course, I understand. I should apologize – I have a nerve, asking about your private life.' He moved a little away on the tram's wooden slatted seat. 'What must you think of me? We've only just met and I'm prying like some old busybody!'

'It's all right, Brett, honestly, I didn't mind.' She laughed. 'I mean, I could ask you something the same, eh? Is there someone special for you back home?'

'Well, I can tell you that there isn't. My brother's married, but I've no girlfriend at present.'

'I find that hard to believe. You must know you're very handsome.'

His smile was wide. 'If you think so, I'll be very chuffed.'

They reached their stop and on their way on foot to Baxter Row, Brett had his first view of the Dean Bridge from below. 'My word, that's some structure!' he cried, staring up in wonder. 'And you live underneath? Doesn't it kind of – dominate you?'

'Oh, yes, it dominates the whole place, but you get used to it. See, it's always been there. I mean, for pretty much a hundred years.'

'It's certainly lasted well, from what I can see.'

'Carries more traffic now than when it was built, with all the cars and lorries. But there aren't so many suicides, thank goodness.'

Brett's eyes widened. 'Suicides?'

'Yes, seemingly when the bridge was first built, folk were always jumping off it. The engineers raised the parapet and that made it more difficult.' Shona shivered a little. 'Awful to think of it, though. Wanting to end your life like that.'

Brett quietly tucked her hand into his arm. 'Best not to think about it, I'd say. Now, show me where you used to live.'

Pointing out her old home, Shona's voice still shook a little, even though there had been tenants there for years. Brett's face in the lamp light was sympathetic. In fact, he took her hand and held it for a moment until they moved on to halt outside Mrs Gow's.

'Would my mother have known this street?' he asked softly, but Shona shook her head.

'No, our grandparents lived in a tenement in the Old Town. It's been pulled down because I tried to find it once. It was my dad who came from the Dean Village, so when Ma married him, she came here too.'

'And you're in lodgings with this Mrs Gow? What's she like, then?'

'Sweet. Very motherly. A bit nosy, though she swears she's not, but we get on very well.' Shona smiled. 'Hope you won't mind, but she's very interested in you. Soon as I told her you were here, she asked me to bring you round for a cup of tea.'

'Why, that's so nice! When can I come?'

'How about tomorrow? I can show you round the village and then we'll have tea. Mrs Gow's planning to make her soda scones already, and her coconut cake!'

'People are so kind here,' Brett said seriously. 'You know, Mom said to me that sometimes Scots people are slow to get to know you, but I've found the opposite.'

'I'm glad.'

Standing outside Mrs Gow's door, their eyes met as the time came to say goodnight. There would be no attempt at kissing, of course, for they were just cousins who'd met for a meal, not two people who were attracted to each other. Wasn't that true?

Of course, but Brett's dark eyes seemed loath to leave Shona's face, and Shona's heart was beating fast.

'See you tomorrow, then,' she whispered. 'Hope it doesn't snow.'

'Snow or no snow, I'll be here.' He took her hand again and pressed it before letting it go. 'What time?'

'Oh, middle of the afternoon, when you're ready. It was a lovely evening, Brett. Thank you.'

'For what? I didn't even pay. You'll have to let me live that down next time.'

'Don't worry about it,' she told him, laughing. 'Goodnight, Brett.'

'Goodnight, Shona. It's been wonderful, meeting you.'

'Next, I want you to meet my boss. I'm sure he can fit you in somewhere. I'm going to speak to him on Monday.'

'I'd be so grateful.'

He was walking away, still looking back, until she finally went into the house, preparing herself for her landlady's excitement at the news of Brett's visit next day.

'I've made the cake already,' Mrs Gow told her. 'And that means I've just the soda scones to do tomorrow. Your cousin will like 'em, eh? Real Scottish scones. That's what foreigners like.'

'He isn't a foreigner, Mrs Gow. He's from Canada – it's a British Dominion.'

'Aye, well I just hope I understand him!'

Shona lay awake for half the night, for no good reason that she could see. Or so she told herself. Next morning, however, she was relieved to see that her looks had not suffered, that she seemed, in fact, to appear quite radiant and had to be careful that Mrs Gow didn't notice. After all, Brett Webster was only a cousin, even if he was very handsome. And he would certainly not be staying for ever, even if he did find a job.

But I will speak again to Fraser tomorrow, Shona promised herself. He'd seemed so much more reasonable when she'd last seen him, and he knew, too, that Brett was only her cousin.

Forty-Eight

There was no snow the following day. It was cold, yes, and frosty, not the weather for sightseeing but, as Brett said afterwards, he'd never enjoyed a walk more. As he'd been fascinated by the city, so he was charmed by one of its villages, which he described as being so different from Toronto, it was like being in another world. And another time.

The narrow streets, the gaunt mills, the old houses all of distinctive character, some bearing panels set in by the Baxters, with dates going back to the seventeenth century and beyond – these all made Brett feel he was moving through a period from long ago. Yet there were more recent buildings, such as the Dean Church and Shona's school; also Well Court, designed for the workers, where there were flats and a club room, rather than the individual little houses of Baxter Row.

Perhaps most attractive of all was the Water of Leith, flowing between houses, or green banks and trees where, as Shona told Brett, she had loved to walk as a child. 'You could walk all the way to Stockbridge, following the water,' she told him, 'and that's another place that was a village but is part of Edinburgh now. So many places are like that, but the Dean's kept its character, that's the difference.'

'You can say that again,' said Brett as they leaned over the old single-arch bridge in the village. 'I've never seen anywhere that's so distinctive. I want to thank you for showing it to me, Shona.'

'I love showing it, Brett. I love just being here. And there's lots more to see, but we haven't time today.' Shona paused. 'Maybe, another day, I could show you my mother's grave? It's in the Dean Cemetery and that's quite famous.'

'Sure, I'd like to see it. Pay my respects.'

'I've got a stone for it now and go there when I can.' She brightened again. 'But now we'd better get back for Mrs Gow's soda scones.'

'First, there's something I have to give you.' Brett was taking from his pocket a small package. 'It's from my mother.'

'For me?' Shona asked, amazed. 'Aunt Mona's sent something for me?'

'Yes. I was going to give it to you in the café but it was too full of people. It's better here with just the two of us.'

'But what is it? Brett, tell me!'

'Why don't you unwrap it?' he asked with a smile, putting the tissue-wrapped package into her hands.

'What can it be?' she was still murmuring, as she tore away the paper to reveal a small well-worn box, and was reminded of her excitement when Fraser, too, had given her a package with a little box like this. But this was a different kind of gift.

Glancing up at Brett's watching dark eyes, she slowly opened the box. And stared. 'It's a watch,' she whispered. 'A ladies' silver watch. It's beautiful.'

'It's special,' he told her. 'It's not just any watch. It was our grandmother's. Granddad had saved for years to give it to her and she wore it on her dress for best, but when Mom left to be married, Grandma gave it to her. Now Mom's sent it to you.'

'Oh, Brett!' Tears were welling into Shona's eyes as she held the watch. 'Oh, I can't believe it. Grandma's watch! And your mother's sent it to me? Why? Why would she want me to have it?'

'I think to make up for never taking you. She's always felt bad, but this was something she felt might make up for what she didn't do. It's a family piece – she was sure you'd like it.'

'A family piece . . . Brett, I'll treasure it. I have so few. Oh, I can't tell you what it means to me! I'll write this very night to thank your mom.'

She reached up and lightly kissed his cheek, at which he slightly flushed, then took her arm as they turned their steps towards Baxter Row.

Naturally, Mrs Gow was thrilled by Shona's grandmother's watch, but even more so by Brett's looks, Brett's voice, Brett's manners, and everything about him. And not just because he had presented her with a box of chocolates when he'd first arrived for the walk, which had had her blushing like a young girl. No, Shona could tell, as her landlady called them to her table on their return, that this visit from such an amazing young man was turning out to be a red letter day for her, and that she was somehow astonished that Shona, poor Emmie Murray's lassie, should have a cousin such as this!

After tea, so extravagantly praised, they moved to sit near the range and Shona, at a request from Brett, brought down her photographs to show him.

For some time, he studied them. Emmie, smiling, on a day out at the seaside – Portobello, perhaps? Shona had never been sure. And Jim in his uniform, taken before he went to France. Then Brett looked up at Shona. 'Yes, you're like your mother,' he told her. 'I can see the likeness plainly. Your dad looks fine, but you're not like him. And you and your mother are not like my mother. Strange, how heredity goes, eh?'

'I always say we all get different packages,' Mrs Gow remarked. 'Nobody knows which way a babbie will turn out, eh? Same goes for character as for looks. Like father, like son, the saying goes, but it's no' always true.'

'My dad was a very law abiding citizen,' Brett said with a smile. 'I hope I am like him.'

'I'm sure you are!' cried Mrs Gow.

A short time later, when the January afternoon was already closing in, Brett said he must be on his way. No, no, he really couldn't stay, he had shirts to iron, amongst other things, but he'd had a really wonderful day; he'd always remember it. Now he just wanted to say thank you for the lovely tea and the lovely walk.

'You have to iron your own shirts?' Mrs Gow was scandalized. 'Why ever didn't you bring 'em here? We'd have done 'em for you, wouldn't we, Shona?'

'As though I'd do that!' Brett grinned, as Shona found his coat and handed him his hat. 'No, all the fellows at the Y do their own laundry. It's no trouble. I'm a dab hand at it, anyway.'

'Well, I never heard of men doing the washing,' Mrs Gow declared. 'My husband never ironed a shirt in his life; he wouldn't have known where to start.'

Shona, scarcely listening, was touching her grandmother's watch that she'd pinned to the front of her green dress, and was taking such pleasure in it she almost shed tears again. Aunt Mona couldn't have given her anything she'd value more, for this was a family gift, a link with those who'd gone before that she'd never thought to own. Already she was thinking out her letter of thanks and planning to get it into the post tomorrow, as she knew it would take a long time to Canada.

'See the laddie to the door, Shona,' Mrs Gow said kindly. 'I'll clear away.'

Finally, Shona and Brett were alone in the tiny hallway before the door.

'Shall I call in at the shop tomorrow?' Brett asked, his gaze on Shona soft and melting. 'Just to see if you have any luck with your boss. You did say you'd speak with him?'

'I did, I will. So, yes, look in later on.'

They exchanged long looks, then quickly hugged and moved apart.

'Thank you for today,' Brett whispered.

'And thank you for bringing Grandma's watch to me. It's so wonderful to have it; I'm so grateful to your mom.'

Shona opened the door and gazed out at the wintry evening. 'I'm sorry you have such a trek back, Brett, and in such miserable weather.'

'It's OK. I told you, I'm used to much worse than this. All I'll be thinking of is the good time I've had today.'

Touching his cap, he left her, pausing to wave once then walking strongly away, while Shona, having watched him out of sight, ran upstairs to her room to replace her photographs by her bed and add to them her grandmother's watch in its worn little box.

Forty-Nine

If Shona had hoped for a sympathetic response from Fraser when she tried a second time to plead Brett's case, she was disappointed. As soon as she'd explained on Monday morning why she wanted to see him, his welcoming expression changed; even his dimples vanished with his smile, to be replaced by a dark frown.

'Shona, you're not on again about this cousin of yours, are you?' he asked in exasperation. 'I've already explained, I can't help. I have an accountant. Your relative will have to find something for himself.'

'I know you did say you didn't need him,' she persevered, 'but with the new shop and everything, surely Mr MacNay could do with an assistant? Brett's no' asking for a top job, just something to keep him going while he spends time here.'

'Stuart MacNay is very efficient; he doesn't need an assistant.'

'But you must admit there is a lot to do,' she pressed. 'And it would mean so much.'

'To him? Or to you?'

'Well, to him of course, but he is my cousin. I'd like to see him get a job he'd enjoy.' Shona's look was earnest. 'And I'm sure he'd enjoy working here.'

Fraser heaved a deep sigh. 'I don't know, Shona, you're a terrible girl, eh? Won't take no for an answer. Tell you what, if this paragon comes in tomorrow at about ten with all his references and such, I'll agree to see him. I can scarcely recommend him to anyone unless I know what he's like.'

'You will recommend him?' asked Shona, brightening.

'Depends how he shapes up.'

'But you could suggest to Mr MacNay that he might like to have someone to help? I bet he's already thinking about the extra work when we open the new shop.'

'And maybe not just the new shop,' Fraser said, suddenly relaxing. 'I'm seriously considering opening a café at the market garden.'

'A café?' Shona raised her eyebrows. 'But who would want a café at a place like that?'

'Families. Folk on Saturdays looking for a place to take the children. I see them taking a trip out to Kyle's to choose some plants, then having tea or a light meal while they're there. It's something new but it could take off, Shona. A place like that – it's wasted. So much more could be made of it.'

'If you say so,' she said, shaking her head. 'Honestly, Fraser, you have me in a whirl. I never know what idea is coming next.'

'That's where money comes from,' he told her. 'Ideas that work. Now, I've to get on. You tell your cousin to come at ten tomorrow and we'll see how things go.'

'I'm really grateful, Fraser. Thank you very much.'

'Don't need thanking – haven't done anything yet.' He moved with her to the door, where he laid his hand on her arm. 'You're looking particularly pretty today, Shona. Have you done something new to your hair?'

She laughed. 'Just washed it.'

'Tell me, does this cousin of yours look like you?'

'No, not at all. He doesn't look like my side of the family; he told me he was like his father.'

'H'm. Well, I'll see him for myself tomorrow. Listen, are you going to spare me some time later on this week? When you're not acting like a tour guide for your cousin, I mean.'

'I have to show him round, Fraser. I'm the only person he knows here.'

'Yes, yes, agreed, but what about me? I'm still waiting, you know.'

There was a significant silence between them as they stood face-to-face at the door. 'I do know,' Shona said at last. 'I'm sorry, Fraser.'

'Well, there's a Gilbert and Sullivan concert at the Lyceum. Maybe we could go to that? I'm quite a fan of theirs. How about Thursday?'

Agreeing to meet, Shona left Fraser, pausing for a moment at the door of Stuart MacNay's office next door. Poor chap – he'd probably be dosing himself with peppermint, or some such medication, as he worked on his books. Everyone knew he was a fanatic for work, but surely he would be glad of an assistant? If she could only pop in and put the idea to him . . . No, no, she'd better not annoy Fraser, doing something like that, for he would surely find out. Better just leave it to Brett himself to convince him he was needed.

She was turning to go down the stair when Stuart surprised her by coming out of his office, a cup in his hand. 'Good morning, Shona,' he said with one of his faint smiles. 'I'm just off to make my tea. Miss Elrick's in Peebles today.'

'Hope you're feeling better?'

'Och, I just take things as they come.' He shook his head. 'Sometimes think I've no digestion at all, but if I'm careful I get by.'

'Must be hard for you, with so much to do,' Shona couldn't resist saying. 'With the new shop coming soon.'

'I know. As it is, I've to spend time over at the market garden, doing their accounts. How I'm going to manage with the Morningside shop, I've no idea.'

In for a penny, in for a pound, thought Shona. 'My cousin from Canada is an accountant, you know. He's seeing Mr Kyle tomorrow to see if there's any hope of a job.'

'A job? Here? It's news to me that Mr Kyle is thinking of taking on another accountant.'

'Oh, he isn't! My cousin's just hoping he might be given something temporary. But he might well be a help to you, eh?'

'He might at that,' Stuart said thoughtfully. 'I wonder if I should have a word with Mr Kyle?'

'If you do, don't tell him I said anything,' Shona said hastily. 'He wouldn't be pleased to think I was interfering.'

'No, no, of course not. He might ask my opinion, anyway.'

'He might.' Shona, already beginning to have regrets that she had, in fact, interfered, said she'd better get back to work, at which the accountant nodded abstractedly and walked slowly away to make his peppermint tea, obviously deep in thought.

What have I done? Shona asked herself, hurrying down to the workroom, feelings of guilt now consuming her. Hadn't Fraser once said she was one who had the success of the business at heart? Yet here she was, working to get Brett a job in it when she hadn't the faintest idea how good he was, not actually thinking of the business at all. And pretending as well to be thinking of Mr MacNay's health, when again she only had Brett's interests in mind. As for her treatment of Fraser, she was ashamed of herself for keeping him dangling and not telling him of her true feelings.

What sort of a person was she, then? Just somebody carried away by a good-looking face? Somebody who accepted presents from a man who wanted to marry her and hadn't the courage to tell him she never could?

Whatever else, she must return the bangle when they went to the Gilbert and Sullivan concert on Thursday, even though her heart was already sinking at the thought of sitting through the witty songs and jolly music while knowing what she must say to Fraser. Unless she said it first? No, that would be even worse.

It was a relief to find that there was no one else in the workroom, and she stood for a moment looking at her reflection in the long mirror on one wall. Where was all her colour, the radiance that had been hers lately? Only a subdued young woman gazed back at her now, hazel eyes so sad, short bright hair only emphasizing the paleness of her face. Perhaps she'd feel better when Brett looked in? The girl in the mirror did smile at that, but it was only when the real Shona turned to the flowers she had earlier left in water that her low spirits revived.

To be with flowers usually had that effect, their scent and texture cheering her on the bleakest days, and those she had selected for a customer's engagement present didn't fail her now. Fine lilies, roses, antirrhinums, gypsophila, all filled her with new enthusiasm for creating a truly handsome bouquet the young man wanted for his new fiancée. The foliage framework was ready to hand, as well as all the tools she needed and the satin ribbon for tying. All she had to do was get to work and as she settled down to it and grew totally absorbed, her troubles faded and she was, at least for a while, herself again.

When Brett came to the shop in the afternoon, the bouquet had long been despatched for delivery by Dan and Shona was ready to greet Brett with her news.

'Ten o'clock tomorrow I see Mr Kyle?' he murmured, keeping his voice down as Cassie and a customer were close. 'Shona, you're a marvel! How'd you fix it?'

'I'm no' even sure, but it's just to check your qualifications and that sort of thing. There's no promise of a job.'

'I know, but still, I'm in with a chance, eh?' Brett's eyes were shining. 'Gee, I'm glad I ironed a shirt last night – I guess it'll be best bib and tucker tomorrow, do you think?'

'Oh, I should say it'll be just very informal.' Shona smiled. 'You'll do well, anyway.'

'I hope so, as you've got me this chance. Shona, I'm truly grateful. Could I not take you out tonight – to sort of celebrate?'

'I think we'll save the celebrating until we've something to celebrate,' she told him, moving with him to the door. 'I have to go now: there are more customers coming in.'

'Everything all right?' he asked anxiously. 'You seem – I don't know – a bit less cheerful somehow.'

'I do have a few things on my mind – nothing to do with you. I'll see you tomorrow then, after your interview? Don't forget to bring all your documents.'

'You bet. I'll be getting 'em all in order tonight.'

Looking slightly worried but no less handsome he left the shop, while Shona, avoiding Cassie's questioning stare, turned to serve a customer who wanted something nice and easy. 'Daffodils!' she cried. 'Do you get these from the Scilly Isles?'

'From Peebles, as a matter of fact,' said Shona.

'Your cousin didn't stay long today,' Cassie observed when they had a free moment. 'What's up, then? You're looking down again.'

'Nothing's up, Cassie. There's good news, as it happens. Mr Kyle's going to interview Brett tomorrow. Just to see what he's like – in case there's any chance of a job.'

'Mr Kyle is?' Cassie gave a knowing smile. 'Your doing, eh? You can always wrap Mr Kyle round your little finger.'

'I didn't say he was taking him on.'

'Took me on,' said Cassie. 'Oh, it'd be lovely if your cousin came to work here! Imagine seeing him instead of Mr MacNay!'

'No' instead of Mr MacNay, Cassie. He'd just be Mr MacNay's assistant, if he'd be anything at all.'

'As long as he ends up coming,' sighed Cassie. 'Why, it'd be like working with a film star, eh?'

'A film star who can do accounts?' Shona managed a smile. 'That'd be a change.'

Fifty

At a quarter to ten the following morning Brett arrived at Maybel's. He was wearing his winter jacket which he removed to reveal a dark suit of good material and cut, with an immaculate white shirt, and seemed a little under strain when Brigid said she'd take him up to Mr Kyle's office. Naturally he was looking round for Shona, but she was keeping in the background, trying to convince herself that what she'd brought about was really nothing to do with her. His dark eyes found her, though, and as hers sent the message – *Good luck!* – he smiled.

'Oh, my,' sighed Cassie when he'd left the front shop, a briefcase under his arm, to follow Brigid. 'If it just went on looks he'd be given a job, eh?'

'His looks won't cut any ice with Mr Kyle,' Shona said quietly.

Cassie's blue eyes rested on her and she nodded. 'Think it might go the other way? He'd rather your cousin doesn't look like he does?'

'All I'm saying is that Brett will have to show that he can be useful. Mr Kyle's a businessman – he won't want to spend money taking on somebody who doesn't know what he's doing.'

'See Brett's briefcase? I bet it's full of his qualifications and good references.'

'I just feel so sorry for him,' put in Isla. 'Interviews are so horrible, eh? I hated mine with Mrs May.'

'Never mind, you got the job,' Cassie said comfortingly, and Shona, moving to attend a customer coming through the door, wondered if that might be a good omen. On the other hand, of course, there was no job actually involved. Unless Mr MacNay had had a word, as he'd said he might. As she sold yet another bunch of daffodils, Shona felt she must be looking as strained as Brett himself.

Upstairs, Fraser was rising from his desk as Brigid showed in 'Mr Webster', trying not to show his surprise at the looks and style of Shona's cousin. He'd been expecting someone so different, some sort of unpolished guy from abroad, and here was this fellow in a good suit with matinee idol looks and a charming manner! Hell, he'd said he didn't stand a chance beside him, but that had been a joke. Now it seemed only the perfect truth.

'Come in, Mr Webster,' he said, drawing on his own ease of manner. 'Take a seat by my desk. Thanks, Brigid.'

As Brigid reluctantly withdrew, Brett seated himself before Fraser's desk, settling his briefcase on his knee, and looked expectantly at Shona's boss, whose gaze was so riveted on him. After a pause, Fraser spoke. 'Now, Mr Webster, I'm told you are a cousin of Miss Murray, my manageress?'

'Yes, that's right, sir. Our mothers were sisters.'

'But your family emigrated to Canada, where you were brought up. Did you have any particular reason for coming to Scotland?'

'Well, both my parents were Scottish. I'd heard a lot about the old country and thought I'd like to see it before I settled down.'

'I see.' Fraser shuffled papers on his desk while Brett opened his briefcase.

'Mr Kyle, I'd like to say thank you for seeing me,' he said earnestly. 'It's good of you to give up your time.'

'Not at all. I'm always interested in finding the right staff, though I'm not at the moment advertising for any.'

'I know, sir, that's why I appreciate your seeing me.'

'It was, of course, Miss Murray who told me about you.' Fraser smiled briefly. 'She's anxious to help you find a job, so I said I'd see you.'

Brett had flushed a little. 'Shona has been very helpful to me since I arrived. I'm very grateful.'

'Quite right. Well, have you anything about yourself I can read to begin with?'

'Yes, I've everything here.' Brett opened his briefcase and passed a sheaf of papers across to Fraser. 'The top one's my own details, education and so on. Then there are my certificates of professional exams passed, and two references – one from my college tutor and one from the firm where I was working in Toronto.'

Fraser, leafing through the papers, raised his eyebrows. 'Very impressive, at first glance. I see you have the Canadian qualification of CA – that's good. You did well at college, and three years ago joined a Toronto accountancy firm.'

'That's correct.'

'You weren't worried about losing your place on the ladder at all? I mean, to come over here?'

Brett smiled. 'I take the view you've only got one life, so you should see something of the world before you settle down. I decided to begin with Scotland, my parents' country.'

'But you will be returning to Canada, when you've seen what you want to see abroad?'

'Definitely. My real roots are there.'

Fraser seemed to relax as he laid down Brett's papers. For some moments he considered the young man whose great dark eyes were fixed on him. 'Obviously, I'm going to have to study what you've given me,' he said slowly. 'I did say that I'd no plans to advertise for another accountant, but there has been a possible change in requirements. My present accountant, Mr MacNay, thinks that with the expansion of the business he does need some help. At the moment he's responsible for looking after accounts for this florist's and my market garden, our main supplier, but from the spring there'll be a second florist's here in Edinburgh. We're not a huge concern, of course, but I think now it's likely I might be able to offer you some work, on a temporary footing.'

'That would be wonderful!' Brett cried. 'I'd appreciate that very much.'

'Subject to my study of your application, of course, and possible taking up of references.'

'Of course, Mr Kyle.'

'How long might you be with us, would you say?'

'It would be some months, at least.'

'Excellent.' Fraser rose, his large bulk overshadowing Brett's slender frame as he, too, stood up. 'If you leave your details with me, I'll take you through to meet Stuart MacNay next door. He'll be the one who'll deal with the formal side of things, should you be appointed. Give him your address and we'll be in touch.'

'Thank you, sir.'

At the door, Fraser stood still, studying Brett's face. 'I expect after that you'd like to go down and have a word with your cousin, wouldn't you?'

Brett's eyes softened, his smile was tender, and Fraser's heart gave a sudden stab of pain. 'I can't really say much yet,' Brett murmured. 'Unless it's to say I'm hopeful.'

'You could say that.' Fraser opened his door. 'Yes, just say you're hopeful, Mr Webster.'

Fifty-One

That evening Shona and Brett were, after all, celebrating. Having dinner in exactly the sort of restaurant Shona wanted to avoid, with the haughty waiters and French menus, but Brett hadn't been warned and said when he celebrated he wanted it to be somewhere good.

'But should we be celebrating yet?' Shona asked. 'You said you'd only been told to be hopeful.'

'Yes, but look who said that – the boss himself! He should know whether I can hope or not.'

'All right, it's encouraging, but I'm still no' happy coming out to an expensive place like this, Brett. I mean, you haven't the money to throw around, have you?'

'Throwing money around?' He sipped his wine and laughed. 'I like that idea, sounds great. As a matter of fact, I'm not too badly off. I saved up quite a bit to come here, you know.'

'Savings don't last for ever.'

'But then I've my job to look forward to.' Brett leaned forward, his eyes glinting. 'Listen, Shona, I've something to tell you: I think I know who your special man is – the one you didn't want to talk about.'

Shona drank some wine, frowning over what she considered its sharpness. A waiter came to serve their dessert course – something with meringue and ice cream – and she waited to reply until he'd gone.

'Who is he, then?' she asked in a low voice.

'Well, isn't it Mr Kyle? I'm not prying again, honestly, but it was so obvious today at the interview. His whole face sort of softened when he spoke your name; he couldn't hide what he felt, even from me, just a candidate for a temporary job.'

Shona sighed. She picked up her spoon and began to eat her meringue. It was delicious, but she could hardly taste it. 'You're right,' she said, finally laying down her spoon. 'Mr Kyle is the man I didn't want to talk about. I still don't, but I might as well tell you that he's asked me to marry him.'

Brett sat back in his seat, too taken aback, it seemed, to speak. 'I see,' he said at last. 'Well, that's a piece of news I didn't see coming. Are you engaged, then?'

'No. I haven't given him my answer yet.'

'You're thinking about it?'

'I have been.'

'You've decided?'

'Yes. I'm going to give him my answer on Thursday. We're going to a musical show.'

'I am your cousin,' Brett said quietly. 'If you're going to be engaged, you might like to tell me.'

'Coffee, sir?' a waiter asked, clearing their dessert dishes, but Brett, looking at Shona's face, asked only for the bill.

Outside, in the wintry street, he took her arm. 'Look, don't worry about it. What in hell am I thinking of? You don't need to tell me anything. It's your business and his, nothing to do with me. Please forgive me, Shona.'

'I feel so bad, Brett, that's the thing. I've sort of led him on, never saying from the beginning that we weren't right for each other.' As they walked towards their tram, she was almost crying. 'But one time I did think we could make a go of it. Work together, like he said. Be partners in running the business. That's what appealed, because I am ambitious, I want to get on and make money for deprived children, amongst other things.'

'Sure, you wanted to do those things and you'd a right to take your time making a decision. It's a big one, isn't it, deciding who you'll marry? You've nothing to be sorry about, Shona. Mr Kyle will understand.'

'You're very sympathetic, Brett. Thanks for trying to make me feel better.'

'You shouldn't be worrying, anyway. Happens all the time – someone loving, someone not. Can't be helped.'

How many girls had loved him, Shona, wondered, and had not been loved in return? Had he really not minded, telling them?

'Let's get the tram,' she said tiredly.

'I've got a better idea. Why don't we take a taxi? Just another splash out, eh?'

'No, you've spent enough tonight. And, see, there's a tram coming. It'd be a waste of money to take a taxi.'

'OK, then.' He hurried with her towards the stop. 'Mustn't upset your Scottish soul, I suppose.'

'Hey, you're Scottish too!'

'Would anybody think it?'

As the tram clanked to a halt, she looked at him fondly. 'Maybe not, but whatever you are, you're very kind.'

His gaze on her as they sat together in the tram was very sweet, very tender, as were their later farewells. No kissing, of course, just hugs and comfort, and hopes exchanged for good news soon. Shona even felt a little better after they'd parted, but by Thursday she was as apprehensive as ever.

Fifty-Two

Before the Gilbert and Sullivan concert Fraser took Shona to supper at a small restaurant during which nothing of importance was said. Shona did begin to speak of what was in her mind but Fraser put his finger over her lips and said, 'Not now, dear girl, let's enjoy our meal.' And even when she tried to thank him again for seeing Brett, hoping to get some idea of what his verdict would be, he only shook his head and made no reply.

Supper over, they found their seats at the theatre. The curtains parted and on came the three little maids from school, singing and fluttering their fans so charmingly, with Fraser waving his hand in time and saying, 'Oh, I do like *The Mikado*!' while Shona was just wishing she could be a thousand miles away.

'Coffee?' Fraser asked in the interval, but agreed with her that the crush in the bar would be too great and they'd be better staying where they were. As she stared fixedly at the safety curtain, he suddenly took her hand. 'Shona, you're on pins, eh? Wanting to speak to me?' She turned large, sad eyes on him, and he nodded. 'I can feel it, you see, you wanting to tell me what you have to tell me, but the fact is, you needn't. I know what you want to say. You don't have to say a word.'

'But, Fraser—'

'No, I mean it. I was a fool ever to think you might take me on. It's not just that you're so young, it's more . . . Well, I'm not the one, am I? You never pretended I was, and though I was all for saying it would come, that you'd love me as much as I love you, I knew in my heart it wouldn't happen. So, let's just forget about marriage plans and be good friends. What do you say?'

'Oh, Fraser, I don't know what to say. I just feel so bad—'

'No, there's no need for that. I shouldn't have asked you for something you couldn't give. Let's not say any more.'

'But, won't you want me to leave?'

'Leave? The shop? Are you crazy? Of course I don't want you to leave! You're still going to be my right hand; we're going to work together. For God's sake, don't talk about leaving!'

'And then there's this.' She touched his bangle on her wrist. 'I should give this back to you, Fraser. Things were different when you gave it to me.'

'That was a gift bought for you and for you to keep.' He glanced at people returning to their seats. 'There goes the bell. Better say no more.'

What more could she say? He'd been too nice, too thoughtful for her; she wished he'd been angry. Instead, he'd just been understanding, and sad.

And, oh, God, here came the company to perform excerpts from *The Gondoliers*, and Fraser was putting on his act again, humming and beating time, saying he loved *The Gondoliers*, as tears were stinging Shona's eyes and she was trying hard not to let them fall.

Driving back to Baxter Row, Fraser was full of his plans. Everything was going smoothly with his purchase of the Morningside florist's. Soon it would be his and then he could see about ordering new fittings, for the present owner had allowed the shop to become rundown. The only problem was he'd need an extra supplier for the regular stocking of flowers and plants. The present market garden could satisfy George Street's needs, but for a second large shop he'd have to find another source. A challenge, eh? But he liked a challenge.

'And what about Brigid?' Shona asked. 'You haven't told her yet, have you, that you're putting her in charge at Morningside?'

'Not yet, but it's on the agenda. Think I've been a bit hard on her so far?'

'Maybe. She is very efficient.'

'Yes, well, she'll get her chance now. And then, of course, we'll need more junior staff, plus, maybe, Mrs Henderson, as we said before. If she fancies a return to work.'

'It'd be grand to have Willa back, but being married she might no' want to come.'

'You persuade her, eh? You're good at persuading.' For the first time there was a slight edge to Fraser's voice. Halting at Mrs Gow's, he glanced at Shona and said casually, 'By the way, you'll be pleased to know that I've decided to give your cousin a temporary job. Mr MacNay said he was good, thought we should take him. He was going to write to him today.'

Shona caught her breath, her heavy heart lightening. 'Fraser, that's wonderful! He'll be so thrilled. Thank you.'

'I'm taking him on because I think he'll be an asset. He'll have to prove that he is.'

'Oh, he will, he will! It's so good of you to help him. And you've been good to me, too. I've – well, I've been amazed how good. How understanding. I do appreciate it.' She leaned across and kissed his cheek. 'Thank you again.'

'Goodnight, Shona,' was all he managed then.

Driving away, not waiting to see her into the house, his jaw was set, his lips had tightened. 'So good?' he whispered. 'So understanding? God! But what else can I be? I've always known I wasn't "the one" and I don't want to lose her – anything but that. And now I've given the cousin a job . . . What happens next? She mustn't know how I feel. Thank God for work, for making money. Maybe I'll get over her . . . sometime, maybe . . .'

Staring at the shadowy road ahead, he couldn't picture it.

Fifty-Three

The next few weeks were some of the happiest Shona had known. Having someone of her own family working so close, becoming a part of her life, and for that someone to be Brett she felt as if a dream had been answered. Surely the future could only add more to what she already had?

Brett had slipped so easily into the little world of Maybel's, always looking so well turned out, so amazingly handsome, so easy in manner, it was clear enough that he was the asset Fraser had said he wanted him to be. Of course, Fraser hadn't been thinking of charm or looks, but his ability in the office, and seemingly Brett scored there, too, for Mr MacNay reported him to be quick to learn and very professional. So Fraser told Shona this rather grudgingly, and her heart sang with relief. She felt, after all, a certain responsibility in bringing Brett into the business. If he was doing so well at work, she could relax and think about her own relationship with him, and how it might progress.

After she'd told him of how Fraser had accepted her refusal, she and Brett had seemed drawn together even more closely. They had taken to going out after work two or three times a week, having meals in the city or going to the pictures, while at the weekend they would brave more severe weather in the countryside, for Brett now had a little car.

At first, Shona had been worried. Buying a car, even a second-hand one – how could he afford it?

'Easy,' he'd told her. 'Bought it on the never-never.'

She'd been shocked. 'That means you pay more in the end, Brett; it's never a good idea to do that. Mrs Gow's just bought a wireless on the HP and she's really sick about how much extra she'll be paying.'

'Well, I'm not Mrs Gow – I'm an accountant and I know how much I have to pay, but it's worth it because this way I get the car now and don't have to wait. Look, don't worry about it; I know what I'm doing.'

Shona still wasn't happy about it but she had to admit that, even on a winter afternoon, it was pleasant, driving out, to show Brett the sights of Scotland. The Forth Bridge, the beaches of Fife beyond, St Andrews, Perth and the serene beauty of the lochs with the hills in the distance – which Brett said reminded him a little of Canada, only on a much smaller scale.

'You've no idea,' he told Shona, 'of the size of the lakes we have – all so quiet, so empty, except for birds, or occasionally an Indian in a canoe. Sometimes the vastness can be frightening.'

'You have Indians?' Shona asked fearfully. 'Oh, heavens, they're not like in the westerns, are they? Riding around with tomahawks?'

'Good Lord, no, they're all very peaceful. No trouble at all.' He put his arm round her. 'You know, I think Scotland is wonderful – a place of magic – but I wish you could see my home too. I mean, Toronto, it's a great city. Full of life and action and all sorts of interests. Ice hockey, every kind of sport. terrific university, centre of industry – hey, do I sound like I'm trying to sell it?'

'You sound like you're homesick.'

'Oh, no! No, I think of it, of course, and Mom and my brother – but I'm really enjoying myself here.' He gave one of his beautiful smiles. 'The work's ideal, I like old Stuart MacNay, and best of all, I have you, my cousin, my guardian angel.'

She'd blushed, then, said she was no angel, and they'd both laughed and continued their drive.

They were so happy together, it seemed natural that they should exchange kisses when they could – sometimes while having a winter picnic by a loch, or after their Edinburgh evenings out, when Brett had taken Shona back to Baxter Row. They were sweet, tender kisses, not passionate, and it was hard to tell how much they meant.

Was Brett falling in love with her? Shona wondered. She hardly dared consider the question, although she knew what answer she'd give about her own feelings. Yes, of course she was in love, already deeply committed, and it seemed to her that he did feel the same. He was so often seeking her out at work, his eyes lighting up when he found her; always thinking of when they might meet, delighted when they did. Wasn't that the behaviour of a man in love? She thought it was. Yet he never spoke of a future together. Even when he'd said he'd like her to see his home town, Toronto, he never suggested they might go there some time as a couple.

There came a day when he told her he had some exciting news and her heart beat faster, wondering what it could be. Nothing to do with her, she soon discovered, except maybe indirectly, for his news was that he'd rented an apartment, as he called it. An apartment. A flat. Not a bedsit? Once again, Shona was worried.

'Oh, Brett, what's it like? You're no' going to spend a fortune on rent?'

'No cold water, please,' he said quickly, his eyes glinting. 'I have to get out of the Y, haven't I? And I'm earning a reasonable salary, so I've found myself a nice little place in a block near that big hotel in the West End.' He snapped his fingers. 'What's it called . . . ?'

'The Caledonian?'

'That's it. My place is on the first floor and fully furnished, with a living room, tiny kitchen, bedroom and bathroom, and I get the keys on Friday. When are you coming to see it?'

'Soon as possible!' she cried. 'It sounds lovely. I only worry that you might be spending too much.'

'Leave the cost to me. How about Sunday, then? Come in the

afternoon and I'll make you tea. I've seen a bakery in South Queensferry Street – might offer you some scones!'

'Brett has got a flat?' cried Mrs Gow, when Shona told her where she was going on that February Sunday. 'And you're going there – on your own?'

'Don't worry, I'll be quite safe,' Shona replied sharply. 'He's my cousin, remember.'

Mrs Gow's blue eyes remained concerned. 'Oh, Shona, lassie,' she said softly. 'He's more than that. You're seeing him all the time, eh? Going to the pictures, having meals out, driving on a Sunday. Don't tell me he's just your cousin.'

'I am seeing him a lot,' Shona said reluctantly. 'But we just like being together. It doesn't necessarily mean anything.'

'So what's he after? He's a lovely young man, I really like him maself, but he's no' from Edinburgh, he's no got family here. You've no idea what he's really like, eh?'

'I do know what he's like! He's a good man, and he has got family here, Mrs Gow: he's got me! Now, I'll have to go.'

He was waiting for her in his car when she ran out of the house, her face dark red, her eyes flashing, and as they drove away he asked in surprise what was wrong.

'Oh, Mrs Gow's fussing because I'm going to your flat all on my own! Honestly!'

'She doesn't trust me?' he asked quietly.

'I'm sure she does, really. It's just not what girls do, in her eyes, to visit a fellow alone.'

'Glad you're not worried about it. All I'm offering is tea and scones.'

'We're cousins, Brett; I've a right to visit you.'

'Kissing cousins,' he said with a grin. 'So, maybe I'll make it tea, scones and kisses.'

But the kisses this time were different.

Fifty-Four

Before tea, of course, Brett showed Shona round his new flat, part of a handsome block in Rutland Street, and she admired everything: the fine living room, the modern bathroom and wee kitchen, even his small bedroom with narrow single bed at which they both gazed for a moment, before moving away.

'I'll put the kettle on,' said Brett and as he organized the tea, setting out a tray with cups and saucers and a plate of large, thickly buttered scones, Shona looked on, smiling to see him seeming so domesticated.

'Can I help?' she asked.

'No, you sit in the living room and be waited on.'

'I can't believe how tidy it all is when you've just moved in.'

'That's because I've so few possessions.' Brett made the tea and carried in the tray. 'Wait till I get more stuff and you'll see the real me at home. Now, do you want to pour out?'

Shona, looking round as she ate her scone, was admiring the living room afresh. So spacious, with a high moulded ceiling and fine cornices, good armchairs and mahogany table, pictures with gilt frames. It was, as Brett himself described it, a 'classy joint' and she couldn't help wondering how much it was costing.

'That's for me to know and you not to know,' he said lightly. 'The thing is, as you've gathered, I like the best. Good restaurants, good clothes, a good place to live. Can't always achieve them, but I do what I can.'

'You have to keep within your limits, Brett.'

'True, and I know what they are.'

He stood up and gave her his hand to join him. 'We've had the tea and scones. Now it's time for the kisses.'

For some time they stood together, their faces close, their eyes meeting, then suddenly began to kiss, hard and furiously, Shona returning passion with passion, her hands on his body, his on hers, until they had to stop to draw breath and gazed at each other with shining wonder.

'Oh, God, Shona, I'm up there in the clouds,' Brett murmured.

Leaning against him, she whispered, 'Me, too. I'm up there with you.'

'Did you expect this to happen?'

'I don't know. Maybe. Did you?'

'I guess I thought it would. Sometime.' He drew her to an armchair, setting her on his knee. 'I've been holding back for quite a while. Maybe you knew?'

'I wondered. But why, Brett – why hold back?'

'Well, things aren't straightforward for us, are they? I mean, we're cousins, for a start.'

'That doesn't matter!'

'Does to some. Some say cousins should just be friends. Mom, I think, would be one. She's got some old-fashioned ideas.'

'You go by what your mom says?' Shona asked a little coldly.

'No, I'm just making the point. There are other difficulties for us, you see.' He fondled her hand in his. 'You probably think we should be engaged, but I'm not sure what my future is. My job here is only temporary. Do I want to stay on in Scotland? Do I go back home? Truth is, I don't know what I can offer you.'

Himself, she thought. That would be all I'd want.

'If we're sure about each other, all those things you've said would make no difference,' she said slowly. 'They'd all be sorted out in the end.'

'Maybe, but I'd like to be sure. I don't like to ask you to wait, but couldn't we have – you know – what they call an "understanding"?'

'An understanding,' she said softly, contemplating their engagement. 'Brett, I'd like that.'

'After all, you've your career to think about, haven't you? Mr Kyle thinks highly of you. He wants you to do more for the business, doesn't he? Even though you had to give him some bad news the other day.'

'It's true – I do want to do well. Fraser once said I might become a business partner, and that might still happen.' She hesitated. 'But I don't quite know how that would fit in with our future, Brett.'

'Just another of our difficulties?'

'I suppose so.' Impulsively she kissed him on the lips. 'But I'd always put you first.'

'If you couldn't have both?'

'It's hard for women to have both,' she said with a sigh.

After a while they went out for a walk around the West End, but the day soon began to close in and Brett said he'd drive her home. Shona still had some weekend chores to do and he had an account he'd brought home to check over; it was best they parted. In fact, they both felt so emotionally exhausted they had to come down from the clouds. Outside Mrs Gow's house again they quietly kissed and hugged, and as Shona prepared to leave him, Brett grinned. 'Be sure to tell Mrs Gow we didn't actually go into my bedroom, eh?'

'As though I would say that!'

In fact, Shona had already decided not to tell Mrs Gow anything about the afternoon, except that Brett's flat was very nice and everything had been all right.

'Of course it was,' said Mrs Gow easily. 'Brett's such a fine young man, I canna think now why I was fussing.'

Fifty-Five

It was March and work was going ahead fast to complete the new fittings for the Morningside shop. Brigid, who seemed already like a different, brighter person after her appointment as manageress, spent a lot of time over on the south side, along with Fraser, while Shona, as usual, ran the George Street shop with the welcome help of Willa.

Yes, Willa had returned to work and gladly, even if only part time, telling everyone how bored she'd been at home, how it would all have been different if she'd had a baby, but there'd been no luck there.

'Probably Grant's fault, so the doctor thinks,' she whispered, 'though I don't mean it's really his fault, you understand, but he won't accept it anyway, won't even speak of it, so that's it.'

'Shame,' murmured Cassie. 'But at least he's let you come back to work.'

'Yes, but he's not telling anyone at the bank because they'd think it strange. And as for my neighbours, they're just so disapproving. I'm supposed to spend my time cleaning, or shopping, going to the butcher's or the grocer's. And when Grant comes home he tells me about his day and he asks what I've done and I say, "Well, I went to the butcher's, I went to the grocer's and I cleaned all the windows. Want to swap jobs?"'

The girls laughed with her as they commiserated, all agreeing that looking after a house was very nice if you wanted to do it, but why shouldn't you still go out to work if you'd rather?

'Especially if you've no bairns,' put in Isla, and Willa nodded.

'That's my point. If I'd had a baby to look after it would've been different. But there was just me and my dusters!'

'So lovely that you're back now,' Shona said warmly. 'I've been thinking about it and when I'm married I'll want to work, too.'

There was a silence as Cassie and Isla stared, while Willa looked from face to face in surprise. 'You planning to get married soon, then?' Cassie asked abruptly.

'No, I didn't mean to say I was getting married at all,' Shona cried, colouring furiously. 'I should have said "if", no' "when". Don't know why I didn't.'

'Don't you?' Cassie turned aside. 'We'd better get on.'

'If anyone wants me, I'll be in the plant room,' Shona said coldly. 'Willa, you said you'd make a start in the workroom, eh?'

Oh, how stupid she'd been, Shona thought as she stamped into the plant room, which she intended to sort out. Whatever had possessed her to make that slip of the tongue? Now Cassie's face was like a thundercloud, and what could she do about it?

She was reorganizing the house plants, pulling off leaves, checking on watering when Cassie, looking apologetic, sidled in. 'Sorry, Shona, for upsetting you. Didn't mean it.'

'That's all right. I thought it was you who was upset.'

'No, there's no point in me getting upset. I know I'm nowhere when it comes to – well, even getting Brett to notice me. We all know who he's keen on, and I just thought, maybe you'd got plans to wed.'

'We are going out together,' Shona answered cautiously, judging that now was not the time to mention the 'understanding' between herself and Brett. 'But you and me have been friends too long to have anyone come between us, eh?'

'You're right,' sighed Cassie. She fiddled with the leaves of a weeping fig. 'Guess who came in yesterday, while you were over at Morningside?'

'Who?'

'Archie Smith.'

'Archie?' Shona gave a reminiscent smile. 'I haven't seen him for a while.'

'No, he said that. I told him you were out but he said he'd like a wee chat with me. Seemingly he's been invalided out of the navy – damaged his leg in a fall during a storm at sea. He's working in Leith now, something to do with a ship's chandler's.'

'Fancy. I'm sorry he's had to leave the navy, he really liked being a sailor.'

'Yes.' Cassie was looking rather embarrassed. 'Thing is, he's asked me to go out with him. We're going to the pictures tomorrow night.'

'Why, that's grand, Cassie! He always had his eye on you, I seem to remember.'

'When you weren't around. Of course, typical of Archie, he's picked the film – an old Charlie Chaplin – *The Gold Rush*. Still, I don't mind seeing it with him. He's no' so bad, old Archie.'

'He's a nice lad, even if he did sometimes call me Carrots. You go and have a good time, Cassie.'

When Cassie had left her, Shona heaved a sigh of relief. It looked as though the problem of cheering up Cassie had been solved with no effort on her part, and she was about to return to her work when a customer walked in. And not just any customer. It was Mark Lindsay.

Fifty-Six

Shona could scarcely believe it. Mark coming into Maybel's again? She had quite decided he would not return – at least, not to see her. And then, of course, Brett had come into her life, and even the thought of Mark had moved out of it. Yet here he was again. And she had to admit, she was pleased to see him.

'Shona!' he cried, shaking her hand. 'So nice to see you. Cassie said it was all right for me to come in here – I am a customer.'

'Hello, Mark. Yes, if you want plants or bulbs you're in the right place. If it's flowers you need to be in the front shop.'

'I do want plants, actually. But also to see you. Thought I'd see how you were getting on, and when Jay said she'd like some house plants to brighten up her orphanage, I told her I'd ask your advice what to order.'

Now it was house plants for Miss Ruddick? Without her, it seemed Shona and Mark Lindsay would never meet.

'We have a good selection,' Shona told him coolly. 'I'm sure you'll find Miss Ruddick just what she wants.'

'But which do you think would do best? I mean, not die if they're neglected. Jay wants the children to take care of them themselves.'

Shona laughed. 'Well, you can't go wrong with Spider plants – they survive anything. Then there's the Weeping Fig, the Snake plant, or the Peace Lily – the children might like cacti – they're such strange shapes. People are only just getting interested in house plants, you know. At one time there were only aspidistras but now, as you can see, there's quite a variety. How many would you want?'

'We thought about fifteen or so. Could they be delivered? If you could just send those you think best, I'll pay for them now.'

Mark was taking out his wallet when a dark head came round the door and Brett stepped in, smiling, until he saw Mark, when he halted and began to apologize.

'So sorry, Shona, I didn't know you had a customer.'

'That's all right. I'd like you to meet Doctor Lindsay anyway. Mark, this is my cousin, Brett Webster. He's here from Canada.'

'Shona's cousin?' Mark exclaimed, shaking hands with Brett and gazing at him with wonder. 'This is a surprise. I knew about an aunt in Canada but I hadn't realized there were any cousins. You over here on vacation, Mr Webster?'

'Sort of, but I'm working temporarily as an accountant for Mr Kyle.'

'Doctor Lindsay here is the doctor at the orphanage where I was brought up,' she told Brett. 'He was always so kind.'

'Spare my blushes,' said Mark. 'Mostly what I can remember is showing you the Handkerchief Tree.'

'The what?' asked Brett.

'You never told him?' Mark smiled. 'It was just a rather special tree that made Shona feel better when she was homesick.'

'I see.' Brett's dark gaze slid to Shona. 'Well, I just came to tell you that Mr MacNay's not feeling too well so I've offered to run him home. Mr Kyle's at Morningside at present, but if he comes in and wonders where we are, could you explain?'

'Of course,' Shona was beginning when she was brought up short by the sight of Cassie running in, looking anxious and excited.

'Doctor Mark – thank goodness you're still here! Please could you come up the stair? Miss Elrick's just told us Mr MacNay's been taken very ill. She's sure he needs an ambulance.'

'Where is he?' asked Mark, moving at once into his doctor's role. 'Take me to him.'

'I'll take you,' Brett insisted. 'This way, Doctor. I knew the poor chap wasn't feeling too good, but looks like he's worse, then.'

To Shona, following the men up the stair to the offices, what was happening was something she'd seen before when Mr May fell ill and had had to be taken to a nursing home. They'd thought then that it was a heart attack. Could Mr MacNay's illness be something the same?

Whatever it was, it was serious. Anyone could tell that just by looking at the poor fellow, sitting doubled up at his desk, his face ashen, great drops of sweat lining his brow, hardly able to speak. 'The pain – the pain,' he gasped, but as Mark began gently to examine him he almost screamed. 'Don't touch me, don't touch me!'

'I'm sorry, Mr MacNay, won't take a moment, then we'll get you to hospital. Mr Webster, has someone called for an ambulance?'

'I have!' cried Miss Elrick, visibly shaking. 'I didn't wait; I knew Mr MacNay'd need it.'

'Quite right.' Mark stood up, biting his lip. 'If only I'd had my bag, I could have given him something, but of course I wasn't on duty.'

'It's no' his heart, then?' Shona whispered.

Mark shook his head, looking down at the patient, who had now closed his eyes and had begun breathing in long loud gasps.

'Probably a perforated ulcer,' he said, keeping his voice down. 'But now I think we should clear the room. Shona, if you have a number, could you ring the patient's relatives? Tell them he will be taken to the Western General. Mr Webster, can you inform his employer?' He glanced at his watch. 'The ambulance men should be here any minute. I'll go with the patient to the hospital.'

Everyone scattered as Isla ran in to say that the ambulance had arrived, and it was with a huge feeling of relief that they saw Mr MacNay taken aboard, accompanied by Mark, and then being driven away.

'Thank God,' Brett muttered. 'Just hope they're in time to save him.'

'Oh, you don't think – you don't think Mr MacNay's going to die?' Miss Elrick cried. 'Surely, they'll be able to do something at the hospital? They're the best, everyone says so.'

'I'm no doctor, but Stuart looked pretty bad to me. And I've heard that time is of the essence with these ulcers that burst.'

'Burst?' echoed Shona.

'Well, what else does perforated mean?' Brett ran his hand over his brow. 'Poor devil, eh? All this time struggling with an ulcer! How'd he manage it?'

'He never went to the doctor,' Miss Elrick said in hushed tones. 'Just said it was indigestion and took his peppermint. Whatever will his parents say? He still lives at home, you know. Such a quiet man.'

'I'm going to put the kettle on,' Shona declared. 'Come down to our staffroom. We'll feel better if we have some tea.'

Though the front shop was cheerfully busy, with Cassie and Isla serving customers who knew nothing of the drama that had taken place overhead, the atmosphere in the staffroom was of course subdued. It was true that Stuart MacNay was a quiet man, not someone to be at the forefront of things, but the way he had looked on being taken ill had quite shaken the onlookers, bringing them face-to-face with something they didn't usually have to worry about, which was the frailty of the human body.

Brett, smoking a cigarette, was looking particularly thoughtful. Probably, Shona decided, considering how the senior accountant's sudden collapse was going to affect him. Watching him closely, she knew he'd be waiting now for Fraser to arrive, all decisions being his.

First came Willa, ready for a break from her work on an arrangement for a christening party, who had to be told what had happened, for she had been on her own in the workroom. Though she'd only briefly met Stuart MacNay, she was of course deeply shocked, and as she put on the kettle for her own tea, said it reminded her of what she'd heard about poor Mr May's illness.

'He got better, thank goodness,' Shona murmured. 'We'll just have to hope that Mr MacNay makes it too.'

'Amen to that,' said Brett, and Willa fixed him with her large blue eyes.

'This will make a difference to you, Mr Webster,' she said, putting into words what everyone was thinking.

'Yes, I might have a new boss.' Brett drew on his cigarette. 'Only temporary, of course. It'll be up to Mr Kyle to decide.'

'He's good at that,' Willa returned. 'And quick.'

'The quicker the better. Then I know where I stand.'

'So, this is where you all are!' came the voice they'd been waiting for, and Fraser, still wearing his overcoat, appeared in the doorway, seeming as usual to overpower the whole staffroom with his presence.

'What a thing to happen to poor Stuart, eh? Has there been any news since you phoned, Brett?'

'No news, sir.'

'It's a bad business, I can't get over it, but you'd better come up to my office. We'll need to talk.'

'Yes, sir,' said Brett.

It was some time later, when the girls were almost closing the shop, that Mark Lindsay returned from the Western. Stuart MacNay was already undergoing an emergency operation for a perforated ulcer – there could be no news yet of how he had survived. His elderly parents were at the hospital and his own doctor had arrived and expressed horror that his patient had never told him of his symptoms. All anyone could do now was hope for the best.

'I'm so glad you were there,' Shona told Mark earnestly, when they spoke together. 'You were such a help to us all.'

'I wish I could have done more.' Mark rested his vivid eyes on her face. 'But I'll be in touch with the hospital, and you should know anyway how Mr MacNay is tomorrow.'

'I put your order through, by the way,' she told him as he prepared to leave.

'What order?'

'The plants for Miss Ruddick's orphanage.'

'Good God, I'd forgotten all about them. Don't believe I paid you, did I?'

'We'll send you a bill; no need to pay now. You look all in.'

'I feel it.' He rubbed his hand across his brow and gave a wry smile. 'You know, I did come in here for Jay's plants, but I was also wondering if you and I might have had another of our little get-togethers. Better leave it for the time being, I think.'

'Yes, maybe. Can only think of what's happened to Mr MacNay.'

'And then you have your cousin to look after.' Mark's look on Shona was long and considering. 'Seems a very personable young man.'

'Look after? How d'you mean?'

'Well, he's a stranger here – you'll be taking him round, showing him Edinburgh and so on. When he's got time, that is. I suppose he'll be in charge of the accountancy work for the time being?'

'He is, as a matter of fact – he's just told me that Mr Kyle has asked him to run the office until Mr MacNay comes back.'

'Might have to wait some time for that. Well, I'll say goodnight, Shona. I'll be in touch.'

'Goodnight, Mark.'

It was an ill wind that blew no one any good, Shona reflected as Mark left her, but Brett was certainly benefiting from poor Stuart's collapse. He'd be paid more and have full control, it seemed, for Fraser had told him the last thing he wanted to be bothered with was looking for another accountant at this time, when he was so involved with the new shop. And though not, of course, celebrating, Brett was quietly delighted.

Mark didn't sound so delighted, though. Had his voice taken on a certain coolness when he spoke of Brett? Perhaps not. Would he get in touch with her again? Somehow, as before, Shona didn't think it likely.

Fifty-Seven

Mr MacNay did not die, but his surgeon reported that it had been a near thing. There had been great risk of the complication of peritonitis, but this had been avoided, and with rest and a long period of convalescence, the prognosis could be described as good.

Thank God for that, everyone said, but as Stuart's parents told Fraser, there was no question of his coming back to work any time soon. He was their only child, he meant everything to them and having inherited a little money, they could afford to see to it that he didn't have to worry about a salary until he was completely well and strong again. If it meant losing his job, well, so be it.

'Oh, there's no question of his losing his job,' Fraser reassured them. 'Stuart's entitled to sick leave and his young assistant is perfectly capable of looking after things, so no need to worry. We'll just look forward to seeing Stuart back when he's ready.'

'Looks like I'm safe for the time being,' Brett told Shona. 'Shame about poor Mr MacNay – I hope he does come back, of course, but for now it'll be a wonderful experience for me to run the department my way, as well as earning more money.'

'You're going to be so busy, though, with the business expanding,' Shona commented. 'Shouldn't you have a temporary assistant of your own?'

'Hell, I don't want any strange guy coming in and having to be trained to what we do. No, I can manage. I'm looking forward to it.'

When he and Shona visited Stuart in hospital, however, it seemed that the senior accountant was not so confident.

Looking pale and gaunt and older than his years, he fixed Brett with burning eyes as he lay propped against his pillows, and asked him if he really thought he could cope. 'It's not that I don't have confidence in you, Brett,' he said earnestly. 'It's just that there's so much to do – even more than when I was in charge – and it might be too much for you, you see.'

'No, no, I'm fine, I'm looking forward to it. There's absolutely no need for you to worry, Mr MacNay. In fact, you shouldn't – it's bad for you.'

'Yes, bad for you,' Shona chimed in. 'The doctors want you to relax completely, don't they? Just leave things to other people.'

'To Brett, you mean.' Stuart smiled faintly. 'What I can't understand is why Mr Kyle doesn't find someone to help him.'

'You know what he's like – he doesn't want the bother of finding somebody when he knows I can do the job alone.' Brett smiled encouragingly. 'He's a funny guy – doesn't even have a proper secretary, just keeps track of his own appointments and lets Miss Elrick type his letters when she's the time. But everything gets done, you see, because he knows what he's doing and does it well.'

'Promise me this, then – that you'll stay in post until I can return.'

'Of course I'll stay! I can promise you that with no trouble at all.'

'Thank you, then.' Stuart was beginning to look so weary, Shona knocked Brett's arm and they rose to take their leave.

'You're in good hands here,' Shona said quietly. 'Let them take care of you, eh?'

'She means no worrying,' Brett added. 'We'll be along to see you again soon.'

'Wish I could have attended the opening of the new shop,' Stuart murmured, closing his eyes. 'Have a drink for me on the day, eh?'

'You bet!' said Brett.

The grand opening of the new Maybel's was held on a morning

in late March, before it opened to the public in the afternoon. Fraser had invited a number of businessmen, traders and friends, as well as Shona and Brett from the George Street shop and Mr and Mrs May.

'Well, isn't this amazing!' Mrs May cried as she and her husband came up to Shona and Brett, champagne glasses in their hands. 'Just look at this place – and it used to be so dreary!'

They were standing in the beautifully decorated front shop that was filled with flowers and expensive house plants, all ordered from Fraser's new supplier, and now filling the air with fragrance. 'I never thought Fraser would start empire building quite so soon, did you, Hugh?'

'Never. Always thought he'd take his time,' answered Hugh, who was looking fit and relaxed, 'but he's done a very good job here, hasn't he?'

'And Brigid seems to be in her element,' Mrs May observed, looking across to where Brigid was talking animatedly to someone from Rotary. Standing nearby were her assistants – two juniors and a senior, an experienced florist from the previous shop who had been re-employed. 'So very professional!'

Turning back to Shona, Mrs May's gaze, flickering with interest, moved to Brett and she held out her hand. 'I don't believe we've met. I'm Phyllida May and this is my husband, Hugh. We used to own the George Street Maybel's.'

'Why, of course, I know the name.' Brett was all courtesy, all charm, as he shook the hands of the Mays. 'I'm Brett Webster, at present accountant for Mr Kyle, though I'm from Canada – a cousin of Shona's.'

'Shona's cousin?' the Mays echoed. 'From Canada?'

'And an accountant for Fraser?' Mrs May's laugh was a little sharp. 'And to think I used to do all that sort of thing myself! Business must be looking up.'

'Fascinating news, my dear, that you have a cousin,' Hugh murmured to Shona. 'We never knew you had any relatives, you know. But how well you're looking, as pretty as Fraser's flowers! Life's suiting you, eh?'

'I think so,' she answered, blushing. 'But you're looking well, too, and Mrs May. The East Neuk of Fife must have worked its magic.'

'Too right, though I don't mind admitting, when I see those flowers and smell their scent, the old hands start itching for the twine and the wire and I wish I was arranging again!'

'We wish you were, too,' Shona said warmly, and meant it.

As the Mays moved away to circulate, Brett looked at Shona and grinned.

'My word, she's high powered! Bet she kept you on your toes.'

'Kept everybody on their toes. But she was very efficient, and it's true, she did all the accounting herself, as well as running the business and working with the flowers. You had to admire her.'

'I daresay, but I'm glad Mr Kyle's got different ideas on what he wants to do, or I might be out of a job.' Brett took Shona's arm. 'Which, thank God, I'm not. Let's get some more of that champagne, eh?'

If Brigid was in her element, so was Fraser, who was giving the impression of being everywhere at once, shaking every guest's hand, having a word or a smile for all in his path, totally immersed in his celebration. Except that, every so often, his eyes would search faces until he found Shona's, and then a shadow would fall and his smile would fade. Only for a moment. Then he'd be back, greeting people, calling for the hired waitresses to keep the glasses filled and the canapés passed, and would be in control again.

'Shall we have our own celebration tonight?' Brett asked, as he and Shona took a tram back to George Street. 'I feel like going out for a good meal somewhere.'

'I don't know, Brett – we've had a lot of expensive meals lately. Couldn't we just have a fish supper again? You liked that, didn't you?'

'Sure, but I think you're just worrying about money. There's no need, you know, and it does put a bit of a dampener on things.'

'I suppose it's what I'm used to. Never had any money for dinners out in the old days – still doesn't feel right.'

'Shona, I want you to have the best,' he said seriously. 'Things have changed for both of us. You only have one life – enjoy it when you can.'

'There's more than one way to enjoy life, Brett,' she said firmly, at which he pressed her hand in his.

'You're right about that, and being with you means more to me than any grand meal out.' His eyes met hers that were suddenly shining. 'Doesn't mean you have to have an either/or situation, does it?'

'I suppose not,' she said, the glow in her eyes lessening, but that evening she was in for a surprise. Instead of some expensive place Brett took her back for another fish supper which was so good Shona felt herself vindicated, and Brett agreed that she was.

Didn't stop him booking a meal at one of his favourite restaurants for their next night out, though, which meant returning to the starched tablecloths and formality. But what could Shona do? She set herself out to enjoy it, even though she shook her head at him over their first course.

'Brett, you're incorrigible! That's a word I learned at the orphanage when the staff got exasperated with some naughty boy.'

'And that's me,' he agreed cheerfully. 'But don't expect me to change. A leopard can't change his spots.'

'You're my favourite leopard, anyway,' she told him, her smile a little rueful, and he laughed and said he knew.

Fifty-Eight

With the coming of summer, spirits lightened in the city. As blue skies replaced grey and the sun shone, bright clothes came out again for the smart folk strolling in Princes Street, and in the adjoining gardens nursemaids pushed well-to-do babies in perambulators, joining with the tourists, listening to the band.

Sunshine was good for business, too, and as sales went up in Fraser's shops and market garden, he appeared so much at ease with the way things were going Shona thought she really needn't worry about him any more. Money-making took up so much of his time there was little left for brooding over her, and when he began to talk of opening up in Glasgow sometime in the future she heaved a sigh of relief.

'That will keep you busy!' she told him when he talked to her in the workroom one day when she was alone. 'But surely you won't want to take out another loan?'

'Hey, don't worry. I can do it when I pay off the present one. His narrow eyes were studying her closely. 'Remember when we used to talk of your being a business partner with me? Think that will ever happen? Or will you be far away in the icy snows of Canada?'

'I've no plans for any such thing.'

'That's good news. Until Stuart comes back I don't want to lose Brett. He'll be going home sometime, though?'

'I don't know what's in his mind,' she said with truth, but Fraser suddenly put his hand on her chin and made her look at him.

'Are you all right, Shona?' he asked quietly. 'Are you happy?'

'Yes, of course I'm happy!' She turned her head away. 'Hope you are, too.'

'Oh, don't worry about me.' He dropped his hand. 'I'm just a rubber ball: I bounce back when crushed. Hadn't you noticed?'

'I'd better get on,' she said uneasily, continuing to sort out the flowers she needed and, after a moment, he left.

Was she happy? Shona studied the golden orchids she was combining with yellow roses for a Golden Wedding bouquet, half her mind concentrating on what foliage would do best for her frame, the other half trying to answer Fraser's question. Yes, should be the answer, for she had her love and was sure of him. On the other hand, she wasn't sure of anything else.

The understanding she'd thought would be so lovely was no longer enough. There'd been no further plans, no date for a future to be spent together. Whenever she tried to pin Brett down he avoided straight answers, still claiming he didn't know what would be happening, how he must play it by ear, see how things worked out and other such excuses. Eventually Shona would give up her questioning, until the next time, when she fared no better.

In the meantime, of course, life in the summer was sweet. There were the Sunday drives out into the country, the picnics and walks, the meals at local inns, sometimes sitting outside (always considered such a treat in Scotland), the visits to stately homes, or the seaside in Fife. And then, there was the love-making.

It was not true love-making, of course, but as they lay together in Brett's flat, it almost was. It was what engaged couples did who daren't take the risk of 'going all the way', but it wasn't the real thing, it wasn't what she wanted, which was to have the real thing and not have to worry. That only came when you were married, as she and Brett could so easily be. But weren't. They weren't even officially engaged. No wonder, then, that she didn't always look happy. More often than not she must appear anxious, uncertain. For she was like someone tossed on a wave, thrown by the current, with no idea where she would come to rest. If she ever did.

Brett, though he seemed not to want to discuss a future with her, kept a watch on his own at Maybel's, always enquiring about

Stuart MacNay's progress, sometimes visiting him at his parents' house on the south side where he was still convalescing. On one of her free afternoons in August Shona went too, and sat with Stuart and Brett in the MacNays' large, pleasant garden, drinking Mrs MacNay's home-made lemonade and enjoying the sunshine, although Stuart said he still didn't feel up to enjoying anything very much.

'Just can't seem to regain my strength,' he said mournfully. 'I've been away from work for months – felt sure I'd be better by now, but all I want to do is rest. Ridiculous, isn't it?'

'You're looking much better, though,' Shona told him warmly. 'You've put on a little weight and your face is not so pale.'

'Think so?' Stuart sighed and looked down into his glass. 'I can't see it myself. Sometimes I wonder if I shouldn't just resign.' He glanced at Brett. 'Just leave it all to you, Brett. I understand from Mr Kyle that you're doing a very good job.'

'Come on, you're going to be fine!' Brett's tone was hearty. 'You're probably almost there – maybe just need a little more time in this lovely garden. We all want you back, you know.'

'Nice of you to say so but we'll just have to see, won't we, how I get on?'

'So kind of you to visit our poor boy,' Mrs MacNay told the visitors, when they took their leave. 'He leads a very dull life, really, just waiting to get well. The doctor thinks his recovery could come quite suddenly, but we've told him he mustn't rush back – his health comes first.'

'Oh, quite so,' Brett agreed. 'He mustn't think of coming back until he's really well.'

'Really well,' Shona echoed.

Strolling through Morningside, looking at the shops, Brett laughed shortly. 'Did you hear her?' he asked. 'Mrs MacNay? "We've told him he mustn't rush back"? Does he look like rushing back? He's already been off for months!'

'He has been dangerously ill, Brett. Something like that must take its toll.'

'Oh, I know.' Brett flashed a sudden smile. 'Suits me, anyway, if he takes his time. I'm not complaining over my improved salary!'

'You're certainly spending it,' Shona remarked. 'You've bought some beautiful clothes lately.'

'Only in the sales. I thought you'd be pleased.'

'Even in the sales, Logie's shirts are not cheap, and then there was that linen jacket and the dressing gown.'

'It pays to buy the best, Shona. Cheap stuff doesn't last.' He took her arm. 'What I'd really like is to buy you an evening dress. I saw a gorgeous one – emerald green, the latest style – and well marked down, but I didn't dare to buy it without you. Would you let me buy you a dress, anyway?'

'Brett, it's a lovely idea, but quite unnecessary. I don't need an evening dress, and if I did, Cassie could make me one for a fraction of what the shops charge. When would I wear one, though? That's the thing.'

'I thought we could start going to dinner dances. We've never been dancing, have we? I'm not keen on dance halls and don't suppose you are. But the hotel dances are different, and we could have a good meal into the bargain. What do you say?'

'Brett, I don't know. I've never thought about going anywhere like that.' Shona hesitated. 'I daresay it'd be very nice, but—'

'But what?'

'I don't know – I just feel everything's so unsettled between us, I can't get worked up about dancing.'

'Oh, poor Shona!' In the middle of the street, Brett took her into his arms. 'I'm sorry – I really am. I know you want things to be cut and dried, and I do too, but it's difficult at present, as I've tried to explain. Why not let's just enjoy what we have and see how things work out? I do love you, you know, and if you'll let me kiss you here, I'll make you believe it.'

She smiled and let him kiss her, even if frosty-faced shoppers were staring, then they linked arms and made their way to a tram stop, putting aside for yet another day all that had to be decided.

Fifty-Nine

Summer never seemed to last long. Just as people grew used to long days and short nights, smelling flowers, seeing trees in full leaf, wearing light clothes – no vests, no woollen stockings – along came the winds of autumn and everything changed. September wasn't too bad, could be golden, even if the evenings grew darker and darker, but October – oh, yes, the year was in decline then, when you felt the first real cold seep into your bones and fires were lit, smoke hit the skies, and 'Auld Reekie' was back to normal.

Everything seemed normal, too, at Maybel's in George Street and in Morningside. Business was good, Fraser was cheerful and Brett working hard, still covering for Mr MacNay, balancing his tasks, he told Shona, like a juggler keeping balls in the air. There was no hint of change, no harbinger of trouble, until one afternoon in late October Brett sought out Shona to ask her to come to his flat that evening.

'But we said we wouldn't meet tonight,' she exclaimed. 'I've a load of chores to do at home. Why d'you want to see me?'

'Something's cropped up – no need to worry.'

He smiled easily, but there was a look in his eyes she hadn't seen before. A kind of wariness, or maybe defensiveness – she couldn't quite put her finger on it, but a small alarm suddenly began to ring in her head.

'All right, what time shall I come?'

'Oh – after your tea with Mrs Gow. Thanks, Shona.'

Without saying more he returned to his office, leaving her to look after him with a puzzled look that gradually became one of apprehension.

It was already dark by the time she reached his flat and rang the bell, which he answered immediately. He had changed from his work suit into a sweater and flannels and at first seemed as usual – relaxed, welcoming. After he'd taken her coat and they'd briefly kissed, however, she began to sense that he was more on edge than she'd ever seen him and felt herself tightening in response.

'Heavens, why only one light in here?' she cried, looking round the living room that was full of shadows. 'Have you been sitting in the dark?'

'Hadn't noticed.' He snapped on another table lamp and put coal on his fire which had not yet begun to burn brightly. 'I've been thinking, that's all.'

'And smoking.' Looking at his ashtray filled with stubs, Shona sank into a chair. 'Brett, what's wrong? Why did you want to see me?'

He remained standing, gazing down at her, a cigarette still between his fingers. When he spoke his voice was hoarse, as though he had trouble getting the words out. 'Shona, will you come with me to London?'

She stared up at him, her eyes widening. 'London? What are you talking about? I mean – why?'

'I have to go. Go somewhere, anyway. London would be best, to start with – we can do all the paperwork from there.'

'What paperwork?' She was bewildered. 'I don't understand.'

'Well, we'll need visas of some sort, and you'll need a passport.' He gave a crooked smile and threw his cigarette into the fire. 'And then there's the special licence – for us to get married.'

'Married!'

'I couldn't ask you before when I didn't know how things would go for me. But now I know, don't I?' He sighed. 'And you can make your own decision. Wouldn't want to go to Australia without being married, would you?'

She sprang to her feet and putting her hands on his shoulders, shook him with all her strength. 'Brett, will you stop it? Will you stop talking in riddles and tell me what's going on? I think I deserve something better than nonsense about Australia!'

Slowly he drew her towards him and for some moments held her close, before seating himself in one of his armchairs and drawing her on to his knee. 'I wish it was nonsense,' he said quietly. 'But it's the only place I can think of to try. Like I said, I have to go somewhere. I can't stay here, I can't stay with Maybel's. I might be arrested.'

Shona's heart was beating so fast, her head throbbing so strongly, she felt almost sick, yet she knew she could not give in; she must look into the fine dark eyes fixed on hers and try to understand, try to make sense of what Brett was saying.

'Arrested?' she whispered. 'Brett, what have you done?'

'I'm an accountant, sweetheart, can't you guess? I look after the books and – I've – well, I've been milking 'em. Falsifying the accounts is the correct term. Ever since Stuart went sick I've been playing around with all that lovely money.' He laughed shortly. 'Temptation was there – and I succumbed.' He put his face against hers, he held her close, he would have caressed her but she leaped from his knee and stood looking into the fire, trembling so violently she had to hold her hands together to try to keep herself from collapsing.

'I don't believe it,' she said several times. 'I don't believe you'd do something like that. No, you wouldn't. You wouldn't!'

'I told you, I was tempted and I fell. Happens to a lot of guys like me. We know what to do and we do it. Then we regret it.'

'But did you never think you'd be found out? One day Mr Kyle would be sure to send in auditors. It's a routine thing, isn't it? How could you hope to get away with it?'

'There'll be no need for auditors to find me out now,' Brett said with a strange lightness. 'We got word today that Stuart MacNay is recovered. He's coming back to work on Monday and it won't take him long to smell a rat, I can promise you. As soon as I heard the news, I knew I'd lost out.'

'That was always going to happen, wasn't it?'

'No, because I thought I'd get enough notice to cover my tracks. It's like in Toronto—' He stopped, his cheekbones colouring, as Shona looked again into his eyes.

'This has happened before?' she asked quietly. 'In Toronto? You didn't want to come to Scotland to see the old country, did you? You were forced to come – you had to leave Canada?'

'No, it wasn't as bad as that. I failed to cover things up there and my employers found me out, but I was young and they decided not to prosecute. Just gave me the sack and told me not to try working in the same field again.' Brett shook his head. 'Of course, there was no reference, but I reckoned that people over here might not bother to check with Canada – it takes so damned long and, you see, I was right. Mr Kyle didn't check. He accepted my forged reference on company paper and there I was – in.'

Suddenly Brett took Shona's hands and swung her round to face him. 'But I swear I'd no intention of fiddling the books again. It was just that – well, I knew I could, so in the end I did. Gave myself some extra cash to take you around, buy a few clothes—'

'Oh, don't, don't!' Shona put her hands over her face. 'I thought all that spending was just extra salary, for being in charge.' She lowered her hands and looked at him with huge sad eyes. 'And you were going to buy me an evening dress? With someone else's money?'

'I know it sounds bad, but it was never, you know, deliberate.' Brett put his hands on Shona's shoulders. 'And when you think how rotten the world is, so bloody unfair! Why should some folk be starving and others go swanning around in Rolls-Royces, buying whatever they want, not giving a damn?'

'But you weren't stealing to help folk starving,' she cried, pulling herself away. 'You were spending the money just the way the rich do – on things that don't matter.' Her voice thickened as tears gathered in her eyes and began to fall. 'Brett, it's no good. I can't go with you to Australia – or anywhere. I just – can't.'

'You always said you loved me, Shona. Is this what you call love? Soon as I make a mistake you ditch me?'

'I do love you, I do. How could I just stop? And I don't want anything to happen to you – I mean, if you were arrested – went to prison, even – I'd no' be able to stand it. But I couldn't live like you do. Looking over your shoulder, moving on when you might be found out, spending money that's no' yours.' Her voice trembled. 'My folks had so little, Brett, no margin for anything, but they'd never, *never* take what wasn't theirs.'

'But were never tempted, I'm willing to bet. It's easy to take the high road when you're never put to the test.'

Shona was moving away, her head bent, her face averted. 'Dad once found a pound note on the pavement in the village. It would've meant so much. A whole pound! But he took it to the police station and handed it in because he said it wasn't his. Some time later – I forget how long – they told us we could keep it. It was . . . wonderful.'

'Where are you going?' Brett asked huskily. 'You're not leaving me now?'

'There's no point in staying.' She looked back at him. 'But don't worry, I won't say anything. I won't tell them where you've gone.'

'If you're going home, I'll drive you.'

'I don't want you to, I'll be all right.'

He was moving swiftly into the hall, taking his coat from a cupboard. 'I'm taking you home, Shona. Don't try to stop me.'

Outside Mrs Gow's house, where they had halted so many times before to say goodnight with kisses and hugs, they sat for some time in silence.

'What will you do now?' Shona asked at last.

'Pack my things, get the car filled up, drive down to London tomorrow. I've already cancelled the lease on the flat and my rent's paid in advance, so that's OK. I'll mail the keys to the landlord when I leave.'

'Where will you stay in London? And what will you do with the car?'

'I know a chap from home who's living in London. He'll put me up for a while and probably sell the car for me, too. Soon as I can make arrangements, I'll get a passage on some small boat – not a liner – and make my way to Sydney, Adelaide – I don't mind.'

'And tomorrow,' Shona asked fearfully. 'What will you do about work? Leave a message or something?'

'I'll call in sick. Say I've got a sore throat.' Brett grasped her hand. 'You promise you won't say anything? I'm dependent on you, Shona.'

'I've already said I won't say a word.' She hesitated. 'Except maybe to Cassie.'

'Cassie? My God, why should you tell her? Shona, I don't want you to tell her, or anyone. You promised!'

'She loves you so much, Brett. I think she should know that you've gone.'

'Cassie loves me?' He groaned. 'That sweet, pretty girl? And I only love you.'

Suddenly they held one another, kissing as they'd always done, gazing at each other in the darkness of the car, tears streaming down Shona's cheeks and stinging Brett's tragic eyes.

'I'll write to you,' he gasped. 'I'll tell you where I am. Just in case . . . you change your mind.'

She shook her head, stumbling blindly from the car, running towards the house, never looking back. In case she did. In case she did change her mind.

Sixty

Going in to work on Saturday morning was agony, even though everyone accepted Brett's excuse of a sore throat for not appearing, and as he didn't work on Saturday afternoons anyway there were no problems there. Yet Shona had somehow to conceal her own desolation at parting from him, as well as her fears for Monday when Stuart MacNay came back and still Brett would be absent. What could she say? Folk would be looking at her, expecting her to provide some explanation, which was just not possible.

She began to feel desperate to talk to someone and as she'd already decided to tell Cassie about Brett, arranged to meet her for a walk on Sunday. It would be better than staying in the house with Mrs Gow, for all Shona had told her was that her cousin had left for London, which at least gave her an excuse for her tears which Mrs Gow could accept. But, oh dear, her sympathy had made Shona feel so bad she'd just longed to escape, and was relieved at last to be out in the open air with Cassie.

They decided to walk by the Water of Leith, following its course as far as Stockbridge, where they sat on a bench and looked at each other. Until then they had said very little. Now, Cassie's blue gaze rested wonderingly on Shona's white face and reddened eyelids. 'What's up?' she asked bluntly. 'Have you and Brett had a row?'

'No. But we've parted.'

'Parted? Shona, you're no' serious?'

'I am, then.' Shona's look was indeed serious, and made Cassie seem almost afraid.

'You going to tell me about it?' she whispered.

'If you will promise me you'll never repeat what I tell you to anyone else. Promise me, Cassie.'

'I promise!'

'All right, then. The thing is, Brett's gone to London. He went on Saturday.'

'He's no' got a sore throat?'

'That was an excuse. He's going to make arrangements in London to sail to Australia; he won't be coming back here.'

The colour drained from Cassie's face and her gaze fell. 'Why?' she asked at last. 'Why's he doing it?'

Shona looked away. 'This is the part I don't want to tell you, but there's no way you'll understand if I don't. He's running away, Cassie. He's running away because Mr MacNay's coming back and he's going to find out that Brett's been fiddling the books. He could be prosecuted, you see, so he's gone.'

Cassie was stricken, unable to find words, until at last she cried out, 'I don't believe it, Shona! There must be some mistake. Brett wouldn't – he wouldn't do a thing like that!'

'He's done it before. In Toronto. They let him off then, but who knows what Mr Kyle would do? Brett couldn't risk staying.'

'This is terrible,' Cassie was moaning. 'Terrible, like a nightmare. And for you, Shona. You must be in a state, eh? I mean, he's left you behind. And he never asked you to marry him? Never asked you to go with him?'

Shona bit her lip, her eyes filling with tears. 'He did ask me to marry him,' she said, her voice so low Cassie had to strain her ears to hear it. 'He did want me to go with him. But I said I couldn't do it.'

'Couldn't do it? What are you saying? You turned Brett down? How could you? I thought you loved him?'

'I do love him! I do, Cassie. But he's no' the Brett I thought I knew. They say if you love somebody it shouldn't matter what they do, but I couldn't live his life, you see. I couldn't be living on the edge, worrying all the time if somebody was coming after us.' Shona was shaking her head. 'And the worst thing of all is that Brett doesn't really understand that everything we had would be built on shifting sands. I could tell he didn't really believe what he'd done was wrong. He thinks it's owed to him, to have what he wants, so he might do the same thing all over again. How could I live like that?'

Shona was suddenly sobbing in earnest as Cassie sat staring, her face set, her eyes cold. 'If you truly loved him, you could. But you didn't give him a chance, did you? Supposing he'd said he'd never make that mistake again, couldn't you have believed him? Folk change, you know.'

Change? Hadn't Brett himself said once, 'don't expect me to change'? And 'A leopard doesn't change his spots'? That was about something else, of course, and maybe where more important things were concerned he might have different views. Shouldn't she have given him a chance, then, as Cassie had said? No, Shona decided, no! For he had never said he would change, never tried to persuade her that way. Maybe he knew himself too well.

'No,' she said aloud. 'No, Cassie, Brett's life isn't for me. That's all there is to it.'

'Is it?' Cassie rose and stood looking down at Shona. 'He asked you to marry him, he asked you to go with him, and you said no. If he'd asked me I wouldn't have cared what he'd done, I'd have said yes. That's the difference between us, eh?'

Shona slowly stood up and turned to go back. 'Well, there's no difference between what we want for him, anyway. I can't go along with what you say, but we both want him to get away and no' face arrest. So I know you'll keep your promise.'

'I shan't even reply to that. Let's just go home, it's getting cold.'

'You could come in for a cup of tea at Mrs Gow's if you liked?'

'No, thanks.' Cassie was walking fast, keeping her gaze straight ahead. 'No' today.'

Sixty-One

On Monday, October 21, Stuart MacNay returned to work at Maybel's in George Street. Everyone was, of course, delighted to see him, and looking so well, too – no longer pale and gaunt, enduring pain, but quite filled out, with tanned cheeks and an air of confidence.

'I'm so glad to be back,' he told Fraser. 'Work beats rest any time – but where's Brett, then?'

'Hasn't phoned in,' Fraser answered, frowning. 'May still have the sore throat. I'll speak to Shona.'

'I'm afraid I didn't see Brett yesterday,' Shona answered truthfully, but Fraser was looking at her with eyebrows raised.

'Are you feeling all right, yourself, Shona? You look a bit under the weather.'

'I'm all right, thanks, Mr Kyle.'

'Well, I don't mind telling you I'm a wee bit concerned about this. I don't like an accountant of mine not keeping in touch. I know the firm he's letting his flat from – I think I might give them a ring, see if they know anything.'

With a beating heart, Shona watched him walk away to make the call. This was it, then. Fraser was going to find out that Brett had gone and there was nothing she could do.

It didn't take long for the balloon to go up, as Fraser put it himself. As soon as he was told that Brett had cancelled his lease and left the flat, he came back at once to the workroom to find Shona.

'In my office, please, Shona. Now.' In his office, he pointed to a chair. 'Sit down, please, and tell me what's going on.'

'I don't know what you mean.'

'Where is Brett?'

'I don't know, Fraser.'

His green eyes centred on her face. She had never seen them look so cold. 'If I were to fetch a Bible, would you still tell me that you don't know where he is?'

She flushed, her lip trembling. 'I can't – I can't say any more. Please, don't try to make me.'

'He's gone, hasn't he? Absconded? And what would be the reason for that, I wonder?'

She was silent, her hands twisting on her lap.

'And you haven't gone with him? Another mystery.' Fraser suddenly moved to the door. 'All right, Shona, I'll let you off the hook for now. I've got work to do, and so has Mr MacNay. Surprising, isn't it, that Brett only decides to go missing when his boss comes back to work?'

News of Brett's flight spread fast around the shop, with all eyes on Shona, though no one asked her outright where Brett could be. In fact, apart from Cassie, there was sympathy for her but little for Brett, for it seemed obvious enough why he had gone.

'I always did feel a bit uneasy about him,' Willa remarked. 'So handsome – quite the film star – but too good to be true. Sorry, Shona, I don't mean to upset you. I know he's your cousin.'

Shona said nothing. She didn't feel like talking.

'Wonder what'll happen now?' Isla asked excitedly. 'What will Mr MacNay find?'

'Who says he'll find anything?' asked Cassie, but no one troubled to reply.

For three days, there was no information on the senior accountant's search. While Fraser fumed about and Brigid came over from Morningside specially to get news, it began to look as though Brett had been particularly clever and that nothing would come to light. But Mr MacNay was not one to be beaten, and on the morning of Thursday, October 24, he was able to tell Mr Kyle that his assistant had indeed been falsifying the accounts. Not by great sums, and not enough to make Fraser suspicious, just the sort of amounts he could use to spend on himself and maybe hope to put back at some future date.

'What will do you now, Mr Kyle?' Stuart asked him. 'Inform the police?'

Fraser ran a hand over his brow and shook his head. 'I don't think so. What's the point? We don't know where he is. Probably back in Canada by now, unless he's in trouble there as well. I didn't check his references, did I? What sort of a damned fool does that make me?'

'He seemed such a nice young man,' Stuart said sadly. 'And so incredibly good looking.'

'Handsome is as handsome does.' Fraser stood up. 'Come on, it's lunchtime – I'll buy you a pint, Stuart. You deserve it.'

'No pints,' Stuart said firmly. 'I'm afraid it'll have to be a glass of milk.'

'Oh, God,' said Fraser. 'But come on, anyway.'

Late afternoon, Fraser sought out Shona. 'It's all right,' he told her heavily. 'No need to look so scared. We've decided to write the whole thing off to experience. I won't interrogate you any more.'

She gave a long sigh. 'Fraser, thank you. I appreciate that. But I do want to say I'm sorry I couldn't say anything. I'd promised.'

'I understand.' His look was sympathetic. 'This has been hard for you, Shona, very hard, and it'll take some getting over. But you will, you know, you will get over it.' He paused for a moment, then asked softly, 'Did he want you to go with him?'

She nodded.

'But you didn't. I'm not going to ask why, but I can guess, and I believe you've done the right thing. There's no point in going over what was wrong with Brett, but it's something to remember – if you can't trust a man with money, you can't trust him at all. What you have to do now is let time do its work. Take it day by day and one day, I promise, it'll be over. You'll see.'

'Fraser—'

'No more, no more. As a matter of fact, we've other things to think about. Have you heard the news?'

'What news?'

'It was on the wireless in the pub at lunchtime. The American stock market has crashed.'

'Oh. That sounds bad.'

'If you're thinking, but that's America, nothing to do with us, I'm not so sure. It might have ramifications for us all.'

'But it's so far away!'

'Not these days.' He laughed shortly. 'And what America does the rest of the world often follows. But, you know what this day's going to be called? Black Thursday. For you and me, too.'

Sixty-Two

Time, Fraser had said she would need, just as Mark had once said, too, and time Shona endured, hiding her loss as much as she was able, keeping going, working hard, hoping to get better. Brett never wrote, which was just as well. Somehow she'd known he wouldn't; he was sensitive enough to know that she'd meant what she said and was now making a new life for himself in which she would have no part. No doubt time was working for him, too, as for her, but oh so slowly!

Meanwhile, as she faced her own personal tragedy, a greater tragedy was beginning to play out on the world stage. Fraser had been right – the Wall Street crash in America had had far-reaching ramifications. Maybe only making worse problems that were already there, but as the 1930s began, it soon became apparent that the outlook for the future was bleak beyond belief.

American credit vanished. World trade crumbled. Everywhere there were cuts in expenditure and more and more people began to lose their jobs. Over the industrial and shipbuilding areas, particularly in Scotland, a terrible fog seemed to have descended, and though there was talk of weathering the slump and the hope that the national government might do something to help, no one really believed it.

'Because we're all in the same boat,' Fraser cried. 'Who can bail us out? However many cuts we make, when we reach the bone, that'll be it. No more to be done.'

Not that he was saying Maybel's had reached that level yet, but already there were bad omens, the first casualty being his plans to open a new shop in Glasgow, followed by his idea of starting to open a café at the market garden. Both of these projects being close to his heart, Fraser was deeply affected, though trying to put a good face on things. 'No, haven't reached the bone yet,' he told Shona. 'And if we can still keep the two Edinburgh shops going, we'll manage until the slump is over.'

'Surely folk will always want to buy flowers, Fraser? There are still people with money in this city.'

'Depends if there are enough to keep us going, though. We might have the rich ordering flowers for weddings and dinners and corporate events, but we need a lot of them, and ordinary folk, too, coming in to buy their daffodils and such. If you lose your job are you wanting to buy daffodils, or struggling to buy food?'

Shona had turned away from that conversation with a stronger feeling of dread even than she'd been feeling since the Wall Street crash. She thought of Brigid and her staff, of Isla, Cassie, Willa and Dan, the delivery man – were all their jobs at risk? Was hers? Not yet, not yet. To cheer herself she suddenly decided to go back to Edina Lodge. See her Handkerchief Tree. It was May, it should be looking beautiful. And it had never failed to cheer her yet.

Some days later, on her next afternoon off, having been admitted through the gates to the Lodge, she made her way to the gardens, feeling sudden anxiety that her tree might no longer be there. It was some time since she'd visited the orphanage – maybe it had died, or for some reason been chopped down?

But it was there. Her tree. Covered in its exquisite load of flowers, or leaves, whichever term you cared to use, for there was the tree's strange charm – that you couldn't tell which of the two – flowers or leaves – it bore. How the sight of it took her back to that first sad day at the Lodge! Mark Lindsay had taken her then to see the tree and told her it would make her feel better, which it had. He'd been so astute, hadn't he? For there was no magic about the Handkerchief Tree, only a strangeness that had so intrigued her she'd forgotten her homesickness for a little while. And he'd known that would happen, clever Mark – it was not surprising he'd made such a good doctor.

Hearing a footfall behind her, she turned, half expecting to see him, but was surprised, instead, to meet the interested blue gaze of Miss Bryce.

'Shona, how nice to see you! Haven't seen you back here for some time.'

'No, it's true, I haven't visited for a while. But it's so nice to see you again, Miss Bryce.'

And she hadn't changed at all, except for one or two grey hairs at her temples and small creases at her eyes. Telling her she was looking well, Shona hoped Miss Bryce would see no great change in herself. Perhaps it was only her imagination, but sometimes when she looked in the mirror she thought she did look much older and sadder.

'What a piece of nonsense!' Willa had declared when she'd remarked on it. 'You look exactly the same. Just a very pretty girl.'

Miss Bryce made no comment, anyway. Only said she was out for a breath of air and to take a rest from all the orders from authority to cut costs.

'Cut costs! Now, you tell me where I can cut costs when everything is pared down as much as possible anyway! I told them frankly that under no circumstances would I cut food bills, so now they're trying to make me cut the staff.' Miss Bryce shook her head angrily as she and Shona began to walk towards the house, laughing after a moment and saying she must simmer down. 'How are things with you, anyway? The flower shop keeping going?'

'More or less. But we're all a bit worried, to tell you the truth. Sales figures are down. We're wondering if we'll be having a few cuts of our own.'

'Oh, dear, I hope not. You'd really found your niche there, hadn't you? And Cassie, too. Now that did surprise me.' Miss Bryce pursed her lips. 'Seems she didn't, after all, take to being in service, after saying she was so keen.'

'Had bad luck with her places, I think. But she's been very happy at Maybel's.'

But not with me, thought Shona, for the coolness between her and Cassie had never really melted. There was still surface friendliness, but the old closeness had never returned. Another thing to make Shona feel older and sadder.

'Like to come and have a cup of tea with the staff?' Miss Bryce asked as they moved to the side door of the house. 'We'll be having a break in a moment.'

'I'd like that, thanks. Have there been any changes since I was here?'

'Well, Mr Glegg has retired and we haven't had a replacement yet, and Miss Anderson is engaged but still with us, thank heavens.'

'And Doctor Lindsay? Is he still the doctor here?'

'Doctor Mark? Oh, yes, his practice still looks after us, but he's doing a lot of work in Glasgow at present for a child health clinic. His special interest, you know.'

'That's wonderful, eh?' Shona would have liked to ask about Miss Ruddick, but said no more as she followed Miss Bryce into the house and up to the staffroom, where she was given such a warm welcome she felt decidedly better. At least, for a little while.

There was nothing for it, though – she had to return to work next day, where the same anxiety hovered as before, made worse by Fraser's lack of cheerfulness. Where was the outsize air of confidence that had always been his? Lost, it seemed, with the prosperity he'd once taken as a right. There was nothing for it but to keep going and hope for the best, but as the year wore on that became harder and harder to do.

Sixty-Three

The first real blow for Maybel's came some months later, early in 1931. There had been no improvement in the world situation, quite the reverse, as more and more businesses – shops, mills, factories, shipyards – closed and more and more people became unemployed. In Scotland, where the recession was like an acid, biting so cruelly, families were facing severe hardship, there being so little help in welfare payments and no hope of work. Even the once serene Dean Village suffered when one of the mills was closed, and Kitty's husband was without a job, just as their first baby was due.

'Oh, it's too cruel,' Addie Hope wailed. 'What'll they do, then, what'll they do? We'll help as best we can, but who knows who'll be next?'

'I was thinking of moving out, with Kitty's baby coming,' Cassie told Shona, 'but they're keen for me to stay, seeing as I've got a job and can pay ma board.' Her expression turning bleak, she'd added after a moment, 'Well, I've got a job at the minute, anyway. Don't know how long for, eh?'

'Must hope for the best,' Shona said, though the words rang hollow when Fraser called her into his office and gave her the bad news. He was going to have to close the Morningside shop.

'Oh, no!' Shona took the news like a stab to the heart. 'No, Fraser, I can't believe it. That's such a good district; there must be people who can afford flowers, there must be!'

'Not enough.' Fraser put his hand to his brow. 'It's the loan, Shona. I'm finding I can't keep up the payments without dipping into capital, and that's shrinking fast. I've no choice but to sell up and hope to pay off with what I can get.'

'But if you can't sell?' Thinking of the boarded-up shops seen everywhere, Shona's voice was hushed. 'You might be no better off.'

'I'll be saving all the overheads and, let's face it, wages. Though I'll still be left with paying off the loan, I'll admit.'

'All the girls will have to go?'

'Except for Brigid. She'll be coming back here.'

Shona hesitated. 'Then we'll have one extra?'

Fraser sighed. 'No, I'm afraid Willa will have to go, too. She was last in, it's only fair, and she does have a husband with a job.'

'Oh, but poor Willa! She was so happy to be back at work.'

'As I say, she's better off than some. Though she'll be a big loss, I know, and I'm really sorry to lose her. Sorry about losing them all, in fact.'

'It's no' your fault, Fraser.'

'That's no consolation.' As he walked with Shona to his door, Fraser's look was dark. There was no sign of his usual smile or his dimples, no sign about him of his power to ride a storm. 'What worries me,' he said in a low voice, 'is that I can't even promise you folk here that your jobs are safe. We're on uncertain ground until there's an upturn in the economy and there's no sign of that. What we're starting to get is civil unrest. People ready to fight back. With what? They've nothing.'

'Fraser, about us – we're all prepared. We know the situation. We're just hoping we can hang on, that's all.'

He touched her shoulder. 'Brave lassies, all of you. I'm lucky to have you. I promise I'll keep going as long as I can.'

Brave lassies? Not really, Shona thought, when she'd left him. What else could they do but hang on and hope for the best? Oh, no, she wasn't going to say that any more. There was no point, was there, in hoping? Just get on with the job while it was there. That was all they could do.

As it turned out, Willa's departure was not the sad occasion they'd expected. On the very day she had to leave she arrived at the shop with a face so radiant, everyone was mystified. Until she told them her news. 'Listen, you'll never guess what's happened! Never believe it either! I can't myself.'

'For heaven's sake, put us out of our misery!' Brigid cried. 'If it's good news, spit it out. We could do with it.'

'It is good news. The best.' Willa sat down, her face beaming. 'I've fallen at last. The doctor told me last evening. I'm going to have a baby!'

There were squeals of joy for her, hugs and pats on the back, questions, even a few tears, for it seemed that for once there was something to celebrate. Maybe it wasn't the best time to bring a baby into the world, but everyone knew how long Willa had been hoping for success, and if she'd been the one to lose her job, could anything have worked out better?

'And what's Grant saying?' Shona asked as they all hurried into the staffroom to make their first cup of tea for a toast to Willa. 'He must be over the moon.'

'Moon, stars, planets, he's there, sailing!' Willa answered, smiling. 'Keeps saying he was right, he'd no need to see anybody about it, everything had happened naturally, and now he's the happiest fellow in the world. Of course, we've still got worries – I mean, we don't know if anybody will be made redundant at the bank, but we'll get through, I know we will, and if we've got our Miss or Master Henderson, we'll be happy, eh?'

'Happy's the word,' said Shona, pouring the tea. 'Come on, everybody, raise your cups! Here's to Miss or Master Henderson – and an end to the Depression!'

'To Miss or Master Henderson,' they solemnly repeated, 'and an end to the Depression.'

'You'll never guess what we're giving you for a leaving present,' Brigid told Willa. 'Mind you, if we'd known your news, we'd have made it bootees and bonnets.'

'Wouldn't be flowers, would it?' Willa asked, laughing.

'Madonna lilies, as a matter of fact, and what could be more appropriate? We've got them all ready in the plant room, and Mr Kyle's coming down specially to present them before you leave.'

'Oh, that's so sweet.' Willa suddenly looked sad. 'But I'm going to miss you folks, you know. Expect to see me any time, when I've – ahem – done my chores!'

'As long as we're still here,' Brigid said in a low voice, but everyone pretended not to hear. This was a day for joy and as there was little of that around they wouldn't let anything spoil it. For all they knew, their little world would be collapsing tomorrow, so today . . .

'Have another cup of tea,' said Shona. 'Listen, where do I get a pattern for booties, then?'

Sixty-Four

A few weeks later a telephone call came for Shona at the shop. 'Who is it?' she asked Isla, who'd taken the call.

'I never asked. Sorry. But she sounded Edinburgh – bit like a teacher, I'd say.'

Edinburgh voice. A bit like a teacher. Miss Bryce, then? Miss Bryce it was.

'Good morning, Shona. Andrina Bryce here. I hope I'm not interrupting your work?'

'No, no, that's all right. What can I do for you?'

'Well, I may be quite wrong about this, but I'm wondering if you'd be interested in a job here. I mean, if there's any question that you might lose yours in the near future.'

'A job? At the Lodge?' Shona was astonished. Never had the thought crossed her mind that she might work at the orphanage.

'Yes. Actually, it's a new post. I'm to lose my assistant to the cuts, but they've offered to create a housekeeper's job, at less pay than my assistant, but to be responsible for some of her type of duties. My assistant doesn't want it as she's getting married. Would you be interested? It would mean living here again, of course.'

A housekeeper's job? Shona hesitated, having difficulty seeing herself in that role. Before she could reply, Miss Bryce was continuing, 'Obviously, I'm hoping that your own job will be secure – I mean, that's what you really want to do – but I feel that, if you can't, you might consider working with us at the Lodge. You'd fit in so well!'

'It's good of you to think of me,' Shona said slowly, 'and I don't honestly know if I'll have a job at Maybel's for much longer. But what sort of duties would the housekeeper's job involve?'

'Apart from the usual routines – checking on supplies and general maintenance, managing domestic staff, that sort of thing – there will also be looking after the children's welfare in the way my assistants have done in the past. Organizing uniforms, seeing that they have all they need, know where to go if they need help and so on. That's where you'd be such an asset, Shona – you've been through the system. You know what is required.'

'I see. Well, as I say, I'm no' sure what's going to be happening but I think I would be interested if I need another post. When is the closing date?'

'Probably in about three weeks or so. We'll be advertising next week. Shall I send you details and you can think about it?'

'Oh, yes, please. And thank you, Miss Bryce.'

Feeling slightly stunned at the way a new prospect was opening before her, yet at the same time dismayed that there could even be any question of having to give up her beloved work as a florist, Shona found herself, almost without thinking, on her way to see Fraser. She could do nothing until she'd some idea what might be happening to Maybel's.

He had been closeted with Stuart MacNay, but came out when he heard Shona knocking on his door. 'You wanted to see me, Shona? Go on into my office, take a seat. I'll be with you in a minute.'

Coming to join her, he put on a smile, tried to look his old cheerful self, didn't succeed. 'What's up, then? Nothing wrong, I hope? At least, no more than usual.'

'Something strange has happened. I've been offered a job.'

'God help us, a job? Where?'

'Housekeeper at Edina Lodge. Sort of an assistant to Miss Bryce as well. Of course, I'd rather stay here, so it's no' really an option.' She looked at Fraser hopefully. 'Is it?'

His eyes fell. He took out his cigarettes and slowly lit one. 'You want my advice, Shona? I'd say, take it.'

She sat very still, hands clasped, large eyes fastened on his face. 'What are you saying?' she asked at last. 'You're going to close the shop?'

'Stuart and I have been discussing it. Things are pretty tight for me at the moment, as you know, and we've decided what I could do is close but not try to sell. Put everything on hold. Save on salaries and overheads, and hope to reopen – well, when things improve.'

'Not sell? Just leave the shop empty?'

'It's what's happened already to the Morningside shop. I've never had a buyer for that – probably wouldn't get one here. People are closing shops, not buying them.'

'But what would you do, Fraser? Where would you go?'

'My market garden, of course. We're still getting customers there, particularly for vegetables. I'd aim to cut down on flowers, build up the veg, maybe do more as a seedsman. And, if you remember, I already have a wee flat in Peebles. That's where I'll live, and if I had any takers to rent my top flat here, well, I might consider making a bob or two that way.' He shrugged. 'It's not much of a prospect, what I'm planning, but it's a way of keeping going until we come out of the slump. I'm not the only guy to be hit like this – I might be luckier than most.'

'Oh, Fraser!' Shona was almost in tears. 'It's too cruel, what's happened, too cruel and unfair! You were doing so well . . .'

'Whoever said life was fair?' Fraser ground out his cigarette and rose. 'So, are you going to put in an application for this job, Shona? You can count on me for a reference.'

She gave a sob and after a moment he came round his desk and put his arms round her.

'Hey, hey, none of that. You're one of my brave ones, remember. Look, things'll come right again. It's just a question of waiting and being ready. And if I open up here again you'll be able to come back from the orphanage.'

'I haven't got the job yet,' she said in muffled tones.

'You will, you will. Your Miss Bryce will see to that. And you'll do well in it, too.' He kissed her cheek. 'Maybe you'll come over to the garden some time, eh? See how I'm getting on?'

'You should be finding someone to make you happy, Fraser. I'm sorry I wasn't the one to love you as you deserve.'

'Can't expect to get what you deserve in this world,' he said lightly. 'Unless it's trouble. You get your application off, but don't say anything yet to the others about what's been decided. I'll tell them myself, Mr and Mrs May as well – Lord knows what they'll have to say. Their beloved shop closing, eh?'

'At least they'll know it's isn't your fault.'

'You always think that makes a difference. What matters is what happens, never mind if you're blameless or not.'

Returning to work Shona felt guilty, burdened by news she couldn't tell. Yet it wouldn't be long, she knew, before the news would come out anyway and by then she might be looking at yet another turn in her fortunes. Working as a housekeeper instead of a florist? She couldn't say it was what she wanted, though it might have its compensations. Oh, not Dr Mark, she told herself, don't go down that road, Shona! She had long ago known that there would be nothing between them, but if her thoughts went wandering back, at least that proved one thing: she was better. Fully healed. Finally over her love for Brett Webster.

Sixty-Five

Suddenly it was April and with it came the sad goodbyes. Maybel's, George Street, was closing.

At the end of its last day, after loyal customers had bought the remaining flowers at sale price, sighing over their loss and wishing everyone the best of luck, Brigid closed the door and looked back at those watching. Fraser, Stuart, Shona, Isla, Cassie and Dan Hardie, all so soon to scatter, all trying to put a brave face on things.

'That's it, then,' she said lightly. 'All over.'

'Canna believe it, eh?' Dan muttered, accepting a glass of the wine Fraser had brought down. 'Never thought I'd see this day. Bet Mr and Mrs May are in a state?'

'You're not wrong about that,' Fraser told him, filling glasses for the girls whether they wanted them or not. 'Had 'em in my office yesterday, asking if they could do something to help. As though I'd take money from retired people! But it was good of 'em to offer. Stuart, you going to risk a drop?'

'Might as well.' Stuart allowed himself a grin. 'Live dangerously, eh?'

'This'll not harm you. A good Merlot. Very nice wine.' Fraser, glass in hand, cleared his throat and looked round at those who had been his staff. 'You'll know how I'm feeling today – the same as you,' he said quietly. 'I might add that this is one of the saddest days of my life, and I'm not just thinking of myself. The only bright spot is that most of you folk have got jobs to go to, or something to do. That's a weight off my mind.'

Shona, glancing at those around her, felt something the same. She herself had been lucky, having been appointed to the housekeeper's job at the Lodge, not just because Miss Bryce wanted her, as Fraser had predicted, but because the man from the council in charge at the interview believed her experience as an orphan would be invaluable. It was true, she'd never worked as a housekeeper, but no one else at the interview could offer her sort of understanding and sympathy with the present-day children, and as much of her work would be with them she would be the best person for the post.

It had been a great relief to her to have something to go to, and an equal relief to know that the others were fixed up, too, except for Cassie. Brigid, for instance, had been taken on by Logie's, the famous department store in Princes Street, so large and prosperous it had no fears of the recession, while Isla was going to take a typing course, Stuart was doing private tutorial work and Dan was to be driving for a furniture firm. That only left Cassie, who'd been cagey about what she might be doing and kept fixing Shona with mysterious glances as though she might like to talk – as Shona fervently hoped was true. It would make such a difference if she and Cassie could be good friends again before they had to part.

'You'll let me know if you find something,' Fraser was saying to Cassie now. 'I've every confidence you will, and I've given you a stunning reference.'

'Thank you, Mr Kyle. I'm sure I'll be all right, but you've been very kind.'

'Very kind,' Brigid suddenly agreed. 'It's been grand working for you and we all appreciate that it's been as hard for you as it has for us.'

'Quite right,' said Stuart. 'I second that.'

'And me,' added Dan and as Isla, blushing, said she did, too, Shona stood smiling.

'We all want to wish you the very best for the future, Mr Kyle,' she said softly. 'And say maybe we'll all be back here again one day, working with your flowers.'

'Help, I don't know what to say,' Fraser muttered with a gulp, his broad face even colouring a little. 'You've been such grand folk to work with. I just hope you're right, Shona, and we all meet again one day here at Maybel's.'

There was a chorus of agreement, and after they'd washed their glasses in the staffroom, Fraser said he'd take them upstairs to be packed with the rest of his stuff for Peebles. Then it really was goodbye. They put on their coats, Isla burst into tears, and one by one they shook hands with Fraser.

'Now you all know where the market garden is and my address in Peebles,' he cried. 'I'll expect to see you over there when you can make it, so don't let me down, and in the meantime, let's make this *au revoir*, eh, and not goodbye?'

Au revoir. Seemed strange to say it, but as Shona met Fraser's gaze, she knew for her that he meant it.

'You will try to come over?' he whispered, 'just for old time's sake?'

'I don't know – maybe.'

And then they were out in the street and Fraser had closed and locked the door behind them before going up to his flat. Standing together for the last time, they said goodbye again before they went their separate ways, waving sadly, the men making for one tram, Brigid and Isla for another, while Shona and Cassie set off to walk to the Dean.

'I wanted to talk to you, Shona,' Cassie said hurriedly. 'To say I'm sorry I've been such a pain in the neck, but I'm over it now. I just think now you did the right thing about Brett, and I'm sure you wouldn't have been happy with him in the end. You'd never have known where you were, eh?' She laughed a little weakly. 'And neither would I.'

'That's all right, Cassie,' Shona answered warmly. 'You said what you thought was right at the time. Let's say no more about it and be friends.'

'Let's.' Halting in the middle of the street, they stopped, hugged each other, then set off again.

'There's something else I want to tell you,' Cassie said after a moment. 'I didn't want to tell the others – Mr Kyle and everybody – but the thing is, I'm no' looking for a job, except maybe something temporary. I'm going to marry Archie Smith. We got engaged last week and he's saving for a ring.'

'Cassie!' Shona was stunned. 'But that's grand. That's wonderful. Oh, fancy – Archie and you. Oh, I do wish you all the best!'

'Kitty's no' bothered that I'll be moving out, either, now that she's got the baby and her husband's working for one of the breweries, but I'll be sorry to say goodbye. She's been so kind.'

'Aye, she's like her ma. I'll have to be saying goodbye to Mrs Hope and Mrs Gow, too, but of course I'm no' going far. I'll always be popping back to see them, and the Dean. Mrs Gow's like Kitty, she's no' bothered I'm going because her daughter wants to visit more, seeing as she's got a baby too. Seems everything's worked out well, eh?'

'Worked out well,' Cassie agreed. 'But, listen, good luck for your new job. When do you start?'

'Monday. You'll come to see me when you can?'

'I'd like to. I'd like to see the old place again.'

'All the best to you, then. I still can't believe it – I mean, you and Archie engaged. Remember me to him, eh? Tell him I'm thrilled.'

'I will.' Cassie paused, looking down. 'He's no' got the looks, you ken, he's no film star, but he's a good lad and I think we'll be happy.'

'Oh, you will!' cried Shona. 'Cassie, you will!'

They parted at Kitty's house, waving and smiling, before Shona went on to Mrs Gow's for one of her last evenings in lodgings. From Monday she would again be living in at the Lodge. How strange was that, then? But now she must go and pack, and tomorrow must hug dear Mrs Gow, who'd looked after her so well. She really would miss her. Thank goodness she needn't make a proper goodbye to her, or to Mrs Hope.

Sixty-Six

Was it strange to be back at Edina Lodge? Yes it was. Strange, for everything now was seen from a different perspective from when she'd been a child. And yet familiar, for that child's view was still with her.

Though everyone was so kind, welcoming her back, which made things pleasant enough, she found her work in the early days to be quite hard. There was so much to do and learn – all the ordering of supplies, for instance, and the calculating of how much food would be required, and of how its cost would fit their budget, as well as discussions with the head cook, Mrs Grant, on menus and how to make the meals healthier. (Though Shona had to tread carefully there – not upsetting the cook was the cardinal rule of the kitchen.) And then there was the ordering of the uniforms and other things to wear, including shoes and even slippers, and the organization of the laundry, involving mountains of sheets, towels and all those clothes, of which none must be lost.

Sometimes Shona felt her head was so much in a whirl she longed to be back at Maybel's, sorting out her flowers for an ordered bouquet, smelling the scents again, thinking out a new design – oh, happy days! But then she remembered the children and what she could do for them and was cheered, for that was the aspect of her job she liked best and was the most valuable.

Especially when, in her first few weeks, several new orphans arrived and had to be helped to settle with varying results. Eventually, most managed to accept their new life, but there was one, a girl of nine who'd lost both parents in an accident and who was so stunned with shock she was in danger of becoming quite withdrawn. Only Shona could get through to her, taking her up to her own room, showing her her photographs and her dear old rabbit still with her, asking why Freda didn't take her teddy to bed but kept him in a paper bag in her locker.

'I'm no' wanting the others to see him,' Freda said huskily. 'They'll say I'm too old to have a teddy.'

'Och, that's no' true! Why, I was eleven when I came here and at first I didn't want to bring my rabbit – I called him Master Bun – but then he came and I was so happy. You'll be the same. Why don't we take your teddy out of his bag and put him in your bed? He'll be such a comfort to you.'

'Will he?' asked Freda, agreeing to the idea anyway, and though Shona knew that a long, long time would have to pass before she could know real comfort again, it was a start, it was something, towards accepting normal life.

'Is it true, you were here, just like me?' Freda asked when they'd settled Teddy in her bed, his head on her pillow. 'And did you get to like it?'

'Yes, it's true and I did. Why, here I am back again! I must have liked it, mustn't I? I made a lot of friends, and so will you. Now, what about putting up your pictures?' For Shona knew that in the paper bag in the locker were photographs of Freda's mother and father which Freda would not display. But Freda wasn't ready to do that yet, the sting of grief was still too sharp, and Shona left it for the moment. Later, Freda would be glad of the photos; for now, she must do what was least painful for her.

'Well done, Shona,' Miss Bryce commented, 'Young Freda is looking just a little better since you talked to her.'

'I'm afraid she has a long way to go.'

'Like so many here, unfortunately. We can only do our best.'

'Mightn't it be an idea for all new orphans to have an older child to look after them at first?' Shona asked. 'I know the staff are only too happy to do that, but can't always be around.'

'That's a good point,' Miss Bryce agreed. 'I'll look into it. Thanks for the idea, Shona. But before I forget, could you organize lists of names of the seniors for Matron? Doctor Mark's coming in next week to begin doing ear and eye checks.'

'Yes, Miss Bryce, I'll see to it,' Shona replied with routine calm. Inwardly, however, she was excited. Now would be her chance to bite on the bullet and ask about Miss Ruddick. Was she engaged to Dr Mark, or what? But as Shona took the list of names to Matron, she wasn't sure if she was ready to know.

Sixty-Seven

On the day of the eye and ear tests Shona was in the little room she'd been given as an office, waiting to go along to assist Matron and pretending to herself that she was in full control over the idea of seeing Mark Lindsay again. Nevertheless, when someone tapped lightly at her door she jumped as though shot, though of course she knew it could be anyone wanting to see her; it didn't have to be Mark.

But it was Mark. He was wearing his dark work suit and carrying his bag and hat, his unruly hair slightly damp, his bright eyes on her. 'Shona!' He held out his hand which she shook, remembering its firmness. 'I've only just been told you're housekeeper here – what happened, then? I mean, to the shop?'

'It's closed, for the time being, anyway. Miss Bryce told me about this job – it sort of involves being her assistant as well. So, here I am.'

Now that they'd met and were talking just as usual, she was no longer nervous, just very happy to see him.

'Back at the Lodge,' he said softly. 'And I thought you'd be married by now.'

'Oh, no.'

'Cousin gone back to Canada?' he asked after a moment.

'Gone, but maybe to Australia.'

'I was so sure—' He stopped, his eyes never leaving her face. 'You don't want to talk about it?'

She shook her head. Another moment passed. 'What's been happening to you, then?' she asked lightly. 'Are you married?'

'Me?' He laughed. 'Who would I marry?'

'Why, Miss Ruddick, of course.'

'Jay? Hadn't you heard? She's gone to Africa.'

'Africa!'

'Yes, to look after children in Nigeria. I told you she had plans, didn't I? Those were the plans. To go abroad, do what she could to help the children. She wanted me to go, too. Purely as a doctor. Nothing romantic, of course. That was never for Jay, as I realized. Eventually.'

'You didn't want to go anyway?'

'No. My work is here.' His face darkened a little. 'If you could see some of the Glasgow tenements – well, maybe you don't have to go to Africa to find children needing help.' He glanced at his watch. 'I'm due at Matron's in five minutes.'

'So am I.'

'Let's go, then.'

The rest of the day was taken up by the tests, with Mark conducting them, Matron assisting, and Shona supervising those waiting for their turns. When the work was finished and Miss Donner had arrived to take the seniors downstairs for free time, a welcome tray of tea arrived, after which Matron thanked Mark and Shona and said she must get on.

'What do you think about having Shona back as a grown-up?' Mark asked, at which Matron beamed and said she couldn't be more pleased.

'So lovely to have you, dear,' she told Shona. 'And you're just as efficient as I thought you'd be. But what a shame you had to give up your floristry, eh?'

'Floristry's loss is our gain,' Mark said cheerfully, once again looking at his watch. 'Got to go. But the tests went well and there are only three needing glasses. Will you arrange optician's appointments, Shona?'

'Certainly, Doctor Mark.'

As Matron hurried on her way, Mark grinned. 'Very formal, aren't we?'

'Have to be, I suppose.'

'Not always. But why don't you see me out?'

They made their way to the front door, where Mark paused to put on his hat.

'Been to see the Handkerchief Tree?'

'Oh, yes, but it's no' fully out yet.'

'Will be soon.' His vivid gaze was considering her. 'I was wondering – you must get time off here, don't you? A half day or something?'

'I get every fourth Sunday and a half day on Wednesday, just like at the shop.'

'We never did get that second cup of tea, did we? How about meeting again, then? I can take a Wednesday afternoon if I'm back for evening surgery.'

'That'd be nice,' she said, by enormous effort showing no surprise. 'When shall we meet?'

'Next week? I'll come over and collect you.'

'You mean, come to the front door?'

'Afraid people will see? Let 'em, but if you're worried, I can come to the gates and you can meet me there. Shall we say about three o'clock?'

'Fine. I'll be there.'

As he turned away, he looked back and smiled. 'Shona?'

'Yes?'

'I'm glad you're back.'

That night, Shona scarcely slept. Once she sat up in the darkness and fumbled amongst her possessions in her bedside table. Was it really there? She seemed to remember seeing it when she unpacked. Imagine her keeping it all this time . . . but there it was – Mark's handkerchief. She slipped it under her pillow and lay down again, but not to sleep. Would she ever sleep again?

Of course, she did. But during the day she walked on air.

Sixty-Eight

For their teatime meeting, they chose a small café in Princes Street, Shona having admitted that she would rather not go again to the Tea Box. To walk down George Street and have to pass Maybel's all boarded up – no, she'd rather not.

'Very understandable,' said Mark. 'It's been a bad time for you. Well, for everyone, but Maybel's was special to you, wasn't it? How's the owner taking it?'

'Mr Kyle? He might bounce back. He always says he's like a rubber ball.'

Sitting opposite Mark, meeting his amazing eyes, Shona was being borne along on such a crazy cloud of happiness she really didn't want to think of Fraser. Yet how could she not think of him, and want him, somehow, to find someone he'd feel the same way about as she did with Mark? At the same time, she knew she should be careful, giving way to happiness, when she might in fact have no right to it at all.

Still, there she was, and there was Mark, looking at her so cheerfully over their tea things. It seemed to her that she might as well feel happy while she could, and Fraser's image faded from her mind.

'Well, this is nice, isn't it?' Mark said, passing her a cucumber sandwich. 'You and I together again.'

'I never thought we would be.'

'Why was that?' He was watching her pour the tea.

'I suppose I was thinking of Miss Ruddick.'

'Ah, Jay. I'm afraid Africa cut me out there.'

She passed him his cup, wondering what to say. Sorry? Of course, she wasn't, but said it, anyway.

'It's all right – water under the bridge, as they say. I had to find out that she wasn't interested in love or marriage. A genuinely fine person, quite selfless, only wanting to help people, but not, you see, wanting me.'

He drank his tea, keeping his eyes on Shona's face. 'Once I understood, I had to accept the situation and I did. We'll always keep in touch, be friends, but no more. End of story.'

'I see,' Shona murmured. 'I do believe she's a very wonderful person.'

'Oh, she is, and before I forget, she asked me to tell you she was sorry she hadn't had time to come in to say goodbye, but wishes you all the best. She thought very highly of you, you know.'

'Another sandwich?' asked Shona, flushing, but Mark shook his head.

'One of those delectable little cakes, I think. But, listen, mind if I ask whether you feel like telling me about your cousin yet?'

No, she decided, she didn't feel like telling him about Brett. What could she say when so much was secret? How could she ever tell Mark what Brett had done? 'He had to go,' she answered slowly. 'Felt he had to be on the move. I didn't want to leave Scotland, so we parted.'

'And now?' he asked softly.

'Now?'

'I mean, is it over?'

'It's over,' she said steadily.

'You don't mind that I asked?'

Mind? Her heart was singing that he had. 'Oh, no, I don't mind,' she told him.

He sat back with a sigh. 'Seems we've both had our fingers burnt, then, doesn't it? Both had some heartache. Has it put you off?'

'What do you mean? Put me off?'

'Seeing me. Beginning again?'

She leaned forward, her eyes luminous, her feeling for him so real, she was sure he must recognize it, sense it sweeping over him, as his feeling for her, that she now could truly see, held her in thrall. 'With you there's no question of beginning again, Mark. There's always been something there, right from the start.'

'For me, too.' He took her hand. 'From that first day when I showed you the Handkerchief Tree, there was rapport, wasn't there? But you were so young. I always had to stand away.'

'And you found Jay.'

'And you found Brett.'

'Water under the bridge?'

'Torrents.'

'I'm no' so young now, you know.'

His smile was tender. 'I know. Come on, let's go. I'll take you back to the Lodge.'

On their return he parked near the entrance to the house. 'No skulking round at the gates this time. Why should we?'

'I don't know, really. It's just that people . . . talk.'

'As I say, let 'em. Listen, I've a few minutes, shall we look at the Handkerchief Tree?'

Shona had said it wasn't in full bloom, yet there it was, covered in all its May glory, her special tree that had brought their lives together, hers and Mark's.

'I thought we should both see it again today,' he told her quietly, slipping her hand into his. 'To remember the past. Maybe think about the future? You want to do that, Shona?'

'You know I do!'

'You'll see me again, then? We can meet?'

'Any time, Mark. Any time!'

For some moments they stood looking at the tree, not thinking that anyone might see them, even Shona not caring. There was no one in the garden but themselves.

'You don't think the tree's getting old?' Shona asked fearfully. 'I mean, too old? You don't think it will die?'

'No, it's fine. But if it did, you know where there's another, don't you?'

'In your garden? But that's yours.'

'I'll share it with you, Shona.'

'Share it?'

He did not explain. Perhaps he thought he didn't need to, only suddenly he drew her into his arms so that they might stand together to exchange a long, serious kiss while the Handkerchief Tree looked on.

'Our only witness,' Mark said, catching his breath when they drew apart. 'There's no one around.'

For a moment time seemed to stand still as they stood gazing into each other's faces, but Mark could not forget he had to go. His surgery was waiting.

'Time,' he groaned. 'Why is there never enough? And why have we wasted so much?'

As they reluctantly left the Handkerchief Tree to bloom alone, their free afternoon over, they knew they would waste no more.